HESTOR'S WAY

M. Lee Prescott

Published by Mount Hope Press

ISBN 978-0-9912855-4-9

For my family, always.

CHAPTER 1

The studio's screen door banged behind her, and Beth headed through the gardens toward the house. Passing through the grape arbor at the path's end, she spied her son, Kit, as he raced across the terrace.

"Hi, Mom! Gotta go. See you this afternoon?"

Her eighteen-year-old jumped over the terrace wall and waved as he headed for the driveway and his beat-up Volvo. His father's gift of safe, reliable transportation for the summer.

She marveled at the change in her only son. Where was the round-faced, chubby boy? He had disappeared and now there stood a six-foot tall man in his place! Of her three children, Kit looked the least like his sandy-haired father. Dark curls framed his slender face, the young Shelley, Beth's friend Clarice called him. Although tall, he was slight, almost delicate on first glance until one noticed the powerful legs from years spent on the soccer field. Kit would be playing soccer at Bowdoin in the fall.

"Kit, try to be home early, it's Nanny's birthday."

"Mom, don't worry. We'll probably head to the beach after work, but I'll be home in plenty of time to get the grill going."

"Kit," she called as the Volvo's door creaked open. "I forgot to tell you, Dad's coming. He, well, he asked and I said fine. You know how he is about the grill."

"Well, tough shit, it isn't his house, or his grill anymore."

She came to stand beside him, eyes soft and pleading. "Kit, please, it's a little thing and it's Nanny's night."

"It's not a little thing to me. Who does he think he is? We've been doin' fine without him. Now, he thinks he can waltz back in whenever he wants and take over. God, and you just let him, every single time!"

"Honey, I know it's hard, but it's only one night. I'd never have made it through the last three years without you. We can do this. Have a birthday party for Nanny and be together. You're right about the grill though. I'll have a word with Dad. You should do the cooking. But, Kit, do try to be civil, okay?" She rubbed his shoulder.

Shrugging from her touch, he dropped into the car seat, muttering.

"Beth's heart ached, watching him and remembering the shy, introverted fifteen-year-old who so desperately tried to take his father's place three years earlier.

"It's okay, Mom. I'll be home around five, but don't expect me to be jolly. Is she coming?"

"No Chloe." She closed the car door. "You'll be civil, for Nanny's sake?"

She noticed a glimmer of a smile as he pulled away. "Stinker!" she called as the Volvo tires crunched down the drive.

Turning toward the house, she glanced down at her watch. Nearly nine. Kit was late for work again.

When she entered the kitchen, Kat, her oldest, stood at the kitchen counter, barefoot, in the long tee shirt she used as a nightshirt. Kit, short for Kittredge, and Kat, short for Katherine had been Alan's ideas.

"Hi, Mom." She turned and gave her a sleepy smile as a dollop of strawberry jam dropped from her knife to the floor. Tall and slender like her mother, Kat's hair was also long and straight, lighter than Beth's chestnut color. Auburn tendrils framed her sleepy face as she smiled sheepishly, stooping to wipe up the jam. "Oops."

Beth flicked on the burner under the teapot. "Late night, huh?"

"Kinda. You didn't wait up, did you?"

"I heard you come in, if that's what you mean, but I was only semi-conscious. So?"

"So, Rob took me to Newport and we went clubbing."

"Clubbing, Kat? You're only nineteen."

"Mom, it's not that kind of clubbing. We didn't drink, not even Rob."

Rob had just turned twenty-one and the difference in their ages worried Beth. He and Kat had been dating since her freshman year at Dartmouth. Rob would be a senior this fall, Kat a sophomore. His parents lived in New Jersey, but Rob had found a job painting houses with a local contractor in Windy Harbor for the summer. He shared a house with four other guys who had already thrown several raucous parties.

"Kat, you know I trust you, but I'd rather you stayed closer to home."

"There's nothing to do here. If the Harbor wasn't so dead, we'd stay home, but it is. You worry too much. Anyway, we'll be taking a break next week when Rob goes to training."

A nationally ranked collegiate soccer player, Rob had hopes of a professional career and it looked as though he might have a shot at it.

"Kat," Beth began, her voice tentative as she embarked on a touchy subject. "I know we've discussed this before, but I do hope that you and Rob are taking precautions."

"Mom!"

"I'm serious. I'm not implying that you're sexually active and I don't mean to pry."

"We are, on both counts," Kat replied. "Mom, we've been sleeping together for over a year, but it's okay, Rob uses condoms every time. Want to know what brand?"

"Very funny."

"Don't worry. We're careful." Kat put her arms around Beth's shoulders and hugged her.

She returned the embrace, then turned away, not letting her daughter see the tears in her eyes. "Fine, that's all I need to know."

"Mom, we had this conversation two months ago."

Beth blushed. "Did we? I'm sorry." Relieved and embarrassed, she rushed to add, "Maybe you and I can snatch some time together in the next few days? I feel like I've barely seen you since you got home." Beth played with a lock of her daughter's hair. Even in a ripped tee shirt, with sleep-drenched eyes and tousled hair, what a beautiful woman her eldest had grown into.

"Sure, love it. Let's plan something for my day off. Shopping, a movie?"

"Or a canoe trip up the river or a day at the beach?"

"Yeah, sure, sounds good. This jam you made is great, a little runny, but I love it. Can you save a couple of jars for me to take back to school?"

"Of course. Your brother's already put three aside."

"The pig, he doesn't even like your jams."

"Now, now, stop it and don't be greedy. You both better leave a jar or two for Nanny and me. We like it too, you know."

"Speaking of Nan," Kat whispered, sitting down next to her mother at the long, wooden table. "I haven't gotten her anything yet. What's she want for her birthday? I thought I'd ride up to the Mill shops after work today and get her something."

Beth laughed. "Cutting it a little close, aren't you? You know Nanny; she likes almost anything, especially coming from her older sister. Just surprise her. You always do."

"Dad's coming, isn't he?"

"How'd you know?"

"Nanny told me, plus we ran into him last night and he mentioned it."

"Ran into him where?"

"Thames Street, can you believe it? We go down to Newport to get away from Windy Harbor for a few hours and who's the first person I see after Rob parks the car, but Dad. Chloe was draggin' him around to every shop on Thames. He looked real happy as you can imagine. You know how much he loves to shop."

Beth laughed, almost pitying her ex-husband. "Chloe must have strong arms."

"What an airhead. What he sees in her is beyond me."

Youth, Beth thought, but added charitably, "Chloe is far from an airhead. She's a gifted artist and you know how much that means to Dad."

"Yeah, if you like nihilistic, heavy metal."

Her daughter was referring to Chloe's massive, metal sculptures, welded together with a blowtorch. She smiled, brushing a lock of hair from Kat's forehead. "Now, now. Anyway, your father's coming around six and I thought we'd eat, and then have presents. Supper around seven? What do you think? That way we'll be finished in time for the fireworks."

"Rob is taking me."

"Why don't you have Rob and the kids come to the house to watch them? We can all sit out on the porch and—"

"Thanks, Mom, but we really like to be up close and personal, right underneath 'em."

"Uh, huh."

"We're meeting a bunch of kids in the Commons at nine," Kat continued. "Kit's friends will be there too."

"Suit yourself, but remember, Nanny comes first. Just family till eight thirty."

"'Course, Mom. What do you think?"

Her children treasured the rituals and traditions that accompanied birthday celebrations. The previous September Kat had been despondent when Dartmouth's preseason field hockey schedule had taken her away on her birthday. To make it up to her, Beth and Alan, on one of the rare occasions when she'd agreed to go anywhere with him, had packed the other two into the car, along with a birthday cake, dinner and presents and traveled to New Hampshire. They found a campground nearby where they could grill shrimp, Kat's favorite meal, and have cake and presents on the cool September afternoon, sharing a few precious moments together. When they walked onto the practice field, Kat's face had made every minute of the three-hour drive with Alan worth it.

CHAPTER 2

The light was perfect, or nearly so. A faint mist in the air sprayed the canvas, running the colors slightly, but Beth didn't mind. Not with early morning light like this, clean, soft and pure, filtering through the trees at the edge of the pond, bathing every inch of the grassy woods with warmth. The trees mirrored in the pond's glassy surface stretched their branches from sky to the middle of Echo Lake, their reflections an impressionistic extension of reality.

She was working on a commissioned piece for the Wannamakers who owned the stone cottage at the far edge of the pond. Together they had scouted every inch of the far bank on which she now sat, until they fixed on the very spot where her easel rested, a spot Herb Wannamaker had marked with a white stake. After a week of mornings spent in the shady spot, Beth had nearly completed the picture of the turn of the century cottage dwarfed by the towering elms and fir that surrounded it. Some last minute touches and the painting could go to the framer.

Beth enjoyed working outdoors, but had had little time for it the past six months. Her agent was pressing her to show and she needed at least thirty paintings for a one-woman exhibit. A prestigious local art gallery granted three solo shows a year and chose its artists carefully. Every exhibit at the Lynch Gallery attracted national attention, drawing critics from New York, Boston and California. Rick Gould, Beth's agent for the past five years, had been negotiating with Margot Lynch for six months on his client's behalf, but so far the gallery owner showed no signs of capitulating.

She had tried, unsuccessfully, to tell herself that it didn't matter. Fueled by the influx of summer people, the local market for her work remained strong. She usually sold fifteen or twenty paintings a year and several gift shops carried her prints, postcards and notepaper depicting local scenes, all consistent sellers.

It wasn't that she needed the money. Alan had been very generous in the divorce and had cheerfully divided his considerable assets in half, signing the house completely over to her. "Guilt money," Beth's attorney called it. It wasn't money she needed from her work, but something else, less tangible and much more important. Maybe it was recognition, or perhaps the opportunity to finally emerge from Alan's formidable shadow.

Satisfied with the painting, she packed up her things and called to Jasper. Jasper had been Alan's dog, an old Springer Spaniel, left behind when his adored master had walked out. Chloe was allergic to dogs. Jasper usually went to work with Kit, but this morning he had trailed along with her instead.

The route home took her through the village where she stopped for tea and muffins at Begley's. Upon leaving she waved to Ed Talbot, a lobsterman and father of her son's close friend. Windy Harbor was just as its name implied, a town built around a harbor. Main Street ran north to south, the southern end running smack dab into the water, its long piers stretching for almost a quarter mile into the bay. An old whaling village, the narrow streets were lined with all manner of Cape Cod architecture. A few larger homes were sandwiched in between capes and colonials, some with porches trimmed with lacy gingerbread. Widow's walks crowned a number of the larger homes' mansard roofs.

Beth and her family did not live in the village proper, but in an outlying area known to the locals as Hen and Chicks. So named because of its peculiar topography, a large knoll, the Hen, surrounded by many smaller hills, the Chicks, the area had originally been part of a three hundred acre estate. When the original landowner sold off the rolling woods and fields, he had divided the properties into five-and ten-acre lots. Most of those original boundaries remained today.

Soon after their son's marriage, Alan's parents had purchased a five-acre lot for the young couple and the newlyweds built their home together. Both Rhode Island School of Design graduates, they had definite ideas about the house's design. Their collaboration had produced a comfortable, light-filled home, a sort of "adapted saltbox" with a few extra interesting angles.

As the family expanded from two to five, they added on several times, but each addition succeeded in retaining the shingled charm of the original structure. No longer boxy, the house now crawled out both east and west hugging the landscape that surrounded it. Like the brambles and beach roses growing in wild profusion around the property, the additions appeared to have sprouted from the sandy soil fed by the passage of time and pruned by the winds.

To the north, a freestanding barn served as a two-car garage and woodshop. Alan's summer project their third year in the house, the barn had been built entirely of salvaged wood taken from several city demolition sites. Alan's one request in the divorce settlement had been to have access to the woodshop. While his furniture workshop was attached to his new home, he still kept machinery and an enormous collection of tools in the barn.

The rear of the house faced south toward open fields dotted with fruit trees. Beyond the fields, woods stretched for miles. It was common land held jointly by all owners of Hens and Chicks property. The common land would always remain a wilderness populated by deer, fox, coyotes, and smaller mammals as well as countless species of birds. Situated along the Atlantic Flyway, Windy Harbor played host to thousands of migrating birds with the changing of the seasons. The small pond at the back of their property had afforded them hours of bird watching over the years.

Beyond the pond, in the southeast corner of the property, Beth's studio stood alone, surrounded by fields of Queen Anne's lace and golden rod. Built by Alan as a present on their tenth wedding anniversary, its exterior was weathered shingles like the house. The large, airy one-room studio welcomed light through floor-to-ceiling windows on all four sides; its north wall was one huge expanse of glass. Whitewashed barn board covered interior walls. There was a small bathroom, refrigerator, hot plate and a black slate sink for washing up, but few other amenities. A dilapidated couch and chairs were arranged around an enormous, threadbare oriental carpet that had belonged to Beth's grandmother. Dominated by shades of burgundy and dark blues and yellows, the carpet ran to the very edges of the wide pine floors. The only other furnishings were two bookcases and a massive, white Hoosier cupboard housing her paints and supplies. Two easels supported works in progress at opposite ends of the room. Warm in the winter and breezy in the summer, the studio was Beth's spiritual home. It was here where her soul resided, at peace, while she worked.

The driveway stretched around to the back of the studio so she could bring in supplies by car, but generally she walked from home to the studio along the gravel path through her gardens. A profusion of perennials lined the path: hollyhocks, delphinium, asters, baby's breath, statice, yarrow, coreopsis, foxgloves, and many varieties of flowering bushes. Every year she added a few new plantings and her labors rewarded her with riotous color from early spring to late fall.

As she pulled the car to a stop alongside the house, she heard laughter and shouting coming from the barn. "Fuck you, too, Hadley!" he called, emerging from the side door covered in sawdust.

"Jack? Is that you under all those shavings?"

"Mrs. H., hi," he said, grinning sheepishly as he spotted her. "Sorry about that, the yelling, I mean. We're almost through in there and we were foolin' around. We'll clean everything up."

"Where are you, Talbot? You chicken shit!" Kit called, crashing through the door. "Uh oh, Mom, hey."

"Hey, yourself. Taking a little break, are you?"

"Sort of, well. Really, we're finished, aren't we Jack?"

"Yup." The other smiled a beautiful open smile that Beth returned.

Jack Talbot was Kit's best friend. Both were on the same construction crew and they spent nearly every waking moment of the summer together.

It was an unusual friendship. Jack was fifteen years older, one of the harbor boys who had never grown up. On Sundays, Jack and Kit worked for Beth. Their current project involved cleaning out the barn loft, hauling junk to the dump to clear storage space. In a year or two, she and her sister planned on selling their mother's cottage, Hestor's Way. At that time, she would need the room to store everything from Hestor's Way. Lanie would have no use for it in her Boston apartment, but Beth was certain her sister would not allow Beth to dispose of or sell one stick of furniture, one piece of chipped crockery, one moldy, moth-eaten blanket or one spineless, dog-eared copy of Agatha Christie, at least not right away.

Like Kit, Jack had grown and filled out the past few months and looking at him, Beth experienced the same sensation as when she regarded her son. Where had the teenager gone? With his sandy hair covered with sawdust, broad shoulders straining the fabric of one of Alan's faded blue work shirts, he stood before her a man.

"How 'bout some lunch, you two?"

"Great, sure, Mom. Just let us clean up this mess and we'll be in."

They joined her several minutes later still talking and laughing. Both had changed into tee shirts and swim trunks.

"We gonna head out after lunch, if it's okay. Go out on Pete's boat, fishing or diving."

"Lucky you. What can I fix you? I've got turkey, cheese, avocados, lettuce, tomatoes, tuna fish?"

"What about veggie burgers?" Kit asked, rummaging in the freezer.

Beth watched him, wondering what or who had turned him into a vegetarian overnight. "You might find a package in the downstairs freezer. Run down and check. That what you want, Jack?"

"I'd take a turkey sandwich, if you have enough," he said, coming to stand beside her. "I can make it though."

"Okay, I've got pita bread here and there's whole wheat in the freezer, white and Italian, too." Stepping aside, she continued to assemble ingredients for her own lunch: a pita pocket stuffed with slices of avocado, lettuce, tomatoes, and alfalfa sprouts. As she worked, she popped wedges of luscious, ripe tomato into her mouth. Kit finally appeared proudly displaying a package of soy burgers in hand. "Anyone want a slice of tomato? These early ones are from Wilson's stand and they're incredible."

Kit wrinkled his nose, making a face. "No thanks, Mom."

For reasons Beth could never fathom, all of her children disliked fresh tomatoes. Much as they loved Italian cooking and tomato-based sauces, none would willingly eat an uncooked, "raw tomato" as Nanny called them.

"I'll take one," Jack said, both hands occupied as he constructed a monstrous turkey club sandwich.

Laughing, Beth popped a thick tomato wedge into his mouth. "Here, I'll slice a few more for your sandwich."

"Thanks, Mrs. H.," he mumbled, tomato juice trickling from the corner of his mouth.

"Not too much of a slob, are you, Talbot?" Kit elbowed him as he reached over to pop his soy burger into the microwave.

"People who do not appreciate the sensual pleasure of a fresh, ripe tomato should not call people slobs, dear son of mine."

"There you go again, always taking his side! You'd think *he* was the favorite son." Kit threw up his hands in mock dismay.

"No, but he is a guest."

Her lunch assembled, Beth poured three tall glasses of iced tea and retreated to the terrace. To her surprise, the boys joined her. Pleased at the unexpected company, she rose and made room for Jack at the end of the chaise longue.

"So? I just saw your dad in town. How's the rest of the Talbot family?"

"Great. Dick and Perry are away at camp for two weeks, in New Hampshire, and Caitlin's working at the Marina, in the bait shop."

"How old is she now?"

"Fifteen."

"Amazing. It seems like only yesterday your mom was pushing her in the stroller."

"Mom, you're doing it again. You promised, no more living in the way-distant past."

"Oops, sorry, you're right."

She turned away, hiding unexpected tears. The summer had been a roller coaster side of ups and downs as she anticipated losing yet another of her children. He was right, she had been reminiscing about the past lately, with too many references to her babies and she knew it was wearing thin with Kit. Despite his mother's protests, her son felt guilty abandoning his household obligations and worried constantly about who would take his place when he left in September.

Sensing the tension between mother and son, Jack intervened as he always did, lightening the mood. "So, what project do you have for us next, Mrs. H.?"

"The basement," she replied, turning back to her sandwich. "It needs the same going over as the barn. And there are a bunch of boxes you guys can take over to Mr. Hadley's. Old books, college notebooks, sketchbooks, and things. I'll call and see what he says, but if I know Alan, he'll want them all."

"I doubt they'll fit with Chloe's décor," Kit muttered, taking a last bite of veggie burger.

It was on the tip of her tongue to ask how he knew so much about Chloe's décor when he had supposedly never set foot in his father's new home, but she stayed silent, not wishing to provoke an argument in front of Jack.

CHAPTER 3

"No, Rick," she said for the tenth time. "I'm doing some quick errands, then taking Nanny and her friends to the beach. Period."

"Beth, be reasonable. If I can set something up with Margot today, this might be the break we need, you need. Sweetheart, I'm serious. She'll be making her decision about the gallery's fall schedule soon. They've gotta print programs, get the right people here."

"It's Nanny's birthday. We're having a beach picnic and that's that. It's a perfect day for it by the way. Wanna join us?"

"Just what I need, a bunch of teenage girls screaming in my ear. Thanks, but no thanks. I'll just sit here and weep over missed opportunities. Not to mention all the precious hours you're wasting away from your easel."

"Don't sound so despondent, dear agent of mine. You can always meet with Margot by yourself. You have the portfolio, I trust you. Besides, you'll do better without me. You always do."

"Bullshit. Margot likes to bond with her artists, not their underpaid, unappreciated agents."

Giving up, she sighed, the futility of further argument clear. "Rick's a bull dog," Alan had told her five years earlier when he had recommended that Beth hire him. Alan had been right. "All right, you win, dearest. Set something up with Margot for another day this week. Any day but Friday is fine with me."

"Hmm, I'll see what I can do. I am going to the city tomorrow. Maybe Margot and I can muddle through today alone."

"That's the spirit. And remember, we'd still love to have you stop at the beach for a piece of birthday cake."

"Gritty butter icing, now isn't that tempting?"

"Bring Gary along, it'll be fun."

"Get real, girl. Gary, sand, water? No way. He's working, and besides, he'd spoil the party with all his complaining. Been in a filthy mood lately. Impossible to live with."

The two men had moved in together a year after Beth and Alan's marriage and the occasional separation notwithstanding, their relationship had endured.

"Good luck with Margot," she said hanging up.

He really has gone crazy over this Lynch Gallery show, she decided as she keyed in her friend Clarice's number. It was not the end of the world if Margot Lynch turned her down. A disappointment, yes, but there would be other shows.

"Hey, Clary."

"Who the hell's been talking on your phone?"

Clarice never bothered with hellos.

"I've been calling for hours."

She was a shameless exaggerator.

"Sorry, Rick's been haranguing me about the Lynch show."

"Time for you to invest in "call waiting," dearie, or keep your cell phone charged and on. With three teenagers you need to be reachable at all times. What's the story with Miz Margot? You're a shoe-in for that show. The gallery would be lucky to get you for Christ's sake. Besides, I have it on good authority that Miz Margot no longer makes the decisions."

"Oh?" Beth sat back, waiting for the gossip sure to be forthcoming. Clarice despised Margot Lynch. The two strong-minded women had served on too many committees together, usually taking opposing sides of whatever issue arose. There was no love lost between them.

Beth and Clarice had been roommates at Rhode Island School of Design and had stayed in touch over the years. After years in the Midwest, Clarice and Ben had moved back east to Providence, Rhode Island, where Ben had grown up and where they'd both gone to college.

They had taken a small apartment in Providence, an hour's drive from Windy Harbor, but six months later they packed up again. Like Beth and Alan, they had wanted to start a family. Clarice, a very successful freelance silversmith, whose studio was at home, convinced Ben that a move to Windy Harbor "was best for the children" so Ben commuted to his graphic arts studio in a converted mill building in the south end of Providence.

"That's right," Clary continued. "Margot, the magnanimous, has ceded all decision making to the prodigal son, returned from the wilds of Chicago."

"You mean Graham?"

"None other. I'm surprised Rick didn't mention it. Surely he knows? Maybe not; I know 'cause we ran into him the other night. Better call Rick, hon, or he'll waste a lot of time sucking up to the wrong person."

She laughed. "I'll let him find out himself. At least he'll be off my back for a while. Graham, you say? I had no idea he was back. Why, it's been years since I've—"

"He's still gorgeous, by the way. We saw him at the Butler's last night. Salt-and-pepper, but otherwise he looks the same. It's been how many years since he was back in the area?"

"Well, Nanny's fourteen so that's it, fourteen, at least as far as I know."

Several weeks after Nanny's birth, Graham Lynch had come to see Alan. Her body hidden under a shapeless muumuu, Beth had excused herself immediately and left the two men to catch up. Graham had been Alan's best man, but as the years passed, the two friends had drifted apart. That had been just fine with Beth because, from the moment she met the shy, slightly awkward friend of Alan's youth, she was inexplicably drawn to him. Despite the fact that she and Alan were wildly in love, the unreasonable, surprising attraction persisted and she never completely trusted herself to be alone with Graham. Some years later, she had greeted the news of his marriage to a high-powered Chicago attorney with a mixture of relief and jealousy, glad at least that they would be living halfway across the country.

"From all the reports, he's home for good," Clarice continued. "So you're a sure bet for the show no matter what Mommy Dearest says. You guys go back a long way, don't you?"

"I'm sure that will have no bearing on his decision. After all, the Lynch is not the Guild."

She referred to the Harbor Arts Guild founded by herself and eight other local artists. The group had pooled their resources and purchased a small garage in the village center, which they had converted into a small gallery where they could exhibit and sell their artwork. Alan was not a member of the Guild. His furniture, too pricey for Windy Harbor, went directly to the gallery in New York City. Even so, Alan had provided much of the capital and completed the lion's share of carpentry work for the building's restoration.

"That's right, it's not as cool or prestigious as the Guild!"

"Very funny, the Lynch has a national reputation. They can't be handing out favors to old friends."

"Beth, get real. Who are they gonna get who's more talented than you?"

"Thousands of people. Almost anyone. Let's drop this, okay? I've got a lot to do and I'm calling about Carrie. Want us to swing by for her on our way to the beach?"

"That'd be great, I'm swamped here. Probably won't make it down to the beach after all, I'm sorry."

"That's okay," Beth said secretly glad. Once the girls were fed, they would run off and leave her with her book for an hour or so. "I'll catch up on all your news tomorrow night. Hope it's good weather. We're all looking forward to our first beach cook-out of the summer."

"Ben's dragging me over there tonight to watch the fireworks. Just the two of us, because the kids are going in four different directions."

"Mmm, romantic."

"Yeah, the two of us and several hundred horny teenagers."

Beth laughed. "You'll fit right in. If I know Ben, he'll find a secluded spot."

After thirty years of marriage, Ben and Clarice were still honeymooners.

"Ha. See you in a few minutes, then." The change in the voice she knew so well told Beth her friend was blushing.

Two hours later Beth was serving chicken salad rolls and sodas to Nanny and four friends under the shade of an enormous blue-and-white striped umbrella. She had brought china, a linen tablecloth and napkins, and they were sipping soda from Beth's best crystal. Nanny had requested an "elegant beach picnic" and she was getting it.

"Thanks," Chrissie Moniz mumbled through a mouthful of chicken salad.

Dark-skinned, raven-haired, Chrissie's voluptuous body stretched her tiny, lime green bikini to its limits. Her dark eyes twinkled as she added, "This is the best, Mrs. Hadley. Nanny is so lucky."

"Mom's gonna be pissed she missed this," Carrie Rollins added, smiling at Beth.

She had her mother's enormous blue eyes, but otherwise Carrie was the image of her father. Her easy smile a mirror of his own, her complexion, while not the deep chocolate brown of Ben's, was still a far cry from her fair-skinned mother's. She, too, wore a bikini, hers looser, less well defined, on her flat-chested, boyish frame. Her long, reddish hair cascaded in ringlets to her waist and was tied back in a loose ponytail with a twist tie she had borrowed from Beth.

"I'll catch up with her tomorrow night, but, I don't think I'll bring these wine glasses across the river. Beth referred to the spot across the harbor's channel reachable only by boat where they went for summer cookouts.

After the sandwiches, a small marble cake appeared which the girls devoured down to the last crumb. Then, hopping up, they declared themselves ready for a walk. As Carrie and Chrissie headed off, Nanny lingered behind.

"Thanks, Mom. It was great!"

Beth smiled. "Having a good day so far?"

"The best!"

"There's more coming."

"I know. Thanks for having Dad. I know you'd rather not."

"Nonsense. I'll enjoy every minute of your party. Tonight's focus is on a certain fourteen-year-old, I believe, not on a couple of old divorcees."

"It still hurts, doesn't it?"

The question startled Beth and she peered into the blue eyes, wondering at the reason for her daughter's question. Nanny had never wanted to talk about the divorce and Beth and Alan hadn't pressed her. Three years ago, the two older children had had endless questions, demanding almost continual updates, but Nanny had said little, seeming to accept the divorce like she did everything, with an easygoing affability. An almost innate sense of security seemed to carry her through the crisis; however, recently Nanny had had her first boyfriend and subsequently her first heartbreak.

Beth brushed errant strands of sandy hair from her daughter's cheek. "Yes, it does sometimes, but not like three years ago. It's much smoother sailing now."

"You'd still rather not see him. I know that."

"Sweetheart, this is different," she replied, cupping the smooth, soft chin in her hand. "This is your birthday. Remember Kat's last fall? We had a great time, didn't we?"

"Yeah, except you looked like you were gonna throw up all the way up and back in the car."

Laughing at the idea of vomiting all over Alan, Beth said, "Don't worry. We're not traveling by car tonight and I'm going to have a great time at your party. Honest. Dad, too."

"Not Kit."

"Of course he is. You know Kit, he's still angry with Dad."

"Hates him. He does, Mom, so don't even try to deny it. Chloe too, especially Chloe."

"Nanny, your brother doesn't hate Dad. He's just going through a rough time. He's about to leave for college and he's worried about us and who'll take his place. He's tried so hard the last three years to fill Dad's shoes."

"I'll say. Thinks he can boss me around worse than Dad ever did."

She leaned over to hug her. "Well don't worry. He'll be fine tonight. He's just tired out from his job and you know when Kit gets tired he gets a little testy."

"Plus he stays out till dawn with Jack and the guys."

"You better scoot off and catch up to the girls. Remember, this is your party. We'll have a great time tonight. Don't worry."

If Dad behaves, she thought, watching Nanny run down to the beach after the others, her compact, sturdy frame in sharp contrast to her taller, more shapely companions. All except Nanny wore skimpy bikinis leaving little to the imagination, especially from the rear. Nanny, who declared bikinis to be uncomfortable and silly, wore a navy-racing tank. She swam two miles every day of the summer.

Yes, Beth thought again, pulling out her book and leaning back in her beach chair. If Dad behaves, we'll have a lovely time. Miracles can happen.

CHAPTER 4

Alan did behave, through most of the evening, at least. A preemptive call from Beth in the afternoon had resulted in his abdication of the grill and her sharp looks, which he usually ignored, had forestalled intervention as Kit struggled to cook the steaks and swordfish. Always the peacemaker, Nanny had requested "surf and turf, the turf for her brother, the surf for her dad. The rest of the family enjoyed either, although Beth rarely ate red meat.

Kat set the table on the back terrace with a blue cloth and a basket of daisies in its center. Alan had built the terrace, stone by stone, during their fifth summer in the house. He had laid out the sunken flower beds and curving walkways with the same precision with which he crafted his furniture.

Beth fixed a huge garden salad, parsley new potatoes, and corn on the cob. Kat made popovers, Nanny's favorite food. By the time Kat appeared with the cake, glowing with fourteen candles, they were all stuffed, unsure if they could eat another bite.

After cake and ice cream, they retreated into the house to escape the mosquitoes. "What's happened in here?" Alan said, gesturing around the beamed family room.

Since his last visit, Beth had recovered both couches and rearranged the furniture. The massive cherry sideboard he made for her on their first anniversary had been relegated to a corner. Its original spot along the east wall was now occupied by a maple shelving system that Beth, Kat, and Kit had built from a kit. Lined with books, the unit also housed a new stereo system as Kit was taking the old one to school. Amongst an eclectic assortment of books, the shelves displayed framed photographs, small sculptures and knick-knacks, most of the latter created by their children in art classes over the years.

"Like it, Dad?" Kat beamed. "We built it. Mom, Kit, and me."

"I helped too," Nanny chimed in.

"That's right," Beth said. "Your baby is a world class sander."

"Why didn't you tell me? I could have helped."

Giving her ex-husband and Kit a sharp look, Beth sat down on the couch. "Let's not keep the birthday girl waiting."

Kit glowered, but remained silent, the words "you don't live here anymore" repressed with great effort. Alan shrugged, hiding his embarrassment behind a façade of cheerfulness. "Where's my Nana-banana!"

"Right here, Daddy!" She jumped onto the sofa beside him and gave him a hug.

As Kat reappeared with an armload of presents, the tension eased and Nanny dived into her gifts. From Kit there was a new tack brush and blanket for Willie, the horse she leased from a nearby stable. Beth gave her a sweater, some shorts and several summer tee shirts as well as a gift certificate to a music store. Kat's gift was a shimmering necklace of green-and-blue beads set between tiny silver beads.

She smiled at her mother. "I went to Clarice's after work."

"I love it!" Nanny cried, running to the mirror to admire the necklace.

"My turn." Alan rose with a flourish and disappeared out the side door. He always saved his presents for last. Several minutes later, he reappeared. "All right, everyone, it's ready. Come on."

They followed him outside to find a four-poster bed on the grass next to his truck.

"The mattress and box spring have been ordered. Had to be made specially, but they should be here soon." Beaming, his hand caressed one of the exquisitely carved posts.

"Wow! Dad! Thanks," Nanny cried, running down to touch it.

"Alan, it's gorgeous," Beth said.

"The wood is nice, isn't it?"

"That's not what I mean and you know it. Why, it's one of the loveliest pieces you've ever done. All the detail, you must've been working on it for…"

"Six months. Came out nice, didn't it?"

"Amazing," Kat said.

They all ran their hands over the smooth, flawless finish, the delicately carved headboard, and the intricate patterns on the turned posts. So lost were they in silent reverence to Alan's prodigious talent that they failed to hear the car.

He called from the far side of the truck, "Hi, guys."

"Yo, Jack," Kit said, his whole body relaxing as he spied his friend.

"Hey, Talbot," Alan said, extending his hand. "Long time no see."

"Yeah. Hi, Mr. H., good to see you. Mrs. H…" Reaching in front of Alan, he shook Beth's hand, rough carpenter hands that held hers in a firm grasp.

"Jack." She smiled, returning his handshake. "Here to see the birthday girl, are you?"

"Sure am." He grinned, turning to Nanny. "Happy Birthday, peanut." He hugged her and Nanny blushed crimson.

"We were just admiring Alan's present to Nanny," Beth said.

"It's unbelievable, Mr. Hadley, really. My parents are always saying how they want to save up and get one of your pieces someday. What an amazing present."

"Thanks. Your parents know there's a local discount, don't they? Twenty percent right off the top."

Jack smiled. "I'll tell 'em, but your New York prices are still a bit in stratosphere, even with a discount."

Alan smiled as he placed a hand on Jack's shoulder. "You never know, but listen, son, we're still having a family birthday here."

"Oh, sorry," Jack stammered, blushing. "I'll take off and come back later."

"No sense in that. No, no, stick around. I've just got one more thing for our birthday girl. Hold on, everyone."

As she watched Alan play Lord of the Manor, Beth glanced at Kit who was rolling

his eyes and motioning to Jack to join him on the steps.

At the cab of his truck, Alan reached in and produced a box wrapped in shiny paper and covered with ribbons and streamers. Beaming at his youngest, he said, "This is what you really wanted, pumpkin."

"Oh, Dad," she screamed, pulling a new riding habit and shiny leather boots from the box.

"You'll have to go back and get the right sizes. I'll give your mom the slips or I can take you."

Nanny hugged the clothes, and then ran to hug her father.

He laughed. "Guess you like 'em, huh? Maybe we can work on your mother and finally get the horse to go with them."

"Alan," Beth warned.

"Okay, okay, just saying."

"Let's go back inside," Beth said. "Maybe Kit and Jack could put the bed in the barn? We'll store it there till the mattress comes. I know you all want to go to the fireworks."

As they headed inside, Rob and a carload of Kat's friends drove up honking the horn.

"Mom?" Kat whispered.

"Go ahead, sweetie. Give Nanny a hug first, okay?"

Soon after, Kit and Jack disappeared, leaving Nanny, Alan, and Beth to watch the fireworks from the porch facing south. Alan made noises about leaving, but then stayed on, helping himself to coffee and an aperitif. For Nanny's sake, Beth hid her irritation.

It was a perfect night, with a clear, starry sky and just a sliver of a new moon, a flawless canvas for the Fourth of July fireworks. The three had just settled into Adirondack chairs with blankets over their knees, when the rattle of bicycles in the drive signaled the arrival of Chrissie, Carrie, and three other girls.

"Nanny, hey, Nanny!" A chorus of voices called, bikes clanging as they dismounted.

Nanny dashed off the porch to greet them and returned almost immediately. She whispered to Beth, "Mom, everyone's going down to the beach to watch the fireworks."

"Sweetheart, you're the birthday girl. You get to do whatever you want.

CHAPTER 5

As the girls rode off, the reality of her situation sunk in. She was now alone with Alan for the first time in almost three years.

Jasper settled into his master's lap as the first of the cascading lights burst above them. Finally, Alan broke the silence. "So, how have you been?"

"Fine."

He ruffled Jasper's fur. "I miss you, old boy. But I miss your mistress even more."

"Alan, please don't. You're welcome to stay for the fireworks, but please don't dredge up the past and say things you don't mean."

"How can I help it, Bethie? We've been together for over thirty years."

"Please don't call me that, and don't be absurd. We haven't been together for the past three years."

"You know what I mean. We have a history together and that can't just be erased."

"I don't think about our history anymore. I've put it behind me and that's where it's going to stay."

"How can you just erase the memories of the kids and all that we shared?"

"I didn't erase the memories of the kids."

"Just me?"

"Alan, enough. Please." She rose from her chair and turned to face him. "What do you want me to say? That you were a good father? You were the best. That you provided for us and gave us a spectacular home? You did, but, you also walked out on us, on me, and that's the end of our history, yours and mine. Nothing will ever change that. Ever."

"Do you ever think about getting back together?"

"No, and I can't believe we're having this conversation. You're married, remember? What about Chloe? What about the 'incredible woman who made you feel alive again? The woman you simply couldn't live without? Tired of her already? Better start scouting the incoming freshmen. Must be some nubile young thing to take her place."

"Beth!"

"I'm sorry, that was horrid. This conversation is over. This is exactly what I didn't want to have happen tonight. You're here, Alan. I accept that. The kids need to see you and therefore I will see you. I'm fully prepared to be civil, but I won't do this. You're out of my life. I don't want to be friends. I don't want to be your confessor. I don't want to hear about your marriage. And, most of all, I don't want to talk about getting back together. My love for you is in the past and that's where it will stay. I care about you as the father of my children. Period."

"Fine." He sniffed. "Sorry. Sit down. Please. I won't say another word, but I do consider you a friend, whether you like it or not. And, I wish you well. I can help with this Lynch thing too. I know Margot well and I could put in a word."

"No, thank you. Rick's handling it."

Relieved that they had moved into less dangerous waters, she let out a sigh. His meddling she could handle. It was irritating, but at least it didn't open up painful wounds and dredge up the feeling of icy numbness she had experienced in the year after he left. It was only this past year that she had begun to emerge from her cocoon of grief to "walk among the living" as Rick put it. She was not going to return to the aftermath of his desertion.

During their early years of marriage, she had lived in Alan's shadow. His extraordinary talent, and, in her eyes, well-deserved success, made her painting seem no more than a hobby, a quaint diversion for a bored housewife. Then she began to sell and her own career took off. This gave her a measure of independence and freedom she had not experienced since the heady days at RISD. While her income would never approach his, she was finally able to support herself.

Alan had always been her biggest fan and most ardent promoter. Alan found Rick through his own agent and encouraged Beth to hire him. Alan had urged her to make time for her painting. Just as he had done with countless students, Alan encouraged and nurtured her talent and had helped her to believe in herself.

Theirs had been a passionate, loving relationship until Alan hit fifty-nine, with sixty lurking just around the corner. It was during that time that Chloe Barnard had landed in Alan's introductory wood sculpting course. The bright, blond-haired southerner had already attracted the notice of half the male faculty. When he met Chloe, Alan told Beth he felt young again, happy, and strong. Alan sacrificed his family and his marriage to have her.

"Rick's a good man, don't get me wrong, but Margot and I go back a way. I could drop by the gallery for a chat."

"Alan, please don't. Rick will handle it. Besides, according to Clarice, Margot's not making the decisions at Lynch now, Graham is."

"Oh?"

"Yes, he's back in the area."

"Someone told me he was around. Have you seen him?"

"No. I'm surprised he hasn't called you."

"Yeah, well, Graham was pretty pissed at me over the divorce. Didn't I ever tell you?"

"No."

"He came down a couple of weeks after I left home and read me the riot act. Called me every name in the book for leaving you, then stalked out. I haven't seen him or heard from him since. He was always crazy about you."

What seemed like an eternity passed until the booms of the grand finale shattered the silence. Reds, greens, yellows, and blues showered across the black sky in rapid succession. As the last lights withered their waning tails, drifting down to earth, she rose.

"I'm going in. I'm tired and ready to curl up with my book."

"Sure, hon. How about the clean-up? Can I help?"

"No. Kat and I took care of most of it. I'll get the rest in the morning, thanks."

"What about the kids?"

"They're fine. They'll check in with me when they get home."

"But?"

"They're fine, Alan. They're growing up, you know. They never, well, hardly ever, give me trouble. They're great kids."

"Sure are. You've done a great job with them."

"You, too."

"Thanks for tonight. It was fun."

"It meant a lot to Nanny to have you here. The bed is lovely. She was thrilled."

"With the new riding duds, yes. Couldn't have cared less about the bed, but that was for posterity anyway."

"That's not true, Alan, she loved it."

"Guess now wouldn't be a great time to discuss the horse? She should have one, you know. She's a skilled rider. Why, with her own horse she could—"

"Goodnight, Alan."

"Beth, I'm sorry if I upset you earlier. I didn't mean to."

"It's okay," she lied.

"Let me know if I can help with the Lynchs. Then again," he continued, speaking more to himself than her. "Maybe I better stay out of it till Rick sees what he can do. Might screw up the deal if Graham's involved."

"Goodnight, Alan."

"Night, babe." Before she could pull away, he leaned forward and kissed her on the cheek.

After several minutes of pacing and feeling unsettled by Alan's kiss, Beth headed up to bed. An introvert by nature, she ordinarily enjoyed the peacefulness of having the house to herself; however, tonight, the solitude offered neither peace nor comfort. As she reached the second floor and gazed out the hall window across darkened fields, Beth's chest constricted and her heart ached with loneliness. She had forgiven Alan for the affair, but it was hard to forgive him for leaving her with that loneliness. At fifty-eight, a whole lifetime of loneliness loomed ahead of her.

Shaking herself, she took a deep breath and tried to let go. So much had happened in three years. She would not choose to go back to her old life, even if she could. Nowadays, when she looked at Alan, she felt nothing but a vague familiarity and, of course, the ever-present irritation. No love, no anger, no hurt, just indifference. That's what the years of grieving had left her with, complete indifference to the father of her children and the man she had loved with every fiber of her being for over half of her life.

CHAPTER 6

Beth and Clarice lay on the beach in the warmth of the late afternoon's sun, fishing boats chugging past on their way to the docks.

"Weird," Beth said, referring to her evening with Alan. "It was weird, but okay. I never thought I'd get to a place where I could say that. If I just keep focusing on what an incredible pain in the ass Alan is, I can take him in small doses. And, I have to admit, he's still my best critic and supporter."

"Oh, please." Clarice brushed sand from her sunburned thighs and reached into the cooler for a beer. "There are so many people who could give you that. Me, for instance, or Ben."

"Ha."

"I'm serious. Want one of these?" She held up a Sam Adams, which Beth declined.

"I value your criticism, Clary, really, I do, but it's not the same and you know it. Alan knows painting and he knows me. He pushes me in ways I need to be pushed. He forces me to stretch and grow in ways I'd never think of on my own."

"Bullshit. It's time to get a new guru, dear friend, or if not a guru, at least a boyfriend."

"Fat chance around here." Beth rose, slipping out of her shorts. "I'm going for a swim. Wanna come?"

"A lot of exertion on such a beautiful night. Oh, I suppose so." Clarice set her open beer bottle into the ice at the side of the cooler. "Kids will knock this over the second they arrive, but I can't guzzle or I might sink."

They waded at the water's edge, shielding their eyes from the fiery rays of the sinking sun as they gazed west across the channel at Windy Harbor. A half an hour earlier, Ben had deposited them on the sheltered beach at the end of a long stretch of land known as the Spit. Every week or two, the group gathered and crossed the channel to the Spit for a cookout. There, they could watch the sun set behind the rooftops of the cottages around the harbor and feast on overdone hamburgers and salads, gritty with sand. Behind them the dunes stretched eastward to a smaller channel leading to the east branch of the river to the south; the mouth of the river yawned into the vast blue of the ocean beyond.

Silhouetted against the backdrop of the setting sun, the two women provided a sharp contrast to passersby. Beth, tall and slender, looked almost gaunt beside her pear-shaped, shorter friend.

"What a perfect night." Clarice sighed, echoing Beth's thoughts. "Let's float. The tide is coming in. We'll reach the docks about the time Ben heads back with the kids. What do you say?"

"I'm game," Beth replied, diving into the cool water. Tendrils of eelgrass tickled her stomach as she swam to deeper water. Turning back to shore, she saw Clarice still standing at the water's edge.

"Come on, Clary. It's delicious once you're in."

After hemming and hawing, Clarice eased in and paddled out to join her friend. Both strong swimmers, they swam hard to the middle of the channel and slipped into the current as it snaked its way around the river's neck and slithered inland. They stretched out and surrendered themselves to the current, letting the swiftly moving water carry them along. "The river's escalator," Nanny called it.

As they neared the docks, they spotted Ben's whaler pulling away from the pier so they swam hard to escape the current's grasp.

He waved and turned the boat in their direction. "Hey, you two!" Slowing down, he pulled up beside them. "What do you say, kids," he called over his shoulder. "Do we have room for two gorgeous mermaids?"

A chorus of "yeahs" rang out, but Beth wasn't convinced. "I don't know, Ben, you're pretty low in the water already. Why don't you take the kids over and come back for us?"

Her protests fell on deaf ears as hands reached over to hoist Clarice into the boat.

"Mother of God, woman." Ben groaned, as he heaved his wife up beside him.

"Not another word," Clarice said through clenched teeth, clearly forestalling any further reference to her weight.

"Come on, Mrs. Hadley. There's plenty of room."

Beth grabbed hold of the side of the boat and felt hands under her arms, lifting her easily from the water. Before she knew what was happening, Jack Talbot had deposited her on the side of the boat and Ben was calling for her to hold tight.

"Thanks," Beth said, smiling at Jack, her skin tingly as if he still held on to her.

"No problem."

For an instant, his gaze confused her. If he had been her age instead of thirty-something Beth would have sworn he was flirting with her. Ridiculous, she thought, surprised at herself.

"Hey, Talbot, you've been workin' out," Ben yelled over the engine's roar. His muscular body clad in a tee shirt and bright orange swim trunks, Ben turned the wheel and the whaler shuddered under the uneven weight of too many bodies. A full head taller than his wife, Ben still looked like the high school athlete he had been before giving up a promising football career. "You wait," Clary always said. "Gray hairs notwithstanding, when we're sixty, people will be mistaking me for his grandmother!"

CHAPTER 7

"He's desperately unhappy, you know," Clarice remarked as they pulled on sweatshirts.

Beth stared at her friend. "Who?"

"Alan, the stud," Clary said, resuming their previous conversation as if the swim and boat ride had never taken place.

It was one of her friend's habits, picking up discarded conversations, sometimes days later. Beth found it slightly disconcerting, but also endearing, as if their thoughts were entwined in the way of dear friends.

Clarice had never liked Alan. She thought him arrogant and full of himself, and he did have the irritating habit of critiquing people's work whether his opinion had been solicited or not.

"Ben tells me Chloe's practically living on campus. Spends all day and night there with her friends working on her "art." What a joke. Those monstrosities should have gotten her committed a long time ago."

"Clary, can we please not talk about Alan? We've been divorced for three years, remember? He's out of my life. If you want to gossip, can we please pick some other topic?"

"I'm sorry, hon. I do get carried away. Now, let's see, my mind is a blank, but hey, I almost forgot. How 'bout going to dinner with Ben and me Friday night? We're taking a friend of his from out of town to the Club. He's single, too. Mid-forties, cute as I recall."

"I don't know, Clary."

"Never mind thinking up an excuse, you're coming."

Beth laughed. "All right, if you put it that way. I'd love to."

"Just look at them," Clary said, watching a group of teenagers horsing around at the water's edge.

Ben had taken Nanny, Carrie, and some of the younger ones for a boat ride so the older ones were left ashore. Kit had brought six friends and Kat and Rob had two other couples in tow, one of them Clary and Ben's older son, Mike, and his girlfriend, Janelle.

Although he favored his mother in appearance, light-skinned, with reddish hair, Mike had his father's rugged athleticism. Beside him, Janelle, a lithe, dark-skinned beauty, looked fragile, waif-like, one bird-like arm wrapped round her boyfriend's bare-skinned waist. With the delicate features of the model she aspired to be, Janelle's short, cropped Afro highlighted her high forehead, prominent cheekbones and heart-shaped mouth. "Kissable," Clary called her. Affectionately, however, as she loved Janelle like a daughter and fretted constantly that the couple might break up and she would lose her.

After wolfing down burgers, the entire group walked up the beach, snatching a few beers as they departed. Clarice, self-proclaimed guardian of the cooler, had pretended not to notice.

"They're gorgeous, aren't they?"

"Sure are," Beth agreed. "Mike's really filled out this summer and Janelle, why, she's breathtaking. Can you believe, in a very short time, they'll be gone?"

"Speak for yourself, hon. I've still got younguns," she said, referring to their youngest two, Robert, who had just turned ten and Clark, eight years old. Clary and Ben had had their "bonus kids" well into their forties and Clark when she turned fifty.

"Oh, Clary, it's gonna be so hard when Kit goes, never mind when Nanny leaves and I have no one. Most people our age have grandchildren."

"You'll have me, dear heart. I'm not going anywhere." Clarice reached over and squeezed her arm. "Besides, they'll be back. Your kids are pretty attached to their home."

"I hope so," Beth whispered, more to herself than to Clary.

CHAPTER 8

Dinner Friday night proved more fun than Beth had anticipated. It had been months since she had dined in the Club's chintz and white wicker Summer Room. The food was delicious and Ben and Clary were two of the most engaging, articulate people she knew.

Their friend Frank from Syracuse, was a quiet, considerate dinner partner and good- looking, too. His longish, brown hair was perfectly groomed, a slight receding hairline adding, rather than detracting from his appearance. Alan and Ben favored wrinkled cotton summer shirts and Birkenstocks, but Frank wore crisp tan poplin, a blue dress shirt, conservative, striped tie and brown-laced oxfords. There was something solid and stable about Frank.

They were midway through the main course, chatting about her work, when Beth was startled by a familiar voice behind her.

"Well, hello."

"Hey, Graham." Clary rose to hug him, while Beth sat awestruck, unsure of what to do. "Two sightings in one week. Good to see you again."

"You, too." He shook Ben's hand, then Frank's.

Clarice stepped aside. "Of course, you know Beth."

"Yes, hello," he stammered, facing her at last.

"Graham, so good to see you. It's been a long time." As he bent, she stretched to kiss his cheek.

He towered over her, his lanky, awkward posture betraying the timidity lying beneath the carefully polished exterior. Her kiss appeared to embarrass him and he turned back to the others immediately engaging Ben, whom he knew only casually, in animated conversation. After several minutes, Graham apologized for interrupting their dinner and excused himself without as much as a glance in her direction.

"Wonder where Mary is," Clarice said, referring to Graham's wife. "He looks good, doesn't he? A little thin, but I hear he's quit drinking. Thank God. Last time we saw him in Chicago he was incredibly obnoxious. Seemed a little awkward around you," she whispered conspiratorially. "What gives? I thought you guys were best friends?"

Beth shrugged. "Graham's always been shy with women. Besides, he was Alan's friend, not mine."

As they drank cappuccino on the restaurant's terrace, everyone seemed to have forgotten Graham Lynch, except Beth. Tired of making small talk, she found herself unable to shake the hurt she felt at Graham's cold greeting. She wondered what she had done to deserve such an icy reception. Did he blame her, in some way, for Alan's desertion, or perhaps it was the awkwardness Graham had always exhibited around her? Why had she kissed him? Stupid, stupid, she thought as Frank took her arm and escorted her to the car.

"You okay?"

Beth realized that he had been talking for several minutes. "Sorry, just tired, I guess. It was very nice meeting you."

"Same here. I asked you a few minutes ago if you'd like to go out with me again sometime, but you were lost in thought. I get down this way every couple of months, what do you say?"

"Sure," she said, hopping into her car. As she backed the car out, tires crunching along the Club's long clamshell drive, she called, "Ben and Clary know how to reach me."

CHAPTER 9

Her sandals slapped the bricks like quacking ducks echoing over the fields. "Whoa, Mom, what's up?"

Beth paused at the grape arbor to wait for Kit to catch up. As he came alongside, she resumed her pace, walking faster than before. "You're welcome to come out to the studio, but I've got to get started. Nanny's at Carrie's and I have a full day of work ahead of me. I'm determined to be productive."

"I know, Mom, but can we talk for just a minute? I've got to go to work, but I need to ask you something." He took hold of her arm. "Please, I can't go all the way out to the studio or I'll be late."

"I'm sorry, Kit, I'm driven by unseen demons today. Of course, come on, sit. She settled on one of the stone benches that lined the path and he came to sit beside her.

"So, what's up?"

"Well, Kat was supposed to ask you, but she's gone to work."

The urgency of a moment ago seemed to have dissipated and Beth recognized the familiar hedging. He wanted something.

"It's about tomorrow night."

"Yes?"

"We thought, well, I mean, we were thinking we might, you know how you're always trying to get us to have the kids over and all? Well, we thought we'd take you up on the offer. You know, have a party here? No drinking, well, maybe just a few beers, but then no driving. Everyone lives close by and we'd be really careful.

I mean, I don't drink, but some of Kat's friends are over twenty-one so they'd probably have a few beers."

"I don't know, Kit. I'm happy to have the kids over, you know that, but the drinking is worrisome."

"We'll be okay, Mom. We've got it all worked out. You can take all the keys and check everyone before they leave."

"What about food?"

"No sweat; Kat and I'll do everything. We'll pick up some burgers and dogs, chips, sodas. That'll be easy. What do you say?"

"I suppose it's all right, but not too many people, okay? Don't go opening it up to the world like Pete did. What a mess that was."

Kit's friend Pete Cotter had hosted a party several weeks earlier that had drawn crowds from miles around. Over a hundred teenagers showed up, half of whom Pete had never seen before.

"Thanks, Mom. Gotta go. We'll talk more tonight, okay?" A quick peck on her cheek and he hopped up, headed for the drive.

Sucker, Beth thought, strolling now, all urgency gone. Rick would have to be satisfied with what she had. There were at least thirty paintings that might be worth showing and although she would probably complete a number of pieces over the summer, she wasn't going to kill herself for him or anyone. Besides, after Graham Lynch's chilly greeting the other evening, she didn't hold out much hope for a Lynch Gallery show.

As she entered the studio the phone was ringing and she ran to pick it up. "Hello!"

"Hello, yourself. Getting a late start, aren't you? What gives?"

"My life. How are you, agent extraordinaire?"

"Awful. Caught a bitch of a cold. Been nursing it, but still feeling punk."

"What about the trip to New York?"

"Postponed. We're goin' tomorrow instead."

"Well, I hope you're feeling better by then. Want me to cook up some chicken noodle soup and drop it off when I do errands later?"

"I most certainly do not. You're not to do anything but paint, paint, paint!"

"What about talking on the phone?"

"Ha-Ha. Just checking in before I take off tomorrow. Sniffles or no, we've got tickets to the Met, and Gary would never speak to me if we didn't go. "Aida." That's where I belong today, in a tomb.

"Now, what was I saying? Oh, yes. I'm gonna stop in Greenwich and see about a show there in October. Hedge our bets a little. Maybe we can get at least a few of your pieces in. Never got together with Margot Lynch, but now that junior's in charge, I'm getting ready to sink my claws into him. He has to be easier to deal with than his bitch of a mother. I've left him a slew of messages and when I get back I'll drag him out to take a look at your stuff."

"I don't know, Rick. I'm not hopeful about that. Maybe we should forget about Lynch."

"No way! Junior is gonna look at your work and beg for the opportunity to show you. If he doesn't, well, then fuck 'em. I'll arrange everything, sweetie. Don't you worry."

"Uh-huh."

"My other phone's ringin', doll. Get right to it now, will you? No sipping tea or chatting on the phone. And whatever you do, stay away from that Clarice. She's a terrible time waster. As for your ex, well you know how I feel about him. Beth, he's been calling me night and day for the past week and I need you to call him off."

"Bye, Rick," she said, setting down the phone.

CHAPTER 10

She was working on a landscape, a view across the harbor she had discovered on a walk with Nanny near the south shore. Working from photographs and numerous small studies, she was slowly bringing Stone Hill Farm's fields to life on her canvas. Two thirds of the painting was sky, a towering expanse of blue punctuated by fluffy white clouds. The vast blueness both embraced and dwarfed the meadow below it and the boundaries of earth and sky seemed to grow fuzzier as one gazed at the painting. Beth had always favored "big skies," which is how Rick described them. They gave her landscapes a unique perspective that critics often remarked upon.

At around one, she took a break to go up to the house for lunch and a fifteen-minute rest. After a bowl of yogurt and fruit, she stretched out in the sun on her favorite chaise with its soft green canvas cushions. She always napped at midday, just for fifteen minutes. It was a habit she had gotten into after Nanny's birth and she relied on the brief respite to collect her thoughts, dozing in a kind of half-sleep, as she planned the remainder of the day. Alan teased her about her "siestas," but her naps enabled her to work well into the night, if need be. When her children had been young those evening hours had been precious.

As her mind inched back toward consciousness, she felt cool, realizing with a start that the sun had disappeared. Expecting to see a cloud above her, she jumped as she opened her eyes to find someone standing over her. "Jack. My goodness, you startled me." Heart beating, she stared for a moment unsure if she was awake or dreaming.

"I'm sorry, Mrs. H., I didn't mean to scare you."

He blushed, but rather than staring at his toes as Kit would have done, the dark eyes returned her gaze. There it was again, that look. Beth sat up, feeling exposed and vulnerable. What was it? Longing? Flirtation? Impossible, but what *was* happening between them?

"Jack, why aren't you at work?"

The moment passed and he shifted his gaze. She was back to being his friend's mom and Beth breathed a sigh of relief.

"Oh, sorry. Kit sent me to get his, I mean Mr. Hadley's skill saw. Can I go out to the shop and grab it?"

"Of course. You probably know better than I where to find it. Do you mind going alone? I've got to get back to the studio."

"Sure, no problem." Still he stood over her.

As Beth rose and grabbed her empty glass and sunglasses unease crept over her again. "Okay, then," she said, smiling. "Is that all you need?"

"Yup. Thanks. Sorry if I woke you." He blushed again. "It's just that you looked so peaceful and I was trying to figure out whether to just go out to the shop and take the saw or disturb you."

"That's okay. I needed to get up anyway." Just how long had he been standing there? "Be sure to tell Kit to be careful with the saw. His father's very particular about his tools. He'd better bring it home tonight, even if you need it again tomorrow, okay?"

"Yeah, sure. Thanks."

He turned away. Beth watched until he disappeared around the lilacs at the side of the house, noticing his strong back and broad shoulders.

Late afternoon sunlight played along the studio's west windows as she cleaned her brushes. A soft knock at the side door of the studio startled her. As she approached the door with a handful of dripping brushes wrapped in a terry cloth rag, she spied Graham Lynch standing in the shadows.

"Hello, Beth."

"Why Graham? I mean, how did you? Oh, so sorry, come in!"

"Thanks. I know you're working, so I won't take but a few minutes."

"It's fine, really. I'm just finishing up for the day. Please, sit and I'll get rid of these. Would you like iced tea, juice, and seltzer? I'm afraid there's not much out here."

"Tea would be great, if it's no trouble."

She rooted around and unearthed two marginally serviceable glasses, which she rinsed and filled with ice and the bottle of sun tea she kept in the fridge during the summer months.

She handed him the tea and settled in a chair across from his. "So, what brings you here?" Although she had slipped off her painting shirt, she was acutely aware of her disheveled appearance and brushed back wisps of hair, all the while trying to be nonchalant about the unexpected visit.

"Your paintings; Gould has called at least twenty times a day. Where'd he come from anyway? I don't remember him."

Reference to the past reminded Beth that she had never been alone with Graham. She had never trusted herself to be alone with him. In those days, his eyes invariably found hers in a sea of friends. Even across a crowded room, their attraction to each other had been palpable. Most of the time she would look away, but now, sitting beside him, it wasn't so easy.

"Alan found him, of course." She laughed, endeavoring to ignore the unspoken messages flying between them. "How's Mary?"

"I'd really like to see your work. Have you a few minutes now to show me? If not I can make an appointment to come back."

That was Graham, no superfluous conversation, no small talk.

"Of course." Hopping up, she bumped her glass and he reached forward and caught it, his hand brushing against her side.

"They're all here. Not in any special order or arrangement. I'm afraid I haven't many. About thirty, but there are probably a number of them that aren't worth showing. I have a couple at the framers and Rick has two or three."

He spent the next half hour slowly making his way through the stacked canvases lining the walls of the studio. He made a few comments, took an occasional note, but did not invite further conversation. Beth followed him for a while, and then left him alone and busied herself with straightening up her work area.

Finally, after studying the paintings that hung on the walls, he said, "Any more in the house?"

"A dozen, maybe, but they're not for sale."

"You could show them anyway, if they're recent. What are they, portraits of the kids, a few decorator still-life pictures?"

His sarcasm made her angry. "It doesn't matter. I don't want to sell or show them."

"Fine. So?"

"So you tell me."

Suddenly, he was smiling, genuinely smiling. For an instant, his nervousness, the combative insecurity that had fed his alcoholism and which he masked behind the well-practiced façade of indifference, disappeared and Beth caught a glimpse of their friend from long ago. "That's right, almost forgot. I'm the gallery director, aren't I?"

"That's what I hear."

When he smiled, his gaunt, chiseled features softened. In his sixties, he was still a very handsome man.

"How's November for you?"

"You mean you'll have me?"

"Right now I can give you a qualified yes. There are probably fifteen paintings here, maybe twenty, which are worth showing. The rest seem a little flat and lifeless. The one on the easel shows promise, but we'll need to see more depth to justify a one-woman show. What are your summer plans?"

"Painting, painting, painting."

"Good, so let's wait till early fall to decide, okay? I mean, we'll have you either way, but there's a woman, Joan Pilmer, who does watercolors too. Do you know her?"

"Yes." She hated Joan Pilmer's work, all pastel seashells and windswept beaches.

"Well, perhaps you could exhibit together? Mother tells me she sells remarkably well. Pretty insipid stuff from what I've seen, but tourists will buy anything."

"In November?"

"We'll see. My preference is to give you the show alone. I'm not too keen on Joan's stuff as I said, but she's one of Mother's pet projects. We'll need to reassess in September. Mother's pretty adamant about profits right now and not as willing to take risks with all the advance publicity, engraved invitations, and glossy brochures, whatever. The show's got to pay off at the other end."

"I'll see what I can do."

"Great, now I will get out of your hair."

"Did you park up at the house?"

He nodded.

"I'll walk you back."

As they passed under the arbor at the edge of the backyard, he said, "This is an incredible place you two created. It's changed since the last time I was here, the fruits of all you labor paying off."

"Lots of upkeep."

"How is he?"

"You know Alan, nothing gets him down for long. He'd love to see you."

"Probably not."

"Yes, he would, Graham. Really. He only recently told me about your falling out. I'll bet he's missed you since he—"

"Walked out on you for Suzie Coed?"

"Her name is Chloe, and she's not bad, once you get to know her. She'd love you, too. You're just Chloe's type."

"A broken down alcoholic? Doesn't speak very well for her." He stared at her for several seconds, and then said quietly, "He was an idiot for leaving you."

Don't start, please. I cannot have this conversation, especially with you. "Have you moved back to the Harbor for good?"

"Maybe. I'm still back and forth to Chicago, kinda feeling this out for a while to see what happens."

What about Mary, she thought, but kept the question to herself.

They had reached his silver gray BMW looking sleek and spotless in the drive. "Call Alan. He'd like to hear from you. It would mean a lot to him."

"Maybe."

"Graham, please don't continue this vendetta against Alan on my account. I'm fine and you two were friends long before I came along."

"He's an asshole, Beth. He's always been a self-absorbed prick. He really screwed up leaving you and the kids."

"Believe it or not, it's worked out for the best." Startled, she realized that she finally believed the words she had uttered so many times over the last few years. "I'm happy and the kids are great. Kit took it the worst, predictably, but everything's better now. Alan and I had drifted apart before Chloe. You hadn't seen us much during the years before the break-up. Things had changed. We'd gone our separate ways. We've made it work. The first year was terrible, but we've settled into a kind of civility. It helps keep the kids even and happy."

"Sounds idyllic."

Sarcasm again. His words cut deeper than she would have expected. "It's not, but, it's the best we can do. I've found I like the solitude, most of the time anyway."

"You're lucky."

"Give Alan a call, please."

"Keep painting. I'll put you down for late November and check in from time to time. As I said, my preference would be for you to show alone, so let me know if you need anything, will you? Also, do let me know if you change your mind about the paintings in the house and I'll come take a look."

CHAPTER 11

I can't believe you're sitting here so calmly while sixty or seventy teenagers rampage through your house." Clarice waved her glass of iced coffee, sloshing some down the front of herself.

"Twenty is more like it, maybe thirty," Beth replied. "They're responsible kids. Besides, I have all their keys right here in my purse. I can't stay too long. Let's order, okay?"

They sat in a booth in the back room of the Common's Lunch, a favorite meeting place when neither wanted to cook. When their children had been small, the two families would often meet and cram into three or four booths, completely taking over the restaurant's small back room. The "Lunch" as the locals called it, was situated at the edge of the village green, next to the post office and the Ogden's General Store. Despite its name, the restaurant was open for breakfast, lunch, and dinner.

It was unusual for the two women to be there on a Saturday night. Saturday was Ben and Clary's date night, but he was out of town, staying the weekend in Providence to care for his ailing father and give his mother a much-needed break. Ben and his siblings knew it would be only a month or two before they moved their father to a nursing home, but they were giving their mother time. She wasn't quite ready to let go. The siblings had been taking turns helping her and this was Ben's weekend.

They ordered lobster rolls and were sharing a warm spinach salad. As Betty, the waitress, arrived with the huge bowl of greens, Beth asked, "How is Ben's dad anyway?"

"Anything else, girls?"

"No, but since you called us girls, we're doubling your tip." Clary laughed. "Thanks, Bet, this looks great."

Clary waited for Betty to turn away before answering. "It's a nightmare. Mama Rollins is about to have a breakdown and Ben's relationship with Alexis and Pat is starting to get strained. Old Ben yells, screams, wets his pants constantly and refuses to wear diapers. He's completely demented, but unfortunately his abuse is right on target. He hits people where it hurts most. Patty is so sensitive about her weight and he's been calling her a "fat cow" and every horrible name you can think of. Ben seems to fare the best since he just gets up and walks out of the room when his father starts in."

"Is he still having little strokes?"

"Constantly, but there's nothing the doctors can do. He is on blood thinners and all kinds of meds, but half the time he refuses to take any of them."

"How awful for Ben. I hope I go like my dad. This lingering on, the dementia taking everything from Mother is horrendous."

"How is Hestor?"

"Same. Lanie and I still go every Sunday and the kids go when they can. Kat usually goes twice a week and sings to her, braids her hair and keeps her company. They've always been very close. I'm not sure she knows any of us anymore.

"She's always asking, "Where are Bethie and Lanie?" That's about all she says anymore, that and "chocolate." She still loves Reese's Peanut Butter Cups. They allow her to have two a day so we bring the week's supply with us and they dole them out each day. She's still so beautiful, Clary. Even at ninety-two, her skin is flawless, barely a wrinkle. Her hair is white, but it's still so thick." Beth let out a sigh.

"I've already told Ben to slip me the cyanide capsule when I start to fade. These lobster rolls are amazing, aren't they? Why don't I order this every time we come here? Uh oh." Clary set down her fork, eyes darting from Beth toward the front of the restaurant. "Guess who just came in?"

Beth didn't have to look. "Alan."

"Afraid so. Headed right this way with Barbie doll in tow."

"Well, if it isn't Betty and Veronica hanging out at the soda shop. How'd you get away from Ben tonight?"

"He's in Providence helping care for his dad."

"How is Ben Senior anyway?"

"Not great."

Never one to be ignored, Chloe popped her head around her husband. "Hi, Clary. Hi, Beth." She wore skin-tight leggings in shimmering, metallic silver and a diaphanous mauve silk blouse knotted at the waist to reveal several inches of firm, bare flesh. Her long, blond hair fell loose over her shoulders offering a slight concession to modesty, as she was clearly not wearing a bra. Shiny black ankle boots completed the outfit, which although garish and slightly out of season, looked great on her.

"Hello," Beth said.

"Mrs. Hadley." Clary nodded taking a bite of her lobster roll.

"Haven't seen you and Ben for ages," Chloe continued. "You'll have to come for dinner with Alan and me real soon."

"When are you ever home for dinner?" Alan's eyes blazed for an instant, then softened as he turned back to them. "Artists, you know how it goes. We'll let you two get on with your dinner. Come on, hon, let's sit up in front."

"But I wanted to—"

"Come on." He grabbed hold of her elbow.

"The honeymoon appears to be over," Clary whispered, winking at Beth. "Did you see the look he gave her?"

Beth nodded, but said nothing. In all the years she had known Alan, she could never remember him looking at anyone the way he had just glared at his young wife. It almost looked like hatred.

Later, they made their way to the door and nodded goodbye to Alan and Chloe, but did not stop to chat. On the sidewalk, they ran into Lily Babcock sweeping out of Harbor Video, her chauffeur waiting at the open door of her powder blue Lincoln Town car.

"Caught ya," Clary called, waving.

"Why, my dears, what a pleasant surprise. Of course, these are all educational documentaries," she said, winking as she handed a stack of videos to William, her driver.

"We know, don't we, Beth? Cruising that adult section again, finding the few steamy flicks you haven't watched?"

"Clarice, you are quite rude and naughty. Come give me a kiss. You, too, Beth dear."

"Hello, Lily," Beth said, stooping to kiss the wizened cheek. "How are you?"

"As well as one can be at ninety-two dear. I get by; let's put it that way. But, I've recently heard some news that'll keep me going until November anyway."

"Oh?" Beth asked, taking the bait.

"I've heard about your show, my dear, so deserved, and so late in coming. Why, that Margot Lynch doesn't know art from garbage."

"Lily, who told you about the show?"

"I have my sources."

"Well, it's not definite, so your sources are misinformed."

"Oh, my dear, no need to play coy with me. I own six of your paintings already. You don't expect your nice Mr. Gould would pull my leg about such a thing now, do you?"

Thinking she would certainly wring Mr. Gould's neck next time she saw him, Beth smiled. By the end of the week, thanks to Lily, the whole village would know.

"Lily, try to keep it to yourself, won't you? It really isn't definite, despite Mr. Gould's assertions, and it will be very embarrassing if it doesn't happen."

"Of course, my dear. You know I can keep a secret. Now, William and I better toddle on home before I catch my death standing out here in this breeze."

They waved as the Lincoln inched smoothly away from the curb, Beth muttering about the slow death she planned for Rick.

CHAPTER 12

Clary announced that she needed a peek at the party so they drove to Beth's together. Strains of Police and *Roxanne* boomed out of the windows as they mounted the steps from the drive. Beth wondered where the kids had positioned the stereo's speakers and hoped Bob and Edna Dailey, their closest neighbors, had removed their hearing aids for the evening. As they stepped onto the terrace, the music was almost deafening. Beth spied the speakers set into the windows that faced the back yard. Bodies were everywhere, lying on the chaises, sitting on the walls, stretched out on blankets on the grass. Most were talking and drinking, a few held plates of food and several couples had long since abandoned food for more interesting pursuits. The grill still smoked, but appeared to be abandoned so she replaced the lid and closed the vents. Neither Kit nor Kat were in sight.

"Hey, Mrs. H.," a voice from the grass called and Beth turned to spy Mike and Janelle sitting on a blanket, half-eaten plates of food at their sides. "Uh, oh, you, too, Mom."

"In the flesh, buster, so you'd better be behaving."

"Jesus," Mike muttered, rolling his eyes and turning back to Janelle.

"Clary, you don't always have to embarrass him to death, you know."

"I know, but he loves it. Besides, I won't stay long, just long enough to make the rounds."

Beth thought she heard "thank God" as they made their way indoors.

A quick survey of the family room told her kids had respected her wishes. People were sitting around listening to music and talking. She had made them promise not to use the living room and the upstairs was also off limits. She noticed Kat and Rob on the couch and waved.

"Hey, Mom; hey, Mrs. R. Couldn't stay away, could ya?"

"You better believe it, Katie-Kins! Rob, watch those hands. Her mom and I are packing tape measures."

They laughed, but Beth noticed Rob's arm slid from around Kat's shoulders into his lap. She poked Clary and rolled her eyes at Kat. "Everything under control?"

"Sure. It's great."

"Where's your brother?"

"In the kitchen."

The kitchen had not fared quite as well as the family room. Food was everywhere: open bags of chips, vegetable peelings, slices of tomatoes, ice cream cartons open and melting, dirty dishes, platters dripping with meat juices, wads of damp paper towels, and empty brown bags scattered over the counters and floor, some with food yet unpacked, already mixed with the trash. Kit stood by the sink, slicing a huge watermelon in the company of at least a dozen teenagers. They were spread out at various spots in the large, open room, perched on stools at the horseshoe-shaped counter, preparing food, eating or just standing around talking.

"Mom, hi! I know it's a mess, but don't worry we'll clean it up."

"I'm not worried," she lied.

"Hi, Mrs. H, Mrs. R." Jack sat at the counter a paper plate piled with food before him. "Just got finished cooking. Time to eat."

"I covered the grill. Are you done with it?"

"Yup, thanks, Mom."

"Well, we'll get out of your hair. Tell Kat I'll be out in the studio. If anyone needs keys, they'll have to come out and talk to me. And, Kit, be careful with those speakers, will you? You better turn them down a little or Mr. and Mrs. Dailey won't speak to us tomorrow."

"Look." Clary nudged her, pointing toward the open door. "They're dancing out on the grass. What 'dya say? Wanna help me embarrass Mike a little more?"

"No."

"Come on, you chicken." Clary was already dragging Beth by the elbow out to where a dozen or so dancers moved to the Rolling Stones' *Dead Flowers*. Beth had barely stepped onto the lawn with the CD random playing, when Clary elbowed her saying, "Move, girl."

Giggly and nervous at first, Beth soon gave herself over to the rhythm of a song she hadn't heard in many years.

"See, it's great, huh?" Clary yelled, dancing around her, clapping her hands.

Mike and Janelle had disappeared. Bruce Springsteen's *Rosalita* followed *Dancing in the Dark* and the crowd grew to thirty or forty wildly gyrating bodies.

As the song reached its crescendo, Beth started inching toward the edge of the crows, deciding she had had enough. Clary grabbed her back into the fray just as the Temptations came on with *My Girl.*

"Great music," Clary yelled in her ear, grasping her firmly around the waist. "I'll lead."

Beth laughed, draping her arm over her friend's shoulder. They seemed to be the only couple not plastered to one another.

"Relax," Clary bellowed, just as a hand tapped Beth on the shoulder.

"Can I cut in?" Jack stood behind them grinning. "Do you mind, Mrs. R.?"

"Not at all, although I am a bit insulted. I'll just have to round up that son of mine, now where did he get to?" Clary disappeared, leaving them alone.

Beth considered declining, making her escape while Clary was otherwise occupied, but instead she held out her hand and he clasped it, shyly bringing his other to rest on her waist.

Conscious of every one of his fingers pressing into her side, Beth brought her hand to his shoulder and they began a slow, tentative turn neither looking at one another. Although she held him at arm's length, his body heat washed over her like liquid fire and Beth found herself suddenly weak in the knees. What was happening? This was Jack Talbot, the boy she had raised right along with her own children.

The undulating crowd grew thicker, dancers all around them now, lost in the heat of passion. Each time they were bumped or jostled, he drew a little closer, his hand moving from her side to the small of her back, his chest finally brushing against her breasts. As his cheek grazed her own, his hair damp as it tickled her temple, the song ended and Beth pulled away, breathless.

"Thanks, Jack." Flustered, she turned away, not wanting him to see her expression. "I'd better go find Mrs. Rollins before she gets herself into trouble."

Grateful for the darkness that hid her blushing, she hurried off. What had just happened? Had it been so long since she'd been with a man that a boy could arouse her with a touch? Craziness, that's what it was. What would Jack think if he knew his shy, tentative shuffle had brought her to such a feverish state?

"I'm jealous," Clary called, intercepting her at the edge of the crowd. "I'd stay, too, and make Jack dance with me, but I've got to get home. Unless of course you'd like to take another turn?"

"Thanks, but I've had enough."

Beth laughed, recovering herself. Standing next to her friend, watching the pulsating throng, she shrugged, deciding that her overactive imagination had taken a weird turn. Nothing more.

"Well, I'm off, then."

"What are you talking about, I brought you! I'll go get my car keys and drive you back."

"No, no. I'm taking the jeep. My darling son was holding a beer can last time I saw him and I've instructed him to either find a ride home or sleep on your floor. He's supposed to call if he stays here, okay?"

"Fine with me. I have his keys in my bag. I'll check on him at the end of the night."

"Don't worry. I have a key on my ring." Clary hugged her. "I know as soon as I leave you, you are heading right back to the dance floor, you party girl!"

"Goodnight, Clary."

She waved to her friend, then retrieved her book and a sweater from her room, grabbed her purse filled with keys and headed out to the studio, glad to escape the crunch of bodies and deafening music. She would give them until eleven thirty, and then head back to survey the situation. If things weren't out of hand she intended to allow the party to go until one, then shoo everyone out who could drive. The remainder could stay and sleep on the floor.

Halfway along the path, she stopped and sat on a bench. The first chords of Jimi Hendrix' *Purple Haze* drifted across the fields. She gazed up to a clear sky blanketed with stars. Alan was always dragging them out to the garden to star gaze. An amateur astronomer, he could identify almost any constellation in the sky. He would point from star to star as Beth and the children huddled in blankets listening. Beth's contribution, when she could get a word in edgewise, was the occasional telling of a myth, about the hunter, Orion or Castor and Pollax.

Closing her eyes, she could hear Alan's voice, "Come on, Kit, remember that one? I showed it to you last time we were out? That's right, Cassiopeia." Despite all that had happened, her memories of those evenings were happy ones. She wondered if Alan still took Nanny out to "watch the stars" when she stayed overnight. Nanny was the only one of their three children who spent the night at "Chloe's."

Finally, she stood, stretched and wandered slowly along the path to the studio. The wind had changed direction and a gentle breeze thick with the scent of honeysuckle and wild roses rustled through the miniature dogwood trees on either side of the path that led to the studio's side door. She breathed deeply before stepping inside. Flipping on the lights, she was relieved to find that the music was muffled to a whisper inside her sanctuary. Before settling down with her book, she circled the room and gazed critically at the paintings hanging on the walls. Graham was right, they were flat. Flat and safe, not a hint of passion or fire. She had tried so hard over the past few years to repress the hurt of Alan's rejection that she seemed to have closed the door on all of her feelings. Turning away in disgust, she plunked down on the sofa and lost herself in her detective novel.

CHAPTER 13

So engrossed was she in the exploits of Ricky Steele, the female private eye in her favorite series, that she didn't hear the knock at first. As the rapping became more insistent however, she set down her book and went to the door assuming it was one of the partygoers retrieving their keys.

"Jack, what are you doing out here? Is everything all right?"

"Yeah, everything is fine."

"You're not ready to go home this early, are you?"

"No, of course not! I promised Kit I'd stay and help clean up. No, I just wanted to…can I come in?"

"Of course." She stepped aside to let him pass. He smelled of hickory smoke from his stint at the grill. As he brushed by her the smell was chokingly sweet and Beth wondered why she had failed to notice it while they were dancing.

"Want a soda or some tea or something?"

"No, thanks."

"And why aren't you over there, enjoying the party?"

As she spoke, Beth sat on the sofa and shoved away thoughts of their dance and the feel of his hands moving along her back, pulling her closer and closer and closer.

He sat in the rocker several feet away, momentarily losing his balance as the chair tipped backwards. "Careful." She laughed. "That's one of Mr. Hadley's earlier pieces and it's a little unsteady. So, what brings you out here when you should be back having a good time with the others?"

"I just needed a break, that's all. I know everyone thinks I act like I'm eighteen but sometimes it doesn't quite fit, you know? Everyone is pairing up and I'm not. I mean, I don't have a girlfriend."

"Is that why you asked an old lady like me to dance?" Her nervous laugh echoed in the silence of the room.

He shrugged.

"What about Kit?"

"Well, he and Karen took a walk. They're somewhere around."

"Karen? I didn't know."

"Yeah, well she's kinda been chasing him."

Jack blushed and Beth decided to change the subject rather than test the bounds of friendship with further inquiries concerning her son's love life. "How are your parents doing? I haven't seen your mom all summer."

"She's fine. They both are. Summer is Dad's busiest time and my mother's either at work or in her garden."

Jack's father, Ed Talbot, was a lobsterman and his mother, Sue, the Town Clerk. They rarely took vacations and even more rarely indulged in the harbor's familiar leisure time pursuits like golf, tennis or sailing. They kept to themselves, their social life revolving around a large extended family.

"How's the lobstering?"

"Great. He's had record catches most weeks. Says it can't last though."

"One of your brothers works with him, doesn't he?"

"Jimmy. They have two boats. Over a hundred pots now."

"Not you though?"

"No way. Dad and I do fine on land, but we've never been too compatible in a boat."

Beth laughed and watched him, still wondering what had brought him to the studio. Clary was right, like all his contemporaries, he was beautiful. Beautiful, yet still young enough at thirty to be awkward.

"Mrs. H., can I ask you something?"

"Of course."

"There's a big age difference between Mr. Hadley and Mrs. Hadley, the second Mrs. Hadley, I mean?"

"Yes," she replied, surprised at his question. "Chloe is still in her twenties. In other words, younger than me, and Mr. Hadley is sixty-something, right?

"Why do you ask?"

"No reason, just curious." He blushed, suddenly interested in the paintings on the walls. There it was, that look again.

"All set for college?"

"No, but I guess I'm going. It's going to be weird, you know, being a freshman and so much older than my fellow students."

"I'm sure you'll find peers. It's a big pool. Kit told me you were all excited about Harvard; that you'd already spoken to your roommate?"

"Yeah, nice guy, older like me. We're getting together in a couple of weeks. He lives on the Cape in the summer. I'm okay about going, it's just, I don't know. I'm not like the others. I've never been away from home except for a week at soccer camp. I mean, my parents can drive me crazy sometimes, but I don't even like going away for the weekend."

"Kit's never been away either."

"Yeah, but he meets people so easily, it's harder for me. And I don't know if I'll be able to handle the work at Harvard. I mean, I thought it was what I wanted, what I've been working for these past fifteen years, but now I'm not sure anymore. It means so much to my parents, but I'm not sure. I feel like I got pushed and shoved into something that's not going to be right for me."

"You're not alone. Almost everyone feels that way before they head off to college, no matter what age. It's new, lots of unknowns, but you'll be fine once you get there. You've got a wonderful scholarship. Once you're in the swing of things, Harvard won't be any harder than anywhere else."

"I don't have a clue what I want to do. You'd think after all this time I'd have a plan, but I don't. I've been taking courses for years at UMass Dartmouth, trying to figure it out, find my passion, you know? But, I find myself in the same place I was at eighteen with no idea what I want. So why go to college?"

"To discover, to try out new things, to learn and maybe to find your passion. Harvard is an amazing place and to be in Boston will be incredible."

"You know what's amazing? Your paintings."

"Thanks."

"I like to draw. I've never tried painting."

"You should. Kit tells me your drawings are really good."

"Do you think two people who are very different ages could have a meaningful relationship?"

"Are you talking about Alan again?" She knew he wasn't.

"Actually, I'm wondering about a man and an older woman." His eyes met hers.

"Depends on the people, I guess. Jack, it's getting kind of late. I'd better get over to the house. Wanna walk me back?"

"What I'm asking is about you and me. If we could ever be together?"

"Jack, be serious." She knew he was. "I'm Kit's mother."

"You're also the most beautiful and interesting woman I know."

"That's why you need to get out of this small town and meet more people."

"I think I'm in love with you."

"It's very nice of you to say."

"No, I know it, I'm sure of it. I'm in love with you."

"Jack, I am flattered, but it's out of the question."

"Why?"

"Because you are my son's dearest friend, and *I* am not in love with you. Now, we really should get back. You don't want to miss the rest of the party and I've gotta get these keys back. Her hands trembled as she reached for the light switch next to the door. As she switched off the light, he came alongside her and pushed open the door. She stepped ahead of him, hoping the cool breeze might sharpen her senses and clear her head.

Half running, half walking, she had just passed under the grape arbor leading into the back yard, when he grabbed hold of her arm.

"I was serious."

Low and urgent, his voice startled her. Beth felt as if her knees might buckle beneath her. An instant later, he let go and she hurried on, afraid to look back.

After catching her breath, she hurried into the house to find Kat and Rob wrapped around each other on the living room sofa.

"Sorry, Mom."

Her eldest popped up, pulled down her tee shirt and adjusted her shorts. Another few minutes and she would have been naked. "We're the only ones who've been in here, honest. Where's Kit?"

"Don't know, but it's time to start cleaning up. Everyone out in an hour or so, okay?"

The next hour went by in a haze of faces as Beth checked people's condition before returning keys or arranging rides for those not up to driving. Kit and Kat, with Rob's help, were still cleaning the kitchen when she said goodnight and headed up to bed. Jack had vanished.

CHAPTER 14

Sunday morning. Cooking smells, bacon and hazelnut roast, wafted up from the kitchen rousing Beth from a fitful sleep. All night she had tossed and turned, pushing away thoughts of the previous evening. What had happened with Jack? He must have been drunk, yes, that was it. His condition, however, did not explain her feelings and she wondered if her attraction was a subconscious need to hold on to Kit. In the light of day, the entire episode seemed surreal, as if her imagination had been playing tricks on her. Much as she had tried to chalk the experience up to imagination, her feelings lingered. She felt a strange, aching desire not unlike the early days with Alan.

Dressing quickly, she realized how much she needed Meeting for Worship. An hour of silence among Friends would restore her equilibrium and help her to think more clearly. As she descended the stairs, she could hear conversation from the back of the house and considered slipping out the front door. Then, Kat's irresistible laugh rose above the hum and she turned toward the kitchen.

The room was back to normal, almost. Rob, Pete, Kit, and Ginny sat round the counter, sipping coffee and talking amiably as Kat flipped pancakes on the griddle. Most of them looked a little green around the gills. All except Pete, whom they were teasing for falling asleep at eleven o'clock. Dark-haired with deep blue eyes, Pete towered over his friends at six four. Not entirely comfortable with his recent acquired height, he often slouched as he did now, awkward and unsure standing beside Ginny, Kat's closest friend.

Perky, freckled-faced Ginny was almost two years older than Pete and about to begin her sophomore year at Skidmore. Like many teenage girls, Ginny was too thin, in Beth's opinion. While the others wolfed down their pancakes, Ginny moved hers around on the plate. In designer shorts and matching blouse, her raven hair held back with a tortoise shell headband, Ginny looked many years older than Pete, who wore torn blue jeans and a ripped tee shirt and had the wide eyes and boyish grin of a ten-year-old.

"Hi, Mom, want some? We've got plenty." Kat stood at the stove in a nightshirt, barefooted, spatula in hand. As she turned, pushing her hair from her face, drops of oil dripped from the spatula to the floor. Jasper was right under her ready to lap up the drips.

"Thanks, but I'm on my way to Meeting. Anyone want to come?"

"Not today." Kit groaned, still half-asleep. Of all her children, Kit attended Meeting most regularly. In fact, he had already located an active Meeting within striking distance of Bowdoin.

All her children had gone through the First Day School program and were members of Windy Harbor's Meeting. Kat had begun to drift away after high school. Just recently, Nanny had begun to show impatience in the silence. After a recent sleepover, she announced to her mother that her friend Marcie's Episcopal Church was much more interesting. A birthright Quaker, Beth found great spiritual comfort in the communal silence of the Meeting, but had never pushed her religion on her children. Alan had been raised a Catholic, but supported the children's participation in the First Day School and frequently attended Meeting himself during their marriage. Chloe was a Buddhist so the Meeting House had seen less of him since their marriage.

"Did all you spend the night?"

Reading her thoughts, Rob said, "Don't worry, Mrs. H., I stayed in Kit's room."

"I can vouch for that," Pete piped in. "He took the bed and shoved me on the floor!"

"You would've been there anyway," Ginny Tripp said, elbowing him. Until college, Kat and Ginny had been inseparable. This summer they both had jobs at a local arts camp. Ginny and Pete had spent many of the same nights at the Hadley's and treated each other like brother and sister.

"Probably right." Pete grinned. "If it wasn't Rob giving me the boot, it would have been Talbot. He always hogs the bed."

"What happened to Jack anyway?" Kat asked, turning to her brother. "I thought he was staying to help clean up."

"Dunno. He was acting really weird last night. Then he just disappeared around midnight. Did you see him, Pete?"

"Nope, but I was busy chasing Nancy around the yard at that point."

"That's my exit cue." Beth laughed. "I'll see you all later."

Beth slipped out the kitchen door and was halfway to the drive, her stomach tied in knots at the mention of Jack, when Kat caught up to her for a hug. "Thanks, Mom, it was really fun."

"I'm glad."

"You okay? You look kinda funny. Are you sick?"

'No, just a wee bit tired. One o'clock is past my bedtime, as you know!"

"By the way," she added as Kat turned away, "that nightshirt is see-through!" Kat smiled and disappeared into the house.

CHAPTER 15

The rustling around her told Beth that she wasn't the only uncomfortable person in the room. The heat in the Meeting House was unbearable. Sitting in silence on the straight-backed wooden benches, Beth usually found peace and precious moments of spiritual retreat. Not today. Although the windows were open, not a trace of a breeze stirred the curtains or tickled the flushed cheeks of the worshipers. The press of bodies raised the room's temperature at least ten degrees. Beth gazed around at the elders, convinced that one or more might faint before silence was broken. Only two people felt moved to speak. Their voices almost rippled in the sweltering waves of heat. The first, Sally Butterworth, shared her uncle's misfortunes and her prayers for his family. The second, Richard Paine, a frequent speaker, shared an epiphany concerning grandchildren and the rewards of old age.

Shortly after noon, she emerged damp and fretful, Constance Bicknell at her side. "Don't forget about our business meeting on Thursday next, my dear. By the way, thy look peaked, Beth. Is it the heat? Wilt thou stop back for a glass of lemonade on the veranda?"

"Thanks, Constance, but I'll be fine once I'm in the car with the breeze blowing. The heat was awful though, wasn't it? Like an oven. I don't think I've ever been so uncomfortable in a Meeting."

"Nor I, my dear, but thy face looks troubled. Can I help?"

"No, I'm okay, really." Disconcerted by the old Quaker's perspicuity, she forced a smile. "Didn't get as much sleep as I needed last night, that's all. I'd love that lemonade, but I'm on my way to meet Lanie. We're going up to see Mother."

"Oh, my dear Hestor, how is she?"

"About the same."

"Does she know thee?"

"We think so, but then she doesn't say much anymore. She always seems happy to see us though. That makes the visits joyful."

"Oh, if only I could've kept her." Constance gestured with trembling hands.

"Please don't trouble yourself. She's happy at the home, really she is, and you know how she hates to be a bother to anyone. We made her a promise, remember? You, Lanie, and I promised that we'd take her when she needed overnight care."

"I know, dear, but we loved sharing the apartment all those years. The place seems so empty without her. Marsha and Kenny have been at me to move in with them, but so far I've resisted. I love my grandsons, but you know teenagers."

"I do that." Beth smiled, reaching to take the wizened hands in her own. "You've been such a dear friend, Constance."

Tears welled in the old Quaker's eyes, and she shook her head as if trying to banish them.

"Well, I won't keep thee. Take care, dear, and do get some rest. I was watching thee during Meeting and thy expression was troubled by more than the heat, I fear."

CHAPTER 16

Most Sundays, Beth met her sister at the train in Providence. From there they drove forty minutes to Northbrook where the Friend's Home was situated.

"What happened to you? You look like something the cat dragged in."

Lanie's greeting echoed Constance Bicknell's more politely stated observations.

"Thank you, sister dear. What a boost to my self-esteem. Everyone's been telling me I look like shit today. I must really look awful!"

"What's up?"

"The kids had a party last night. I stayed up late chaperoning, that's all."

"Aren't they a little beyond the chaperoning age?"

"No."

"How are the little devils anyway?"

"Fine. They'd love to see you."

"I'm taking two weeks' vacation in August. Maybe I'll come camp out with you for part of it."

"We'd love it."

They drove out to Northbrook chatting amiably, mostly about Lanie's job. Still single, but not by choice, she was an architect for a big firm in Hartford. After many years with the company, she was now a partner and took only the jobs that interested her. She did mostly residential design and had just finished work on a huge home in West Hartford.

"Billions. These people have billions. They spent four hundred thousand dollars on the bathrooms alone, so you can imagine what the entire project is costing."

"As they neared their destination, talk petered out. They stopped at the Northbrook Pharmacy for their mother's weekly supply of peanut butter cups and arrived at the home a little after two. Beth always brought snacks that they nibbled on in the car. Then, after their visit, the sisters went out for a late lunch or early dinner before putting Lanie back on the train.

Their routine seldom varied although occasionally one or more of Beth's children accompanied them. Nowadays, Kat and Kit drove, so they usually came on their own. Although Nanny sometimes came with Beth, she usually accompanied her father who visited with Hestor every Saturday. Alan and his mother-in-law had always been close. The divorce hadn't severed that bond. In rare moments of lucidity, Hestor was highly critical of his actions in regards to her daughter, but she still delighted in visits from "her boy."

"I hope she's awake," Beth whispered as they wended their way along the wood paneled corridor, their footsteps muffled by soft green carpet. Friends Home was more like a Swiss chalet than a nursing home in ambience and decor. As a birthright Quaker, Hestor had been eligible for residency. When her daughters had begun to seek residential care for her, the decision had been easier knowing she could come to this particular home.

"Won't matter if she isn't. Why do we even bother with these visits anyway? The only reason I come is to see you, so why don't we just start meeting and not put ourselves through this every Sunday? I love Mama, you know that, but my mama died a long time ago."

A nurse passed them in the hallway outside Hestor Whitman's room. "She's up and waiting for you."

"Thanks, Judy," Beth replied and gave her sister a sharp look as Lanie rushed into the room to greet her mother.

Hestor sat in the sun, light streaming through the open window, eyes closed as her skin drank in the warmth. She wore a shapeless cotton housedress, the cabbage rose print faded to a dull mauve after hundreds of hot water washings. Wisps of long white hair framed the beatific face. Her thick, waist-length braid lay serpentine over her right shoulder. A pot of pink geraniums sorely in need of water sat on the windowsill beside her. Beth brought a cup of water from the bathroom and dumped it in the flowerpot before bending to kiss her mother's cheek.

"Hi, Mama."

Silence, a brief nod of the head, a smile, then Hestor slowly opened her eyes and reluctantly turned from the light to her daughters. "Ah, gah, ah gah, aaaah."

"Don't try to speak, Mama," Lanie said, softly patting the gnarled, liver-spotted hand. "We know you're glad to see us. Here are your Reese's."

Lizard-like, the hand darted out and snatched the proffered orange package. Expert fingers unwrapped the chocolate. A drop of saliva escaped the corner of her mouth in anticipation of the sweet morsel.

Lanie wiped away the drool with a tissue. "Mama, behave yourself. Go slow and enjoy it, will you?"

Ignoring her daughter's words, Hestor Whitman gobbled up the first peanut butter cup in the flash of an eye. The second disappeared almost as quickly and she held out her hand for more.

"That's all for today, sweetie," Beth said, touching the paper-thin skin of her mother's arm. There were fresh bruises since last week. Anything, even her daughter's touch, bruised the tender flesh.

Her treat gone, the frail, tired body collapsed. The peace they had glimpsed upon their arrival was now replaced by utter despondency.

Lanie whispered, "Why do this to her? She was so happy before we came in."

Beth didn't answer.

They spent about an hour in the tiny room furnished with an easy chair, an old Boston rocker made by their father, a Whitman family dresser and side tables made by Alan years earlier. Despite valiant efforts to deinstitutionalize the space, a gleaming chrome hospital bed dominated the room. Lanie and Beth had wallpapered the room with a cheerful rosebud pattern that matched Hestor's bedspread. Framed photographs of family and friends covered the walls.

Following a routine that seldom varied, Beth tidied up while Lanie read to their mother, this week from Daisy Newman's, *I Take Thee Serenity*, one of her mother's favorite novels from years past. The staff of the home had suggested that they purchase a television for their mother since she could no longer read or amuse herself in other ways, but the sisters had declined.

Their mother had never allowed a television in the house and they saw no reason to burden her with one now. Hestor had always revered the silence and her daughters saw nothing to indicate that her decline in faculties had altered that reverence. She did have a small tape recorder with a supply of books on tape and a few classical music recordings, but Hestor rarely listened to those, usually shaking her head vehemently whenever they were switched on.

"Okay, sis," Lanie said, rising promptly at four thirty. "Time to go."

Kissing their mother, who had lapsed into sleep, the sisters withdrew, stopping by the nurses' station to drop off the week's supply of treats.

After leaving the home, the sisters usually ate at Leo's, a small café not far from the train station. They chose not to vary their routine today and sat in Leo's back room sharing a salad and pasta dish, talking over the events of the past week. As the waitress served coffee, Beth interrupted Lanie's description of one of her clients' landscaping plans and blurted out, "Have you ever dated someone much older or younger than you?"

Lanie regarded her suspiciously. "Why do you ask?"

"Just curious."

Lanie gave her a piercing look before replying. "Well, there was Buzz, whatever his name was, remember him? He was about eight years older than me. What a dork. That's about the biggest age difference I can think of. You're more familiar on that kinda thing than me though. Look at the generations separating Alan from little Miss Death Sculpture. What is it, nearly forty? Are you asking about this because of Alan?"

"No. It's about me, or someone like me."

"Oh, I see, we're playing the 'I know a person' game."

"No, we're not. I mean, what if I were to be involved with someone younger?"

"Sounds good to me. Have you met someone? If so, it's about time!"

"No, it's not good, Lanie. And I mean much younger, twenty-five years younger."

"What?"

"Doesn't sound so good all of a sudden, does it?"

"Well, now wait a minute, tell me the rest."

"He's thirty-three, Lanie. Thirty-three!"

"Oh my God, you're kidding?"

"No, I'm not. This person has been coming on to me. I can't say that I've never had a younger person flirt with me. The summer I taught one of the college art seminars for instance, there were a couple of kids who were openly flirtatious, but this is different."

"How so?"

"Because, as much as I've tried to push it away, I'm attracted to him. If he were fifty, I'd have already thrown myself at him. Could I be going crazy? Do you think this is my midlife crisis? Am I subconsciously trying to hold on to Kit? Have I become so dependent on him since Alan left that I've transferred my motherly feelings on to someone else?"

"Beth, get a grip! Are you listening to yourself? You're attracted to some guy. Some guy, not Kit and suddenly you've made yourself into a psycho. That's bullshit. If this guy comes on to you and you're game, go for it. That's my advice. Who is he anyway?'"

"No one you know," Beth lied.

Lanie would never betray the confidence, but her younger sister knew Jack and his family well and if nothing ever came of the relationship, which she hoped it wouldn't, she'd rather Lanie not look at the Talbots for the rest of her life and think of her and Jack. "He's here for the summer working."

"All the better. Have your fling and say goodbye to him in September. Do it, Beth, for Christ's sake. What have you got to lose? Guys do it all the time, why not us?"

"This is insane. I can't believe I'm having this conversation. I'm not going to have a fling or anything else and that's that. What could I have been thinking? Please, Lanie, forget I ever mentioned it, okay?"

"Fine, but a chance like this might only come along once in a lifetime, sister dear. Now it's time for me to catch the train."

CHAPTER 17

After dropping Lanie at the train, Beth drove toward the Harbor intending to go straight home. Instead, she pulled off on Atlantic Avenue and parked along Boathouse Road, a dirt laneway bordered on the west by a dozen boathouses. She walked the short distance to the cove, then from the sheltered beach, she took the cliff path to the Point of Rocks intending to turn around as the sun inched closer to the horizon, but she kept walking for almost three miles.

Before turning back, she plopped down on a large piece of driftwood and gazed seaward, waves lapping at her toes. Glassy-eyed, she tried, in vain, to become one with the ocean and sky, the wind on her face, the water tickling her toes, the brilliant sky stretched out before her. It had been so easy in her youth to stay in the present, to breathe in each new experience with one's whole being. Now she felt like an outsider; thoughts intruding like grasping fingers, holding her back from the here and now. Frustrated and tired, she rose and turned back. Alan, Rick, her children, her work, and now Jack Talbot, and this insane attraction to him. What she wouldn't give for a few minutes of peace from it all.

The sky was ablaze with a fury of orange and reds as she neared the car. Her walk on the beach had exacerbated her unease rather than alleviating it. She fumbled with the keys in the growing darkness. Finally, fitting the key into the ignition, she turned it and nothing happened. Not even a click from the starter. The battery had been threatening to die for weeks and apparently chose this moment to give up!

"Damn," she muttered and stepped out, looking up and down the road.

The nearest boathouse belonged to Jan and Steve Templeton. Voices from the deck told her someone was at home. She skirted the shingled dwelling and made her way up the walkway around to the front deck. The deck and most of the front of the boathouse stood over the water and a long, narrow dock stretched twenty feet out into the river.

There were ten such "stilt houses" along boathouse row, all of them shingled, all slightly different styles. Environmental regulations no longer permitted such building over water, so the tiny boathouses were valued far beyond what their modest proportions suggested they were worth. Gently lapping water muffled the voices, but Beth recognized Jan Templeton's as she neared the deck. Jan and another woman sat in chaise lounges, blankets over their knees, mugs of coffee in hand.

"Ladies, hello, excuse me."

Jan, a short, squat woman, trim and tan from a life on the tennis court, turned and gazed up at her, giving her a tight smile, the kind of smile reserved for waiters and lowly tennis assistants.

"Why, Beth, what a surprise."

"I apologize for barging in like this, but I went for a walk on the beach, only to come back and discover my car battery has died."

"Come, sit down. This is my college roommate, Grace Vaughan. She's here visiting. Have some coffee. Ours is liberally laced with Amaretto."

"Thanks, but I don't want to intrude. I'd appreciate the use of your phone. I left my cell phone at home. I'll call and have someone pick me up, then deal with the car in the morning."

"What about Mr. Nickerson? Couldn't he come and give you a tow?"

"No, he's home by now. I'm sure he'd come if I called him, but it's hardly an emergency."

"Why don't Grace and I give you a lift?"

"Thanks, but the kids will come get me."

Appearing greatly relieved that her offer had been declined, Jan pointed the way to the phone. "Right inside on the table."

Kit answered and assured her that he would be right over. Beth returned to the porch, thanking Jan and politely refusing further offers of coffee. Her hostess was clearly as eager to get rid of her as she was to leave. A summer person, Jan was one of those people whom the locals, including her two oldest children, referred to as "skewks," a derogatory term with no apparent derivation save its unpleasant sound.

Alan wholeheartedly embraced the harbor's summer season, so after many years, Beth had met many of the Jan and Steve Templetons as they made the rounds on the party circuit. She had hated the endless mingling with the same people night after night, the same gossip and small talk. She had little enough to say to them once a year, never mind every night.

After the divorce, her name had been omitted from most party lists. Single women, unless they were widows in their eighties, were usually overlooked when party lists were drawn up. They made for uneven numbers and potentially "awkward situations," according to one harbor maven. Beth didn't miss the socializing in the least, but Alan, who had also been crossed off most lists for having married someone "young enough to be his granddaughter" did. The fickleness of harbor society was a bitter pill for him to swallow.

The brief visit with Jan had brought the reality of Windy Harbor's small town ethos into sharp focus. Everyone knew everyone else's business, and had an opinion about it besides. What would life be like for her family if she took up with Jack Talbot? Horrific and unbearable, that's what. The village elders might even decide to oil the locks on the stocks still standing in the village green. Smiling at the image of herself pilloried in the town square, she leaned against the car and wondered what was taking Kit so long.

The Volvo's lights appeared at the head of the road and she started toward them, waving as the car drew near. Kit, reliable and steady Kit, her rock over the past years. What would she do without him this fall? Hopping in, she struggled to close the door, its hinges bent from an accident several months earlier.

"Thanks, sweetie, you're a lifesaver. Can you believe that battery? My own fault, I know. I've known for weeks that it was dying." She turned and their eyes met. "Jack? Where's Kit?"

"He got a call just as he was walking out of the house. From Karen, I think. He was going to hang up, but I said, don't bother, I'd come and get you. His car was behind mine, so that's why I got his Volvo."

Her breath came in gasps, but she managed a muffled "thank you."

He shoved the Volvo into gear and started forward. The road was too narrow to turn around, so he drove to the turnaround at the cove beach. Here the road was deserted, boathouses a good half mile back. The lonely beach stretched before them, its dilapidated wharf reaching out into the river, cloaked in darkness, the starless sky, an inky black ceiling above them. He circled halfway around the turnabout, then stopped and turned off the engine.

Panic swept over her, but Beth willed her voice to calmness, affecting what she hoped was a casual tone. "What's going on?" She could see that his hands were shaking.

"Mrs. Hadley, I mean, Beth, I'm going crazy here."

"No, Jack, please start the car."

"Just let me—"

"No."

"But I love you."

"Jack, that's enough." She put her hand on his arm. Big mistake. The warmth of his body made her want to reach out and draw him nearer, to feel his warmth against her skin.

"I know you are attracted to me. I can see it in your eyes. I tried not to feel like this because of Kit, but I can't help it. I think about you all day, I dream about you every night."

"Not another word. Let's go, before it's too late."

He reached out, his hand gently cupping her chin. "I need you," he whispered, as his lips found her own.

Instead of pulling back, Beth responded and her arms circled his neck as she drew him toward her. Warmth suffused her as his hands moved down her neck to her breast, gently caressing. Moaning softly, she pressed against him, heedless of the shift against her legs. It was then that the flashlight's beam caught her eye and shone through the rear window.

"Oh my God, it's Tom Pelton," she cried, recognizing the crotchety resident's familiar gait with Queenie, his ancient, white Lab at his side.

Tom Pelton owned the largest boathouse and had long ago appointed himself "policeman of the row."

Pushing Jack away, she fumbled with her sweater. "Quick. Start the car. Oh, God, don't let him see us."

As he pulled forward, she ducked, whispering, "Ignore him if he yells at you to stop."

As they passed by the elderly man, he waved his flashlight, shining it in Jack's face. "This is private property," he called as the Volvo roared past him. "You kids go neck somewhere else, you hear!"

In spite of herself, she forgot for an instant whom she was with and laughed. She felt sixteen again. Old man Pelton had been chasing teenagers off Boathouse Road as far back as she could remember.

"Thinks he owns the road," Jack said, laughing, too as he pulled onto Atlantic Avenue. "Now, where do we go?"

"Home, please, take me home."

CHAPTER 18

"Beth, I need to see you today. It's very important."

Everything was always "very important" when it concerned Alan.

Beth didn't attempt to hide the irritation in her voice. If it weren't for Alan, she would never have been necking with a thirty-three- year-old on Boathouse Road. "Couldn't you tell me now, on the phone? My car broke down last night and I've got to go out and get it. And, I have a lot of work to do."

"Where did you break down?"

"Boathouse Road." She explained about the dead battery.

"No problem. I'll come get you, take you there and jump start it. We can talk on the way and you won't have to wait a week or so for Nickerson to get around to towing it.

"Alan, no, I couldn't ask you to do that."

"I want to, Beth, really, it's no trouble. Remember, I'm the one who wants to talk to you."

"Fine," she replied, wondering why she felt guilty. The prospect of spending the morning with Alan was not cheering, but he was right. If she waited for Mr. Nickerson, she'd be carless for two weeks.

A half hour later, she jumped into Alan's pick-up. He gave her a quizzical look. "You okay?"

"Fine."

"Well, you look terrific," he said. "Radiant almost."

"That's a switch. Lately everyone's been telling me I look like shit."

"No?"

"Well, maybe not shit exactly, but old and haggard."

"Never, babe. You look as young as the day I married you."

"Well, I know that's a lie."

"You're too hard on yourself, Beth. Always have been."

Beth didn't reply. She refused to get into a personal discussion with him. Next thing she knew he would be all over her with advice and solicitous comments.

"Can I just pull over for a few minutes before we get the car? I really do need to tell you something."

"Fine, but not on Boathouse Road."

"Is this okay?" he asked, pulling onto the empty beach club lot and parking to face the ocean.

Beth nodded.

Alan spent several minutes staring out to sea, before speaking. Finally, he turned to her. "I have cancer."

Never in his life had Alan been so terse.

"What?"

"It's in my left lung."

"Oh, Alan, how did you—"

"I've been having trouble breathing and catching my breath. I've been coughing a lot, too, so Bob ordered an x-ray."

Bob Ellis had been their family physician for years.

"It's right there in black and white. He called last night with the good news."

"What's Bob say? I mean about treatment?"

"I'm going to Boston Tuesday."

"Oh, Alan, I don't know what to say. How's Chloe taking it?"

"She's a basket case, predictably. Crying and screaming. To tell you the truth, I think she's more worried about herself than me, but don't repeat that."

"Well, with all the new treatments. I mean, we can be optimistic. Can't we?"

He took her hand. "I'm glad you said 'we.' I'm gonna need you during this one, babe."

As his fingers stroked her palm, Beth felt trapped. Gently, she extracted her hand from his grasp. "Alan, you know I'll help if I can, with the kids and all, but I can't be your wife anymore. Please try to understand."

"Hey, no problem. I know that." His expression wounded, he started up the truck. "Just wanted you to know, that's all."

"Are you going to tell the kids?"

"Not yet, let's wait to see what the oncologist says. Now, why don't we see what we can do about that dead battery?"

As Alan fussed and fumed, scraping layers of corrosion from the battery, Beth watched, thinking how healthy he looked. It seemed impossible that his body was sick beneath his strong rugged façade. His thick, sandy hair showed barely a trace of gray and his face was unlined save a few wrinkles around his eyes. Alan looked at least ten years younger than sixty.

Beth couldn't blame Chloe, beautiful, talented and young Chloe, for falling in love with Alan. He was a Renaissance man: bright, handsome, articulate, talented, and rich. Who wouldn't fall in love with him? He was every woman's dream come true.

"Start her up!" he called finally and Beth turned the key and the ten-year-old Saab sputtered to life.

Alan disconnected the jumper cables and threw them into the pick-up. He came around to lean against her car. "So, gonna take this over to Nickerson's right now?"

"I'll go straight over and leave it."

"I'll follow you and drive you home."

"No need. Thanks, I'll walk. I need the exercise. And, thanks for the help. You've saved me several carless days."

"No problem."

"I hope everything goes well on Tuesday. Let me know what you find out, okay?"

"Sure will. And, Bethie, please don't say anything about this to anyone yet. I don't want people looking at me sideways, if you know what I mean."

"Of course."

"I've asked Chloe not to say anything, but she'll probably blab it all over campus." His tone was sarcastic, but the eyes that stared back at her were full of pain and fear.

"Okay, I'd better get along. Thanks again.

She breathed a sigh of relief as she drove away from those eyes, full of fear and sadness.

Chapter 19

By the time she got to her studio, it was after eleven. No sooner had she donned her smock than the phone rang. "Beth, it's me. I'm in the car, only two minutes away!" Crackle, crackle.

"I'm fine, Rick, thanks for asking. How are you?"

"Look, hon, I'll be there in five, okay? Uh, oh, gotta go." Click and the line went dead.

She removed her work shirt, put her brushes aside and walked the path to meet him in the driveway. As the fire engine red Mercedes pulled in, she called, "Lunch" and waved him toward the house.

"Great, I'm starved." He gave her a peck on the cheek and they headed up the walk. "Gary's got me on the macrobiotic diet from hell. It's killing me, I tell you, killing me. Who goes on a macrobiotic diet in this day and age?"

Gary was anorexic thin and always after his partner to "lose a few." While not overweight, Rick tended toward a bulging midriff. Whenever his belt began to disappear, Gary sprang into action and placed the contrite, but miserable Rick on a strict regimen until the weight came off.

Today he looked especially thin, dressed like an ad for J. Crew, in a slate blue silk tee shirt and matching shorts. Tanned and fit from an hour of swimming a day, Rick looked years younger than sixty-two. Beth smiled and took his arm. A good six inches shorter than her five nine, they looked a strange pair walking companionably toward the house.

"I like the hair," she said, poking him.

"Oh, God! It's too much, isn't it? I told Gary it was too much. Just a few blond highlights to hide the gray, that's all I wanted, but no. He has to tell Adolfo to "blond it up," like it's his fucking head of hair!"

"Rick, I said I liked it and I meant it, so stop fretting."

Several minutes later, she stood at the counter filling pita pockets with lettuce, tomato, thick slices of avocado, cheese, and alfalfa sprouts. "How's the cold?"

"Much better, thanks. Now listen, girl. Stop beating around the bush and tell me what you've done to Graham Lynch."

"Excuse me?"

"Don't stand there looking so innocent, Beth Hadley. The man's in a dither about you. I went to see him this morning and he refused to shut up about you. I couldn't get a word in edgewise and you know me, doll, I can always get a word in." She smiled, but said nothing. "He's got your number, hon. You're in."

"That's not what he told me. He made a solo show seem very conditional."

"You mean that bullshit about Joan Pilmer? The woman isn't fit to hang in the garage, never mind the Lynch. As your agent, I would never permit you to hang alongside her. He knows that. I mean, really!"

"Graham told me his mother loves Joan and wants her. Says if I don't have enough paintings to show, it'll have to be a joint exhibit."

"Bullshit. He's just stringing you along. You're in. Do ten or fifteen decent paintings this summer and Joan Pilmer will be relegated to Simpson's Diner where she belongs."

"Ten to fifteen, is that all?"

"Spare me the sarcasm, doll. We both know you can do it. God, is this the greatest sandwich ever! Can I have another?"

"What will Gary say?"

"Fuck Gary. Has Nanny made any cookies lately?"

"You are really asking for trouble."

Agent and artist talked and ate graham crackers and milk, until after one when Rick hopped up with "gotta run" and flew out leaving Beth to her nap.

Chapter 20

It was after two when she returned to work, painting until well into the evening. All three of the kids had plans. Nanny was sleeping at the Rollins'. Kat was babysitting until "at least one," and Kit had gone to a concert at Great Woods with a bunch of his friends. Shortly after seven, she walked back to the house and grabbed a yogurt and apple, which she carried back to the studio to continue working.

Several hours later, finally satisfied, she cleaned up and lay down on the sofa regarding the finished painting. It was the Point of Rocks and the far shore of the Spit at dusk, a number of boats in various spots along the river. She didn't care much for the composition as she had painted it in numerous variations over the years, but this scene always sold well. One of Windy Harbor's most recognizable landmarks, the Point seemed to be the image people most wanted to carry away with them when they returned to their winter homes.

Bored, she closed her eyes, intending only to rest for a few minutes. A short time later she was awakened by a kiss as his thin, lanky body pressed against her. His caresses were awkward and unsure, but Beth didn't care. She rose to meet him, drawing him closer, unsure if she was dreaming or awake.

"I may be thirty-three, but I'm no Casanova." His voice was husky and choked as his hand grazed her breast sending shivers through her.

"I'm here," she whispered in a voice of a siren. "I'm here."

Tentatively, he fondled her breast, then withdrew his hand. Instantly her hand sought his, guiding him back, aching for him to touch her everywhere as she began to explore the trembling body above her. His skin felt rough. His hair, damp from a recent shower, smelled of citrus as she ran her fingers through it.

Opening her mouth to receive his tongue, she realized he had been drinking, probably quite a lot. For a second, she considered pulling away and stopping this insanity while she still could. Sensing her hesitancy, his lips sought to erase it. He kissed her neck and moved down to her breasts, still half covered by her tee shirt. Beth rarely wore bras and didn't have one on, which seemed to arouse him even further.

As they fumbled to strip off their clothes and struggled to contain their ardor, Jack produced a condom, crumbled after months of hopeful waiting in the back of his wallet. He slipped it into place. Moaning, he entered her and she gave herself completely as they rocked in reckless synchrony on the lumpy couch. His frantic desire increased her own until she feared she might lose herself forever in undulating waves of ecstasy.

In her studio, the sanctuary and spiritual home she guarded so zealously, Beth made love to Jack Talbot, forgetting that he was twenty-five years younger and her son's best friend.

CHAPTER 21

They lay, bodies entwined, neither daring to speak. Her head rested on his chest, his beating heart a whisper against her. Panic and guilt mingled with warm euphoria. Finally, the silence became oppressive.

"You okay?"

He rose on one elbow and gazed down at her, his dark eyes, rimmed with tears. "What do you think?"

The husky reply brought tears to her eyes. "Oh, God, what have I done? Jack, I'm so sorry."

"What for?"

"For taking advantage of you. For letting this happen, for everything."

"I'm thirty-three, Beth, not eighteen. You did nothing wrong. Don't talk like that."

Beth grabbed her clothes and clutched them against her naked body, refusing to look at him. Seizing her arm, he tried to pull her back down on the couch.

"No, I need to get dressed and you need to go. Now!"

Releasing her, he dressed awkwardly behind the sofa. Finally, he stood, fully dressed except for the sneakers hanging from his left hand; he said, "So?"

She met his eyes. "I'm sorry. I don't mean to be cruel. This just isn't right. The difference in our ages aside, you're Kit's best friend. If he ever found out, I don't know what Kit would do."

"He won't find out."

"Perhaps not." She pulled on her tee shirt and buttoned her jeans. "Come, sit for a minute, will you? Jack, this is not me. I've never done anything like this before. I don't know what to say or do."

Then as he moved closer and took her into his arms, all rational thought disappeared. His lips moved down her neck and his hands explored her body again, this time more gently. Barely undressing, the awkwardness of the first time vanished, they came together again and she knew she couldn't stop, didn't want to stop, not now, not ever.

Just after midnight, they left the studio and strolled arm in arm along the path toward the house. Under the cover of darkness, his hand around her waist moved continually to her breasts, squeezing her gently, drawing her closer. As they passed through the cover of the grape arbor, they turned for one last kiss before she pulled back.

"Please, Jack, go quickly. Kat will be home soon."

She watched as his car disappeared into the night as creeping tendrils of fear ran down her spine.

CHAPTER 22

Beth spent the next few days in a dreamlike state, her body's heightened sensitivity acutely aware of every breeze, every change in temperature. While she feared running into Jack, her whole being ached for him, for his touch, for the eyes that gazed at her so full of love. But Jack didn't come, not even with Kit. Finally Wednesday morning she knew she had to get away, to clear her mind. She wasn't able to paint and could hardly muster the energy for routine household chores.

Alan phoned Tuesday night to say he wouldn't learn the results of his most recent tests until Friday. Beth decided that he and everyone else could survive without her for a few days. She phoned Clary to ask her to keep Nanny, who was already in residence, having spent the previous night with Carrie.

"Of course, we'd love to have her," Clarice answered immediately. "Everything okay?"

"Fine, just thought I'd spend a few days with Lanie. She's been begging me to come up and see her new place." Beth hated lying to Clarice, but she wasn't ready to talk about Jack and she had given Alan her word that she wouldn't tell anyone about his illness. In Beth's mind, Lanie was different and she desperately needed to unburden herself to someone.

Kat was on a four-day overnight with the camp until Friday, so it would just be Kit at home. She thought he would be thrilled, but when she'd broached the subject he seemed less than enthusiastic. "Why now? Why so sudden, Mom?"

"That's what summer is for, impulsive getaways, right?"

"I guess."

"What's the matter, Kit? You usually love having the house to yourself."

"It's fine. Just, well, I'll be working all day."

"Not partying at night, I hope."

"No, I don't know. I'll be going to soccer camp next week. Why couldn't you go, then?"

Sadly, Beth realized what was eating at him. Like she did, Kit felt the clock ticking down to his last days at home. After all the excitement of his acceptance at Bowdoin and months of waiting to go, as the departure date drew near, he wanted to hold on to every minute. Smiling, she sat beside him at the kitchen counter. "I won't go if you don't want me to."

"No, forget it," he mumbled, shrugging her hand from his shoulder. "It's nothing, go. Tell Aunt Lanie hi for me."

"Why don't you come with me? Take a day off and drive up? Lanie would love to see you and we can put you on a bus tomorrow."

"Thanks, but Will won't let me go. We've been short this week with Jack being out."

"Oh? What's happened to Jack?"

"Sick. He's been out for two days. We're way behind."

"That's too bad. I was going to suggest you get Jack or one of your other buddies to stay here with you while I'm gone."

"I'll get Pete. Jack's been acting too weird lately."

"You mean because he's been sick?"

"No, just weird. Never wants to do anything with us anymore. Disappears at the last minute and won't tell anyone where he's going, like the other night when we went to Jimmy Buffet. We've had the Great Woods tickets for a month and Jack loves Buffet. He's the one that got us to go. Then, he gives his ticket to Lynn Morrell, the afternoon of the concert? What's that about? No explanation, no nothing."

"Maybe there's something going on at home? Something he doesn't feel comfortable sharing?"

"Maybe."

"I'm sure gonna miss you this fall," she said, patting his arm. "You've been my rock, sweetheart."

"That's another thing I've been thinking. I don't know if I should go that far away. I could go to University of Massachusetts, Dartmouth and commute or even URI."

"Oh, no, you don't. Bowdoin's plenty close enough. We can zip up and watch a game now and then, but it's far enough away that you'll have your own life. It's time, sweetheart. Nanny and I are not your responsibility anymore. No more burdening you with our care."

"You're not burdens."

"You know what I mean. And, Kit, please go see your father. He misses you. In fact, I know he'd be happy for you to stay with him this week."

"No way."

"Fine, but at least call him. He'd love to take you to dinner or have you over. Chloe's out a lot these days from what I hear and he's lonely."

"Whose fault is that?"

"Kit, we've gone over this before. It's been more than three years. It's no one's fault anymore."

"That's bullshit and you know it. You're still hurting. Don't think I don't see it."

Stunned, she stared at her son. Of course, he was right. On some level, she was still hurting. Not like before, but the pain lurked in the shadows. She had woven it into the fabric of her life and gone on, but the hurt never completely let go.

"You're probably right, but that doesn't mean you have to punish him. He did what he needed to do for his life. Dad still loves me in his own way. It's just a different kind of love. And, he loves you very much. He's hurting, too, Kit. You're hurting him."

"Tough shit. I don't give a crap about him or his hurt."

"I think you do. I think if you dig down inside yourself, you'll find that you need your father as much as he needs you."

"I'm late for work."

"I'll see you Friday, then?" She leaned forward to hug him, but he pulled away and allowed only a fleeting peck on the cheek. "Don't forget to feed Jasper and give him lots of water with this heat," she called as he banged out the back door, the dog at his heels."

Midway through the morning, Beth realized that in all her preparations, she'd neglected to apprise Lanie of her plans. She dialed her sister at work.

The receptionist informed her that "Ms. Whitman's on-site and she won't be available until the team returns around four. They'll be meeting until around five, five thirty to wrap up, but you can probably catch her after that."

Beth left a message on Lanie's cell and on the office line saying she'd meet her at the office at five and take her to dinner. Hanging up, she went upstairs to pack a small overnight bag.

She left water and food for Nanny's cats and put out a fresh bowl of water for Jasper, then grabbed her things. She was just heading out when the phone rang. It was Graham Lynch.

"Beth? Hi, how are you?"

"Fine."

"Sorry to bother you. You sound breathless."

"No, I'm fine. I'm running around getting ready to fly the coop for two days to Boston to stay with Lanie."

"Oh, then I won't keep you."

"No, it's fine, I'm not in a hurry."

"I'm calling to ask if you'll have dinner with me Friday night."

"I'm not exactly sure what time I'll be home."

"Any time is fine with me. You pick the time and I'll make the reservation."

"Would seven thirty be too late?" Why was he asking her out? What was this about?

"Great. I'll pick you up at seven thirty. Casual or dressy?"

"Casual is always my preference."

"Casual it is, then, see you Friday." He hung up without another word. He sounds much more relaxed on the phone, she mused as she grabbed her bag and headed out.

She arrived in Boston midafternoon and puttered around the city, window shopping and visiting an art supply store. At four thirty, she began her way through the traffic so it was after five when she parked the car and made her way to the lobby of Whitman, Gorham and Peck. Not the largest architectural firm in New England, the century old company was certainly one of the most prestigious. A receptionist in the lobby directed her to the fourth floor where she found her sister slouched in an overstuffed chair reading the latest issue of *Architectural Digest.*

Spying her, Lanie threw the magazine on the glass-topped coffee table and rose to hug her, grabbing a briefcase and enormous black leather portfolio from beside the chair.

"This is a surprise, sis. What gives?"

As they walked toward the row of elevators, Beth said, "Thanks for waiting, Lanie I needed to get out of the Harbor for a day or two. Okay if I camp out with you?"

"Of course, love it. You should've given me some warning though. The place is a pit."

"I won't notice, believe me."

"Are you kidding? Beth, you live in *House Beautiful.* You'll die when you see it, trust me."

Lanie had made reservations at the Union Oyster House, one of Beth's favorite restaurants. They took Beth's car and circled for fifteen minutes before finding a parking space.

Once settled, wine and their selections from the raw bar in front of them, Beth relaxed with a sigh. "Thanks, Lanie, this is just what I needed."

"Okay, sister dearest, what's wrong?"

"That obvious?"

"You look like you want to crawl out of your skin."

"Alan has cancer."

"Oh my God, where?"

"His left lung." Beth related what she knew about his condition, which wasn't much and concluded with, "They'll know more on Friday."

"You poor baby."

"It's all so complicated, Lanie. I feel badly for Alan, but I don't want to get dragged into it. Does that make me a terrible person?"

"Absolutely not. News flash, big sister—you are no longer married to the jerk. I mean, I'm sorry he's sick, but let the bimbette play nursemaid."

"It's not that easy. First, there's Alan, who as you know is annoying, cloying, occasionally helpful. He never completely leaves me alone. Then there's Nanny who worships the ground he walks on, and the other two, who love him in their own way, but it's buried under lots of anger. What am I going to do?"

"Support them as best you can while reminding them that your relationship with their father is over. They know that, even Nanny. Don't go heaping guilt on yourself about this. Please, Beth. He has the type of cancer that will respond well to treatment, right?"

"His father and brother died of lung cancer, Lanie."

"That was a while ago. There've been all kinds of advances since then."

After ordering dinner, the conversation drifted away from Alan to Lanie's job and she spent the remainder of the meal regaling her sister with descriptions of the house she had been working on all day. They were back at the apartment, making up the sofa bed before Beth got around to the real reason for her visit. "Alan's cancer is not really why I had to escape."

"I thought not."

"I mean, it's part of it, but well, there's more."

"It's your younger man, isn't it?"

Lanie always read her like an open book.

Beth launched into a description of the evening with Jack in her studio, leaving little out. She ended her account saying, "It's Jack Talbot, Lanie."

"Oh my God, no wonder you look like Hestor Prynne. Sis, you've gone and done it this time, haven't you? Does Kit know?"

"No. No one knows and no one's going to know. Of course, I'm going to end it. It's impossible, but it's also unbelievable, Lanie. He makes me feel like I haven't felt in twenty years. Loved. He makes me feel loved. Am I completely insane?"

"No, but it's a bit complicated, isn't it?"

"What would you do?"

"Sweetheart, you're asking a horny, single woman with no kids. What would I do if a gorgeous young guy like Jack Talbot came on to me? I'd snatch him up faster than you could blink, lock him up in a hotel room, and screw the hell out of him."

"No, you wouldn't. I'll ask you again when you're sober."

"And, you'll get the same response, baby cakes."

"What about when the flame peters out as it surely will?"

"That's when I'd worry about reality. Think about it, Beth. Think about when you were young and in love. How long did it last? About one semester, as I recall, or maybe a summer? So why not have a bit of fun?"

"I'm not single though, am I?"

"News flash! Yes, you are! This is my point about you; you still think you're married to Alan."

"That's not what I mean. Slip of the tongue. I meant, I'm a mother. A mother who's screwing around with her son's best friend."

"Now, that's a different kettle of fish. We'll have to consider that best friend of son wrinkle aspect a little more carefully, won't we?"

The sisters talked until after midnight. They resolved nothing as they called last minute thoughts to one another through the open bedroom door, until they finally drifted off to sleep.

Chapter 23

As Beth drove home from Boston, rain pelted her windshield. The time with Lanie had done her good and she felt relaxed, the Saab's interior a warm cocoon in the cold dreary day. After two days of discussion, she had resolved that she would be firm and stop things with Jack before both of their lives were ruined. As for Alan, she would listen and be supportive from a distance. She was no longer his wife and she would not play that role.

Sensible, matter-of-fact Lanie always helped Beth to center. From eighty miles away everything had seemed so manageable. Of course, Lanie still insisted the affair with Jack was a good thing, albeit complicated by his friendship with Kit. Her parting comments had been, "I'll be interested to hear how you manage to tear yourself away from that one. Breaking off a casual relationship isn't difficult, sis, but a grand passion is another matter."

Beth had ignored this remark, just as she had Lanie's advice to sever all ties with Alan. Unlike the rest of her family, Lanie had never liked Alan. Both of their parents, especially Hestor, had adored him as "the son they never had," but Lanie always kept her distance. Beth had never understood her sister's feelings, but suspected they had to do with Alan's meddling nature. Lanie resented advice or criticism, no matter how well meaning and Alan doled out plenty of both. His own younger sister, June, barely spoke to him after a lifetime of his brotherly oversight.

As she drove into the village, the façade of control began to crumble with the weather. As the sun peeked out from behind the clouds, Beth swallowed hard and tried to firm up her resolve. He could be sitting in her kitchen right now with Kit.

She stopped at Clarice's to pick up Nanny, listening as her youngest chattered away. As they neared home, her stomach began to churn.

"So what's on for the weekend, Nan? Any big plans?"

"Dad's taking me fishing Sunday in the Wright's boat. He said I could bring someone, but I might just go with him. Just the two of us."

"That'll be nice. Have you spoken to Dad, then?"

"Yup, he took Carrie and me out to dinner and to the club last night."

"Chloe too?" Beth turned to face her daughter. Nanny's cheeks were freckled and sun-burned, her shoulder-length hair tied back in a tangled, unruly ponytail.

"Nope, just Dad. He was acting kinda funny, too, sorta sad. That's why I thought it'd be better for us to go fishing alone. I called Kit and asked him if he wanted to come, but you know how he is."

"It won't last forever, sweetheart. Someday Kit and Dad will make up."

"Maybe, but Dad looks so sad whenever Kit's name comes up. He's lonely, Mom, I can tell. I was thinking I might spend a few nights at his house next week, to cheer him up. What do you think?"

"Up to you. Did he say it was okay?"

"Sure. He is always begging me to move in with him."

This was the first Beth had heard of this. "Oh?"

"Yeah, he's been talking about it for a couple of months. Chloe's never home, that's the reason."

"Nonsense. He wants to be with his daughter."

"Mom, hello? I know Dad. He loves me sure, but if he and Chloe were getting along he wouldn't want me around. You know that. He's not like you. You want me around for me; he wants me around for him."

Out of the mouths of babes. Beth thought sadly. As they pulled into the drive, she breathed a sigh of relief spying neither of the older children's cars in the yard.

"By the way," Nanny said as they threw down their things in the back hall, "Dad wants you to call him right away. He was really upset to hear you'd gone out of town. What does he want anyway?"

"I have no idea, sweetie," Beth lied, irritation rising. The calm control of a short while earlier was slipping away. She found five messages on the machine, all from Alan, each one more frantic than the last, all wanting to know where she was and when she was returning. Her cell had been switched off, but when she checked, a similar number were there as well. Sighing, she threw her bag on the bed and slammed out the back door, calling to Nanny that she would be back in time for lunch.

CHAPTER 24

It was after eleven when she finally put brush to paper. The brush had a life of its own, splaying color wildly across the canvas. It would never work, but it didn't matter. All that mattered was her hand was free from her discipline and Alan's critiques. To be fair, Alan would have been mortified to realize he had such power over her. It had always been her choice to hide in his formidable shadow, not his.

She was working on a painting she had begun over a month ago and had put it aside in frustration. A street scene, it depicted the riotous atmosphere of the village's August flower festival. Working from a number of photographs Kat had taken for her the previous summer, Beth had put many of her friends and fellow townspeople in the crowd, laughing and strolling, arms laden with flowers; snapdragons, heliotrope, hollyhocks, delphinium, asters, zinnias, carnations, and countless others came to life with the swish of the brush.

Just before one, the studio phone rang. It was Nanny telling her she had a babysitting job two houses away. "They want me till nine, okay, Mom?"

"Fine, sweetie, I should be home around then, if not a little later. I'll leave lights on for you."

"Where are you going?"

"Just out to supper with an old friend, Graham Lynch."

"Who is he?"

Graham had been away a long time, Beth mused, remembering that he had left town before Nanny was born.

"An old friend, more Dad's than mine really."

"Oh."

"It's business, Nan. He and his mother run the Lynch Gallery. Rick's trying to get me a show there."

Nanny's voice brightened and she rang off.

Reluctantly, Beth began cleaning up, pouring fresh turpentine into the brush can. The fumes made her feel faint and slightly weak in the knees. Hunger, she decided, and remembered she had not eaten since the previous evening. It was definitely time for lunch.

As she stepped into the kitchen, she found Alan hanging up the phone. "Where in the hell have you been?"

"Alan, what are you doing here? How did you get in? You know our agreement. We said you wouldn't do this, ever. Using the workshop's one thing, but I'm sorry, I can't have you waltzing in to the house anytime."

"Whoa, Bethie. Before you get all worked up, hear me out. Nanny just left. She let me in so I could use the phone to call the studio. I just left you a message. Here, call and check."

He held out the receiver. Beth shrugged it away. "Never mind. I'm sorry, I overreacted. But, finding you here makes me uncomfortable." Arms folded across her chest, she went to the far end of the room then turned to face him.

"Look, Beth. I wouldn't be here if it wasn't an emergency. I need your help."

She sighed, then sat opposite him at the maple table he had built twenty years ago for her birthday. "How are you? Did you get your test results?"

He nodded. "There's good news and bad news. The good news is that my type of cancer is operable and very treatable with chemotherapy. There are so many more options today than they had for Dad and Billy. The bad news is, it has to be caught in time, before it spreads to the surrounding tissue."

"Has it?"

"They won't know until they open me up. If it's spread, the prognosis is pretty bleak."

"Oh, Alan." She reached across and squeezed his arm still unable to meet his gaze. "When will they operate?"

"Tuesday. I'm scheduled for early morning at Mass General."

"We have to tell the kids."

"I know. That's why I've been trying to reach you. Beth, would you tell them? I don't think I can."

For the first time in their life together, Alan looked scared. Terrified would be more accurate. His usually ruddy face was ashen. Deep circles under his eyes told her he hadn't been sleeping. During times of crisis, Alan rarely slept, often staying up for days at a time in a frenzy of activity. He usually collapsed after four or five days and spoke to no one.

"Of course, I'll speak to them. Do you want me to do it today?"

"Whenever you think best. I have to go up Monday night to stay and I'll be in the hospital about a week. Then I'm looking at six to eight weeks of chemo."

"Alan, I'm sure it'll turn out fine, with all the new treatments and you've never smoked. Did they say what might have caused this?"

"Nope, but I haven't led the healthiest of lives when you think about it. Look at all the carcinogens I work with every day, lacquer, shellacs, strippers, you name it, any one of them alone could kill me, not to mention all the crap Chloe uses for her work."

He accepted her offer of lunch and they talked over tuna fish sandwiches. Alan, usually a voracious eater, left most of his sandwich untouched.

Well acquainted with her routine of napping after lunch, he rose soon after she had finished eating. "Thanks, hon, I'll let you get to sleep."

"Talk to you after I've spoken to the kids. I imagine they'll want to call or come by to see you."

"I'm taking Rob and Kat out to dinner tonight. Think you'll have time to talk to her before then?" She nodded, not bothering to ask whether Chloe would be going too. She knew the answer.

As if reading her mind, he added, "Chloe's pretty much out of my life at the moment. I don't know what's going on. She says she doesn't deal well with illness. What a stupid fool I was, Beth."

"Alan, don't."

He left without another word and she collapsed into bed a few minutes later, a restless, uneasy sleep overtaking her.

CHAPTER 25

After an afternoon in the studio, Beth cleaned up early and came in to shower and change for her dinner with Graham. Kat arrived around five, exhausted after four days of camping. She plopped her duffel bag of dirty clothes in the laundry room and ran upstairs to take a shower. A little after six, Kit came in with Jack and Pete, all three of them covered with black dust.

"We're going to the beach, Mom." Kit grinned, his teeth pearly white in contrast to his blackened face.

Beth focused on the task at hand, knowing her lover was standing only inches away. "Guys, could you go on without Kit. He'll join you in a little while, okay? I need to talk to him alone."

"Sure, Mrs. H.," Pete said, immediately shuffling toward the door. "We'll see you down there, Kit."

Jack followed, his expression worried and fearful. *He thinks I'm going to tell Kit about us,* she thought, avoiding his eyes.

After the boys departed, she called upstairs to Kat and the three sat down together at the kitchen table. Both took the news of their father's illness in stoic silence. As they talked, Kat began worrying aloud, what she would say to her father at dinner this evening.

"Just be yourself, sweetie. Let him know you're concerned. Let him know you care. He'll be hospitalized for a week or so. We'll all go up to see him. You can tell him that."

As she reassured her eldest, she turned to spy Kit, tears snaking down his cheeks. "Oh, sweetheart, he's going to come through this fine. You know Dad. He never lets anything get him down for long."

Sobs wracked the slender body and the three of them huddled, holding each other. When they broke apart, mother and daughter were covered with smudges of black dust.

"Remember, guys, Nanny knows nothing about this. I'll talk to her tonight unless one of you wants to?"

They both shook their heads.

"I'll speak to her when I get home. Now come on, you two. Kat's got her dinner and you told the guys you'd meet them at the beach."

Kit protested, his blackened face now striped and streaked, but Beth pushed and prodded, until he finally agreed to go.

As he stood, she took hold of his arm. "You know, sweetie, you can go to see him anytime."

He did not reply, but Beth felt sure father and son would speak before the week was out.

CHAPTER 26

Graham had chosen the Foc'sile, a seafood restaurant at the end of Brayton Point, two villages down the coast. On Saturday nights, the Foc'sile featured live music, usually country western bands, but tonight it was quiet, uncharacteristically deserted for a Friday night in July.

Beth liked the Foc'sile, but hadn't eaten there for five or six years. A favorite hang-out of Alan's artist friends in the early days of their marriage, they had spent many a Saturday night dancing and drinking until the wee hours.

"Good choice," she said as they clinked frosted beer mugs together.

She was drinking dark ale, Graham, a non-alcoholic draft.

"Brings back memories, doesn't it?"

She looked away.

"I'm sorry, Beth. That was a stupid thing to say."

"No, it's fine. I'm a recovering divorcee. What can I say?" She smiled. "I've always loved the Foc'sile. I wouldn't have thought of it, but it's perfect."

"Want to sit outside?"

"I'm happy if you are. Wonder why there are not more people here on a Friday night?"

"Ominous, isn't it? Do you suppose the food has taken a turn for the worse?"

"Probably." She laughed, thinking how handsome he looked, his light blue denim shirt open at the neck, hair curled over his collar. He appeared almost relaxed except for his eyes. Graham had a way of looking into a person, his eyes boring straight to one's soul. His hazel eyes were searching hers now, but for what?

"How's the painting coming?"

"Great. Well, slowly to be honest. My escape to Lanie's didn't help. I did some sketching while I was in Boston, but otherwise I spent two hedonistic days reading, sleeping, and shopping. I put in some time today."

"Gould was in to see me."

"I heard."

"Persistent little bugger, isn't he?"

"Very."

"You know I'm committed to the show, don't you?"

"Are you?"

"When could I ever deny you anything?"

Always. You've always denied me, she thought. Left me all those years ago never knowing if you felt the same way I did. She smiled and hid behind her menu.

"How's Alan?"

"You asked me that last week. We're not married, remember? Did you call him?"

"Not yet. Maybe next week."

"He'd appreciate it." She wondered if she should tell him about Alan's cancer but decided against it.

An ocean breeze blew through the restaurant and she shivered, rubbing goose bumps from her sleeveless arms, chiding herself for not having worn a sweater over her thin blue sundress.

"Want my sweater?"

"Yes, thanks," she said, taking the proffered navy pullover. She started to drape it over her shoulders, and then decided instead to slip it on. The soft cotton felt wonderful against her skin and she was instantly warmer, calmer.

"So what are you going to have?"

"Lobster, I'm paying for my dinner by the way."

"I invited you, remember?"

"Still, I'm going to pay for mine."

He said nothing, studying his own menu, his face flushed with emotion. She wondered if it was embarrassment or confusion he was feeling.

Midway through their lobster dinners, bibs at their throats, he set down his fork and stared at her. "Look, Beth, this is going to sound totally off the wall, but I have something I'd like to tell you."

She returned his gaze, lobster claw in one hand, cracker in the other.

"I want to say it because I'd like to see you again and I need you to know where I'm coming from. Do you remember the first time we met each other?" She nodded. "It was at the Bayside. I'd come down to see Alan for the weekend and you and your friends were there."

"I remember, we'd just come in from a softball game."

"That's right. You had on one of those goofy shirts and your hair was all tied up under a baseball cap."

She laughed. "I always was a stylish dresser. Like now, look at me!" she said, pulling up the corner of her bib. "Tres chic plastique! Oh dear, now I've gotten butter on your sweater."

Ignoring her attempts to distract him, he went on, "Sometimes I've imagined you felt the same way as I did that day. That you were as attracted to me as I was to you. Pretty dumb, huh? What I'm trying to say, is that from the moment I first laid eyes on you, I was head over heels in love. Crazy, huh? You must think I'm nuts to have fallen madly in love with my best friend's girlfriend. Talk about a doomed love affair."

"You weren't, aren't crazy," she said quietly. "I felt the same. I mean, I was deeply in love with Alan, but I was also very attracted to you."

He sat in silence for several minutes before saying, "What about now?"

"You're married now and I'm whatever I am. It's a whole different thing when you're in your fifties instead of your twenties."

He smiled. "Some of us are beyond our fifties. I'm Alan's age, remember?"

"Well, you know what I mean. Thank you. I've lived for so many years with wild fantasies about you and me. I'm embarrassed to say that the thoughts livened up more than a few dull evenings over the years." She laughed.

"Mary and I have split up."

His words fell between them like pebbles scattering off a rock face, the climber frantically scrappling to gain a foothold.

"No words of sympathy? No 'that's too bad, Graham, Mary was such a great gal?'"

She shocked herself. "Of course, I'm sorry. Divorce is horrible."

"It's just a trial separation, but will eventually be permanent. She'll never take me back."

"Why not?"

"I'm a bastard, that's why not." His bitter tone made her blood run cold. "My drinking made life a living hell for Mary for more years than I care to remember. Want to know why I drank?"

"Graham, you don't have to tell me this. You don't owe me an explanation."

"Oh, but I do. I drank to drown out the feelings I had for the woman I loved beyond reason. I thought if I drank enough I might forget the woman I could never have. Mary knew it. She knew from the first and only time she saw us together."

"Then why did you marry her?"

"You were spoken for."

"That's not fair blaming me. You can't blame the drinking and your unhappiness on Alan's and my marriage. You had choices. You must've loved Mary."

"Yes, and fat load of good it did me. Mary's true love is her work. The rush she gets from wielding all that power. That's what sets her frigid heart a pounding, not yours truly. When we talked about kids, it was always, 'let's wait until next year, Graham' or 'we have plenty of time, darling.' All bullshit, of course."

"I'm sorry, Graham, really I am. It all sounds very painful."

"At least in your case it wasn't your fault."

"That doesn't make it any less painful and who's to say. Maybe if Alan and I had been closer."

"That's crap, Beth, and you know it. The guy's a self-absorbed bastard. Always has been, always will be."

"Alan may have left me, but we had some wonderful years together, and he's a terrific father."

"Ouch, kick me where it hurts."

Suddenly tired of the tug-of-war conversation, she reached over and placed her hand on his. "Can we drop this? I'm almost ready to head home. What do you say?" She ripped off her bib and rolled it into a ball, then tore open a moist towelette to clean her hands. The pungent lemony fragrance cleared her head.

"Fine." He turned away and gestured to the waitress for the check.

A study in contradictions, one minute Graham seemed so vulnerable, which she found enormously appealing. He was charming and he was a wonderful listener, thoughtful in his responses, someone who never dominated the conversation. Then, of course, there were his lean good looks and eyes that caressed her with every glance, their gentle kindness drawing her closer, just as the anger and his frightening moodiness pushed her away.

He paid the bill, refused to accept her share, then took her arm to escort her out. As they neared the car, she shrugged out of his grasp.

"I've done it now, haven't I?"

The sarcasm cut like a knife. She ignored him and opened her own door. They spoke not a word on the drive home. Finally, as they drove up her drive, she broke the silence. "I'll wash your sweater and get it back to you."

He stared straight ahead. "No need for that."

"I know."

"Look, Beth. I'm sorry. Please forgive me. Now you see what poor Mary has had to deal with all these years. You are the last person I want to snap at. Mary and I have broken up. It's still pretty raw, that's all."

"Of course it is. I understand," she said in a whisper. And, she did.

CHAPTER 27

Unlike her older siblings, Nanny took the news of her father's cancer calmly. Early Saturday morning, she marched into the kitchen and announced to her mother that she would be spending the next two nights with her father. "I've called and he says it's fine. Chloe's away for the weekend."

LL Bean knapsack slung over her shoulder, jaw set, she looked so much like her father when his mind was made up. Arms akimbo, she dared her mother to object.

"That's nice, Nan," Beth said, smiling at her youngest. "Dad will be so glad to have you. You could ask Carrie or one of the girls to join you, if you like. I'm sure Dad won't mind."

"No, Dad and me want it to be just the two of us. I've gotta babysit for the Sissons this afternoon. Could you drop my bag off at Dad's later if I leave it in the car? I'm just taking my knapsack now so I'll ride my bike there from the Sissons'." Beth nodded, smiling, while silently dreading a visit with Alan.

Kit and Kat were both gone; Kat to work while Kit and his friends were spending the day working for Pete's dad, Wilson Macomber, who ran a charter fishing boat. In exchange for baiting hooks and cleaning fish, they got six hours on the ocean and bluefish for the freezer if the catch was plentiful.

A whole uninterrupted day stretched before her and Beth looked forward to getting to work. After a quick run through the house, taking care of washing and cleaning, she jogged along the garden path, breathless by the time she reached the studio.

After several hours of work, she was satisfied with the flower festival picture despite the dramatic departure in style and composition from any of her previous work. Energized by the success of her morning's work, she was reluctant to break for lunch. Instead she decided to set up for the next painting; canvas propped on the easel, paint tubes assembled, photographs pinned to the frame of the easel, more hanging from a clothesline strung from wall to wall in front of her.

The next painting was to be her first attempt to capture the Spit at sunset during one of their beach cookouts. She had always refrained from painting this particular scene, fearful that if she failed to capture the essence of the place and the spirit of the evening, it might taint the joy of these outings in future. Now she felt ready. Suddenly it was terribly important to paint from experience instead of continuing to crank out the endless string of harbor landscapes that compromised most of her earlier work.

His knock startled her. She expected to find Rick or maybe Alan, anyone but Jack, who was supposed to be fishing.

"Hi. This is a surprise. I thought you were with the guys."

She gazed up, spying desperation in dark eyes.

"I had to see you."

"Jack, listen."

"Why did you leave this week?"

"It wasn't you, if that's what you're asking. Come in."

She stepped aside and he passed, smelling of fresh air and the sea. Suddenly aware of the difference in their heights, she moved away to sit on the couch. She indicated the chair opposite for him, but he sat beside her.

"There's been so much going on. I just needed to get away for a few days to think."

"I heard about Mr. Hadley. Kit told me."

"We're hoping for the best. Mr. Hadley is a fighter."

"I missed you," he whispered gruffly.

"Jack, listen to me. We can't keep this up. What happened the other night can't ever happen again, ever."

"Why not?"

"Because you are too young and you are Kit's best friend. I won't do that to him and you shouldn't either. He needs you now more than ever."

Unable to sit still, he tapped his foot, curled and uncurled his fingers, while his curling eyes darted from her to their surroundings. Finally he stood and began wandering around the studio, studying each painting as he passed. Her work was still propped around the room after Graham's visit. What would Graham think of this, she cringed, watching Jack pace back and forth. Finally, he paused at the recently completed painting of the flower festival staring at it for a long time, before turning to face her.

"That's not true. I'm not too young for you. Look at Mr. Hadley and Chloe."

"I am not Mr. Hadley."

He flopped back on the couch beside her.

"As a matter of fact, at the moment Mr. Hadley is very unhappy in his marriage. Please don't repeat that, but he is. I have to believe their age difference has a great deal to do with their unhappiness. You are my son's best friend. He told me the other day that the guys have been wondering about you and are thinking of following you to see where you go when you're not with them. Just think for a minute what would happen if they found us together."

"They won't. I'll be careful." He reached over and touched her cheek, his hand smoothing back strands of hair. Despite all of her previous resolve, Beth found herself responding as their bodies drew closer until they were entwined. Soon, despite her pronouncements, the rhythm of their lovemaking once again blotted out all reason and sanity. Only afterwards, did she think of the door, standing wide open.

The rashness of her behavior scared her. Dressing hastily, she said, "Jack, we can't do this. We just can't. It's too dangerous and much too easy for someone to walk in or follow you here."

"It's fun." He smiled, pulling his paint-spattered tee shirt over his head. His blue jeans rested on his hips half-zipped.

She stared at him, wondering if he was using her. As if reading her thoughts, he came toward her. The love in his eyes was unmistakable and Beth realized things were not quite so simple. This was much more than sex.

What was she doing? Was she so sex-starved after three years of abstinence that she was using this much younger man to satisfy her uncontrollable urges? Startled by her thoughts, she gazed up at him, endeavoring to compose her words.

"Fun it might be, but, you cannot come here anymore."

"But?"

"Wait." She wrapped her arms around his neck and kissed him. A long lingering kiss that sent shivers of fresh longing through him. "I may be the most despicable woman on earth, but I'm unwilling to give you up."

"I'm glad," he whispered huskily, lifting her up and drawing her to him.

"No, we can't. I won't risk another second of this here." With effort, she pulled away from him. "I won't take any more chances here and we are certainly not going to make this relationship public."

He opened his mouth to protest.

"I suspect you'd rather your friends not know either. Am I right?" She didn't wait for a response. "My family has a small beach house in Sayles Cove. We call it Hestor's Way. It's my mother's actually. You've been out there, haven't you?"

"Yeah, a bunch of us went down there for a weekend a few years ago, remember? You and Mr. Hadley took us right after school let out."

Kit's graduation from junior high, Beth thought, recalling the gangly bunch of adolescents packed into their old station wagon.

She laughed. "Yes, I remember. Anyway, the cottage is empty. My sister and I have been talking about selling it, but right now it's vacant. We could meet there."

"When?"

"This week Alan has his operation, so next weekend? How about Saturday or Sunday?"

"How 'bout both?"

Ignoring him, she said simply, "If you can get away, I'll meet your there next Sunday afternoon around three, all right? Think you can find it?"

He nodded.

"Now go, before Mr. Hadley bursts in here and give us both the third degree."

"I love you," he whispered. He gave her one last kiss then disappeared out the side door.

Dear Lord ,what have I done? As Beth sank back down on the couch and chided herself, the phone rang. It was Nanny reminding her to bring her clothes to Alan's. Beth had forgotten. Scolding herself, she headed toward the house.

She drove into town and stopped at the art shop for paper and other supplies. On the way out with her purchases, she ran into Joan Pilmer.

"Beth, hi. Long time no see."

"Hello, Joan, how are you?" Beth gazed at a short, plump blond, dressed in a bright green skirt and a flowered jersey stretched tight across her ample bosom.

"Fine. I hear we're to be partners."

"Excuse me?"

"Margot phoned and said she's working up a fall show for us. What an honor for me, to be hanging next to the fabled muse of Windy Harbor." Her voice dripped with honey. Beth had forgotten how ingratiating Joan could be. "Love your sandals," she added, pointing at Beth's Birkenstocks.

"Be a real study in contrasts, don't you think? The show I mean, Bohemian artist in clogs and braid, opposite Suzy Prep and her pretty beach scenes. That's what everyone says about me, I know it, no need to feign surprise. I don't care and that's the truth. I love my work and that's what counts."

"I quite agree," Beth said, wondering how to extract herself from the conversation.

"Don't worry, you can stop looking like a cornered squirrel," she snapped, as if reading her thoughts. "I won't take any more of your precious time prattling on. That's what my hubby says; I prattle on. Go on now, make your escape."

"Nice to see you, Joan. Take care."

"See you in the fall, if not sooner."

Reaching her car, Beth breathed a sigh of relief as the door slammed behind her. What an awful woman. While driving the short distance to Alan's, she decided no matter what happened there would be no two-woman show. She rather not show at all than hang alongside catty Joan Pilmer.

Alan answered the door. "Hey, babe, come on back."

"I can't stay, Alan, I'm just dropping off Nanny's things."

"Come in, just for a minute. Chloe's not here." He already had her by the elbow.

Beth allowed herself to be dragged into the front hall.

"Want a drink?"

"Alan."

"Promise not to get serious on you."

"Just for a minute. How are you feeling?"

"Great. How about you?" He set Nanny's bag in the front hall and led the way to the back of the house.

The encounter with Joan Pilmer had squelched some of the euphoria she felt after Jack's lovemaking, but not all of it. "Fine, thanks. I just ran into Joan Pilmer."

He shivered. "Dreadful woman. Had her son, Simon, in my class last year. What a simpering toad."

"Now, now."

"She claims Lynch is staging a joint show for the two of us."

"Don't do it, Beth! Want me to phone Margot?"

Beth was sorry she had mentioned it. She shook her head. "Please don't. Let's change the subject, please."

"Beth, thanks for telling the kids. Kat called me last night and Nanny, my little sweetheart, has been great. It'll be nice to have her here this weekend. Give me something to do so I don't sit and obsess about the operation."

"When does Chloe get back?"

"Monday. She'll drive me up."

That's big of her, Beth thought.

"It's hard on her, Bethie. She's only a kid."

"Your house is coming along," she lied, eyeing the chaos in the yard. Lumber was strewn everywhere, half-finished projects, piles of sawdust. Interspersed between the construction debris were several of Chloe's alarming sculptures, their black fingers pointing accusingly at the mess that surrounded them.

"You were always a terrible liar. The house looks like shit, but I can't seem to get to it. Between classes and commissions and running around keeping Chloe amused, I don't have the uninterrupted time to get out my tools and have a go at it. Got one bathroom done and part of the loft, but that's it. Nanny's bedroom is livable. Don't worry."

"I'm not." She smiled, experiencing a pang of sadness as she remembered the many years they had lived under construction. Alan was always tearing things down and building something.

"You were so patient, Beth. I'm afraid patience is not one of Chloe's virtues. She claims she is not staying here until it's finished."

"What about when you come home?"

"Oh, she'll most likely rise to the occasion. Say, guess who called me this morning? Graham Lynch, can you believe it? You didn't tell him about my cancer, did you?"

"No."

Alan looked disappointed.

"Did you want me to?"

"No, 'course not. I'll tell him. We're having dinner tonight."

"What about Nanny?"

"We're going to the Rollins'. She'll have Carrie to hang out with."

"That's nice," she said, trying to sound cheerful. Instead, she felt left out, thinking back to the many evenings the two families had spent together over the last twenty years.

"Heard Graham took you out last night. Must be his get reacquainted with the Hadleys weekend. Did you have a good time?"

"Yes," she said, bristling under his last remark. "Weekend with the Hadleys" indeed. If Alan only knew.

"Better watch out. He has always had the hots for you, babe."

"I've really got to go." She rose and turned toward the gate in the side yard, an easier escape route than weaving back through the house.

"What did I say?"

"Nothing, I've got a ton of errands to do. Have fun with Nanny this weekend."

"Beth, wait," he called out, but she was halfway down the walk, waving over her shoulder. Another minute surrounded by Chloe's metallic nightmares and the familiarity of her husband's work space and she knew she would burst into tears.

CHAPTER 28

Beth spent the remainder of the weekend and much of the next week painting. On Wednesday, she made her one and only visit to see Alan in the hospital. Chloe was with him when she arrived and clearly resented her presence. She huffed out of the room, muttering, "I need coffee." After a brief visit, Beth said goodbye and told Alan she would see him when he came home. "This is Chloe's place," she added, silencing his protests. "I will not change my mind, so don't excite yourself."

She left Kat and Nanny huddled on a naugahyde sofa with Alan and went in search of Chloe. She found her in a small waiting room at the end of the hall, the picture of waifish dejection.

Beth sat beside her. "You sure you don't mind bringing the kids home?"

"Sure, no problem. Be nice to have the company."

"Chloe, I'm sorry if I upset you by coming. I've told Alan I won't come again."

"Hey, no worries. He's the one's got to get better, right?"

"What does the doctor say?"

"Christ if I know. He treats me like a two-year-old and says stuff like, 'We'll wait until your husband's better, then discuss it.'"

"That's not okay, he should have had you in for a discussion of his care and chemo plan."

"Yeah, well you tell it to the asshole. He's one of the biggest pricks. Oh, hi, Dr. Caffrey."

A tall, gray-haired man in wire rim glasses and pale green scrubs stood in the doorway regarding them. If he overheard Chloe's remark, his expression did not betray it. The epitome of calm detachment, he stepped forward and greeted them. "Mrs. Hadley, how's he doing?"

"Fine." Chloe gazed out the window. "His kids are with him."

"Good."

Dr. McCaffrey stared quizzically from one to the other until Beth was afraid he might ask if she were Chloe's mother.

"How is he, doctor?"

"This is Mrs. Hadley number one, Alan's ex. She brought the kids up."

"Nice to meet you." He smiled, looking from one to the other of them.

What a jerk, Beth thought. "Chloe tells me she hasn't learned much about Alan's condition and the outcome of the operation. Why is that?"

"We were waiting until Mr. Hadley was a little stronger. We've already told him, it was an unqualified success."

"What exactly does that mean?"

"We think we got most of the cancer. We found several very small spots in the lymph nodes."

"Well, why didn't you take them out?" Chloe interrupted, impatient with yet another conversation that didn't include her.

There it was again, the patronizing smile. "We'll leave that to the chemotherapy, Mrs. Hadley. We'd like to save those glands if possible."

"So he has a good chance at a full recovery?" Beth asked.

"Hard to say with certainty, you understand, but yes, I'd say he has a very good chance. All patients react differently to chemo though. Remission isn't a guarantee."

Beth stood, shaking his hand. "Well, it was nice to meet you. I certainly hope you'll keep Mrs. Hadley informed on a daily basis as it is her right. I think Alan's plenty strong enough for a full report and the sooner the better."

She made a hasty retreat before the oncologist had an opportunity to respond. As she boarded the elevator, she heard his voice, dripping with solicitation, as he set up an appointment with Chloe for the following morning.

CHAPTER 29

Alan's week in the hospital had unexpected outcomes for Beth and her children. The first was an easing of tensions between the two oldest siblings and their stepmother. Somewhere amidst the daily trips to Boston and hours spent sharing meals in the hospital cafeteria, long harbored feelings of betrayal gave way to a tentative friendship between the new wife and stepchildren, a friendship of peers since Kat was not much younger than Chloe.

Alan's illness also brought a reconciliation between father and son. Two days before Alan's homecoming, Kit volunteered to make the evening trip to the hospital to give Chloe a night off. Kat and Nanny, who had spent nearly every waking hour with their father since the operation, elected to stay home. Friday after work, Kit drove Beth's car to Boston by himself. He had been in to see his father several times, but always with another person, always staying in the background. This would be the first time in three years that father and son were alone with no siblings or stepmother along as buffers.

Beth never learned what transpired that evening, but the change in her son was remarkable. She was in bed reading when the Saab pulled into the drive a little before midnight. She kept her light on and waited for him to come in to say goodnight. When he popped his head in her bedroom door, the expression on his face was like the cat who swallowed the canary.

"Hi, Mom!" His whole body looked lighter, as if the weight of the world had been lifted from his shoulders.

"You're home late. How's Dad?"

He plopped on her bed, a bowl of tortilla chips beside him. She reached out and took a chip from the bowl.

"Great, he looks great. Doctor told him he can definitely come home Monday."

"That's good news."

"Mom, do you think Chloe would mind if I went up to get him on Monday?"

"Doesn't hurt to ask, she might really appreciate the time at home to get things ready for him."

"Yeah?"

"And he's gotta go back three times a week for the chemo for the next few months. She's got classes, so I bet if you took a day off here and there, she'd really appreciate help with that, too."

He nodded. "I already thought about that. I'm gonna talk to Will tomorrow. I'm working Saturday to make up for today, but I'm gonna cut back my hours. If he doesn't understand, I'll quit."

Beth resisted the temptation to say, "what about your money for college?" So relieved was she for her fatherless son of the past three years. While she felt a twinge of sadness knowing that there would be the inevitable loss of the relationship she had had with Kit since the divorce, she rejoiced for him nonetheless. He had missed his father terribly.

"We made up."

"I'm so glad."

"Me, too. Night, Mom." As he bent to kiss her cheek, Beth resisted the urge to grab hold of him.

"Night," she responded and pecked his cheek as he withdrew, leaving a trail of chips strewn in his wake.

CHAPTER 30

As things turned out, the remainder of Kit's summer revolved around Alan's treatment and recuperation. After each session of chemotherapy, Alan went to bed for two days. Just as he began to feel better, off father and son would go to Boston for another round. After an initial period of stoicism, the old Alan returned. He had never been a good patient.

Kit arranged his work schedule around the trips to the hospital. Chloe gladly ceded the responsibility to him and tried as best she could to continue her coursework. As Alan became more and more demanding, his young wife lost what little patience she possessed and before long, Kit had taken over the home treatment as well.

Concerned about her son's nonstop pace with his college semester fast approaching, Beth finally decided that enough was enough and went to see Alan.

Chloe answered the door.

"Hi, Chloe, would it be okay for me to talk to him?"

"Sure, why not. Better you than me!" She waved toward the back yard before disappearing, presumably to grab a few minutes peace from the invalid's incessant demands.

It was the day before his next chemo session, so he was at his best, feeling well enough to putter outside in the yard and put the finishing touches on a small chair.

Spying him, Beth felt some of her resolve slip away. A Red Sox cap hid the bald head, but the rest of his body betrayed the ravages of illness even from a distance. While they talked almost daily on the phone, she hadn't seen him since the hospital and felt a twinge of guilt. He looked as if he had lost thirty pounds and his jeans hung limply, now several sizes too large. He had cinched the waist with a rope belt, knotted carelessly, its frayed ends dangling in front of him.

He spotted her and grinned, beckoning with a thin arm, his shirt sleeve a cavernous ring surrounding it. "Hey, babe."

Icabod Crane, she thought, waving back.

She gave him a hug and immediately pulled away, sensing he would have held on forever if she had let him.

"Come, sit down. These are dry." He gestured toward two chairs in the shade. "These guys are part of the Pickwick series, recognize them?"

"They're beautiful, Alan. Really lovely. Have they been sold?"

"Yup. Some rich dude out West ordered twenty, if you can believe it. I've only done six so far and don't know if I'll ever get up the strength to finish them."

"Of course you will. Doctor Caffrey says once the treatments are over, you'll be your old self within weeks."

"Do you think Kit would help me if I paid him? I was thinking of asking him, but wanted to check with you first."

"Kit doesn't have the skills to do this kind of work, Alan. He's only used a lathe once or twice in his life."

"Maybe not, but you do." She stared in silence, trying to read his expression. "Just kidding. Don't get panicky on me, Beth. I wouldn't dream of asking you, you know that. No, I figure I could sit right next to him and direct him every step of the way. We could do it together. It'd be kinda fun. Give him a chance to learn the trade so to speak."

Beth shifted in her chair, recalling the real reason for her visit. "Alan, I'm worried about Kit. He's running himself ragged helping you and trying to work, too. He's only got two weeks before Bowdoin's soccer preseason starts and he needs to have a summer. Don't misunderstand me, I'm thrilled that you two are spending time together, really I am, and Kit is happier now than he's been in a very long while."

"Me too," he said quietly.

"He needs a break."

"That's why I thought I could hire him full time. Then he'd be here and wouldn't have to worry about Willie."

She started to protest, but thought better of it, sighing. "That's up to Kit."

"So you don't mind if I ask him?"

"No, as long as you promise not to work him too hard. He needs time to be with his friends, to kick back, read and relax before they all go their separate ways."

"I hear you, Mother. Thanks." He reached over and took her hand. "Not counting you, he's my best friend."

"I know," she answered, extracting her hand as she stood. "Well, I'll leave you to your work."

"Do you have to go so soon? Why don't you stay and have lunch? Chloe can make us something."

Watery eyes beseeched her. Once again, Beth noticed the deathly pallor, the impossible hollow cheek bones. She wavered for a moment before answering, "No, but thanks. I've really got to run. Take it easy on Chloe, too, will you? She couldn't have bargained for all this and rumor has it you've been kind of nasty lately."

He waved his hand. "She's a spoiled brat. Never thinks of anyone but herself."

"Careful, Alan. She's young, but she's been holding things together pretty well."

"The first week or so maybe, but not anymore. Now that the kids have taken over, she's become the invisible woman, again."

"That's a bit harsh, isn't it?"

"You don't know the half of it. Just drop it, okay? Chloe's my problem, not yours. Come on, I'll walk you out the back way."

Hand on her shoulder, he led her around through the side yard littered with Chloe's sculptures in various stages of completion. "Nightmare alley, I call it." He laughed. "How's the painting going?"

"Great. I've completed four new ones, two that I'm very pleased with."

"Graham says they're unbelievable."

"I'd say they're some of my best, if you want a totally unbiased opinion."

"I'm sure they are. What's made the difference, do you think?"

Jack Talbot, she thought, replying, "I don't know. I've been more willing to experiment and push myself I guess. I've even been a little reckless."

"About time! Can't wait to see them. Can I come over for a peek when I'm feeling better?"

"Of course," she said, cringing. She felt sure he would like the paintings, but was also afraid he might see right through them and begin guessing the origin of the passion that had given them life.

CHAPTER 31

They came home to Hestor's Way, making love on her grandmother's quilts laid down on the bare wood floors, sun streaming through curtainless windows. For a few afternoon hours, they shut out the world, ensconced in a magical swirl of dust-flecked light, scattered cobwebs silver gray with age like a canopy above them. Beth forgot that she lay in the arms of her son's best friend. Never mind that she was old enough to be his mother. From the moment Jack Talbot reached out, sending shivers through her body, she forgot everything except the touch of his rough carpenter's hands as they brought her to climax again and again.

At first, there had been little conversation. Their lovemaking consumed every second, but as the weeks went by, their ardor cooled slightly allowing a few languid moments before Beth announced it was time to go. It was during these times when the unease began and the realization that the end of summer was coming, and with it, the inevitable end of their relationship.

During the weekdays, Beth lived in feverish anticipation of her Sundays with Jack. Emotions screamed from her paintings and kept her working well into the night. When she wasn't in the studio, she was out walking the fields and beaches with her camera taking rolls and rolls of pictures for future paintings.

On one of his visits to the studio, Graham had made a suggestion that sent her in a whole new direction. As they sat drinking coffee in the shade of the studio's small, walled terrace on early August morning, he said, "Why not try a few portraits? If you won't divulge the identity of your secret lover, at least put him or some human manifestation into your work." When she stared back, mouth agape, he had added, "I'm kidding, Beth. Kidding? Alan and I both sense a change in you, though, and we both know it's not because of us, so naturally we've been speculating."

Irritated that the two friends had been discussing her, Beth had risen and left, slamming the door of the studio behind her. The conversation had gone no further, but she had nonetheless taken Graham's suggestion and run with it. Portraits of her children and few of their friends were followed by studies of several neighbors. Many were only sketches, but then she chose a few and developed these into paintings. Her first completed portrait was of Nathan Potter, a local farmer. After spending several days following him around with her camera and sketch pad, she finally convinced him to grant her a sitting astride his tractor.

After the old farmer, she painted Constance Bicknell, from a sketch the Friend had allowed her to make one Sunday after Meeting for Worship. Constance sat straight-backed and still on the hard, white bench in the Meeting House, her hands folded on her lap. A hint of a smile played on the thin, pink lips. Soft, wispy-haired Constance with her summer shift and turtle green cardigan sweater, its top button fastened, appeared ready to step out of the picture "a good day to thee" on her lips.

Beth painted her mother and Lanie as they sat together sipping iced tea on a wrought iron bench in the garden of the Friend's Home. On one of their mother's "good days" when a semblance of consciousness lingered in her features, Beth had sketched furiously as Lanie talked, gently combing her mother's hair. Afterwards, she'd taken as many photographs as she dared, careful not to agitate her mother. All her life, Hestor had hated cameras, claiming they separated people from life. Her daughter's caution proved unnecessary, however, for in her current state, the camera was no more alarming than a passing cloud.

There were other portraits began and then abandoned, but her favorite was that of her mother and sister. In it, Hestor Whitman sat clear-eyed beside her youngest daughter looking for all the world as sound in mind as ever. Lanie had already begged her for it, but Beth had held on to it, secretly planning to give it to her sister for Christmas.

She wanted to paint Jack, but she dared not attempt it, particularly after Graham's teasing about her secret lover. She sketched Pete, Sam, and Drew, three of Kit's friends, but she feared a portrait of Jack might reveal much more about her new found talent than she wanted. The question of his portrait prompted one of the first arguments the pair ever had.

It started one afternoon as they lay under a thin cotton blanket in the warm aftermath of their lovemaking. Beth's eyes were closed, his hand caressing hers. Idly she wondered if Jack might be tiring of her, even as she knew it was quite the opposite. Every Sunday he begged her to make their relationship public and pleaded with her to marry him.

He was a thoughtful, sensitive lover. His fingers moved knowingly over her body, gently cupping her breasts, working magic between her legs, drawing her to him, their mutual hunger never satisfied until at last their bodies were joined. Such pleasures were a rarity after years of marriage. Alan had been a wonderful lover, but she could not recall ever feeling as in sync with his body and his flesh. Jack's long, lean body seemed to match hers in a way that her husband's never had.

"So?" he said out of the blue, interrupting her thoughts. "Why won't you paint me?"

She rose up on one elbow and smiled down at him. "Not a good idea, my love. I paint from the heart and I'm afraid if I paint you, my public would see more than I want them to." Her hand played lightly along his cheek, tracing a faint scar just under his eye.

She remembered the day long ago when it happened. Nanny was just a toddler, wobbling along beside her. Together they had skated to the rescue after spying the teenager down on the ice, surrounded by hockey buddies. There was quite a lot of blood. As she helped carry Jack to the car, blood stained the sleeve of her parka, her mittens, and Nanny's fuzzy, white hat. He had required eight stitches. She remembered breathing a huge sigh of relief when Ed Talbot arrived at the emergency room to take her place.

"Then do it here and don't show it to anyone."

Lost in remembering, his words startled her. For an instant she gazed down at him expecting to see the child on the ice, stoic even then, refusing to shed a tear.

"Beth?"

"There's not enough light." She shook herself. "Besides, we have so little time."

"So, all you care about is the sex?"

Staring in disbelief, she sat up. "Is that what you think?"

Shrugging, he grabbed his clothes and moved away from her. "Sure seems like it."

"How so?"

"You grab me the minute I come in and tear at my clothes. When it's over you're up and ready to be gone."

"Jack, that isn't true and you know it. Why, we both—"

"You asked. It's just what it seems like to me."

"Am I missing something? What's happened?"

"Nothing." Staring straight ahead, blue jeans clasped against his chest, arms crossed, he refused to look at her.

She wrapped a blanket sarong-like around her and came to stand in front of him, draping her arms over his shoulders. "Jack, what is it?"

"I'm leaving soon and then what? Your summer fling will be over? You'll bundle up your little college lover and send him on his way with 'thanks and goodbye.'"

"Is that what you want?"

"I don't know what I want, but I'm sick of this sneaking around once a week bullshit. Everyone's paired off now. Kit and Pete have girlfriends and I go around acting gay 'cause I can't say anything about you or us."

"Do you really want to tell them? I mean, it's not as if we could double date, is it? Think about it. Do you really want to tell Kit?"

"No, probably not, but the least you could do is draw my picture. That's all I'm asking. Don't you care about me enough to do that one small thing?"

"It's not a matter of caring," she answered quietly. "If it's what you want, I'll bring my things next week. Okay?"

"Thanks."

He smiled and Beth wondered if the sketch was really what he wanted. For that matter, what did she want and what would happen in a few short weeks?

CHAPTER 32

Dartmouth's preseason began in mid-August. Field hockey players had a week's grace period, but then they too had to report or risk losing their position. Kat debated not playing in the fall and concentrating all of her efforts on basketball, her first love and the sport in which she already enjoyed a national ranking, however, by mid-summer several of her teammates began calling. Finally, she capitulated and called her coach to say she would be there.

Beth dreaded the loss of her two oldest and tried to spend time with each of them. She and Kat went shopping and took long walks on the beach every evening, but she had barely laid eyes on Kit, who practically lived at Alan's. On a warm breezy evening as she and Kat ambled down South Beach she discovered another reason for Kit's absence.

"He's in love, Mom. When he's not with Dad, Karen pretty much monopolizes his time. She's definitely the driving force in that relationship."

Unlike your own, Beth thought. Even though two years older, Rob followed her daughter around like a puppy. "I wish they'd come by once in a while," she said, squeezing Kat's hand. "I've only seen Karen from a distance. I'd love to get to know her."

"Wouldn't count on it. You know Kit, he keeps things pretty close to the chest. I'm sure he'd be embarrassed to have her over unless there was a crowd surrounding them."

"That's too bad."

"Hey, we could always have another party?" She laughed and stepped in front of her mother, walking backwards to face her.

So like her father's smile, Beth mused, returning the grin. "That'd be fine with me. You guys cleaned up and everything the last time. I guess I could take one more late night."

"Maybe. People are kinda scattering. Some have already left for school, others are pairing up, you know? Rob and I have really gotten away from the gang lately. We like to be together, just the two of us."

Translation, the crowd had moved into heavy drinking and Kat didn't drink. Didn't do drugs either. Beth had heard from Clarice that there'd been a fair amount of drug use among the older crowd.

"Besides," Kat went on. "Kit barely sees anyone but Karen. Sometimes they go out with Pete and Sally, but that's about it. Jack's got a girl too, I hear."

"Oh?" Her heart constricted, terrified at what Kat might say next.

"A knock-out, gorgeous girl from East Bay. Lesley someone. He met her a couple of weeks ago at a dance and they're apparently an item. Never thought I'd see Jack with a girl this summer. Did you? He seems kinda elusive. I've always had a little crush on Jack," she continued, oblivious to her mother's distress.

Beth walked on ahead.

"He's cute, don't you think? Mom, wait. Where's the fire?"

"Sorry." Fighting to regain her composure, Beth paused and waited for her. "Let's turn back now, okay, sweetie? Nanny will be home and wonder where we are.

Kat continued chattering away about school, her friends, and her plans, but Beth barely heard a word. Jack had a girlfriend and he had said nothing. Not a single word the whole time he'd been berating her for not painting his portrait, accusing her of wanting him only for sex.

CHAPTER 33

Following the revelation about Jack's girlfriend, the remainder of the week took on a very different character for Beth. Instead of the escalating anticipation of previous weeks, she approached the coming Sunday with a calm detachment she hadn't known since the first evening when Jack Talbot had touched her.

While not heartbroken, she felt betrayed, not by his having a girlfriend, but rather because he hadn't trusted her enough to tell her. What did she expect? How much talking did they do? Actually very little. A part of her was relieved that he was moving away from their doomed relationship into one more appropriate for him. One had only to look at Alan and Chloe to see how impossible May-December romances could be. But, still a part of her ached with hurt. Hurt because he hadn't confided in her and hurt at the thought of losing him. She always knew it wouldn't last, but that knowledge didn't make contemplation of the end any less painful.

He's become another one of my children, she told herself. I love him, but it's time for him to go. Of course, he wouldn't tell me about Lesley. Children don't always confide in their parents about a budding romance.

The all-too-familiar loneliness crept over her as she moved through the days, painting and tending the house and gardens. It was already the second week of August and Kat would be leaving the following Tuesday and Kit less than a week after her. On Friday, she drove Nanny and Carrie home from hockey camp where they had been all week.

After they dropped Carrie off, Nanny turned to her mother. "I'd like to stay with Dad for a while. Not for always, but just for a couple of weeks. He really liked having me there last weekend, and, well, we thought I could try it again, for a little longer?"

As she struggled to hold back tears, Beth thought her heart would break. "Why now?"

"He needs me, Mom."

What about me? I need you. "Whatever you want, sweetie. I know Dad would love it."

"Do you mind?"

"'Course not." Lies, lies. "Just don't stay away too long, okay? It's going to be awfully lonely without Kat and Kit."

"I know, I'll come home before school starts." Nanny leaned across the seat and hugged her.

She didn't smell like Nanny, more like locker rooms, athletic tape and the sweat of days on the hockey field.

As they drove into the driveway, Kit was pulling in, Karen in the front seat beside him.

"Hey, Nanna-banna," he called, waving as they parked.

Nanny ran up to hug him, oblivious of Karen's presence, or her brother's nervousness.

As brother and sister embraced, Karen came around the car. "This is Karen. My sister, Nanny, you've probably seen her around, and this is my mom."

Beth extended her hand. "Hello."

"Hello, Mrs. Hadley, nice to meet you."

Karen gave her a dead fish handshake. Were it not for her dour expression, Karen might almost be pretty. Instead, she reminded Beth of a plucked bird, frizzy hair tied on top of her head, freckled arms poking out of a bright yellow tee shirt. Baby bird thin, she wore shorts that hung limp against her legs.

"We're going to have lunch and hang around for a while. Dad's given me the day off and Chloe's on duty." His cheeks were flushed.

"Great, there's plenty of sandwich stuff in the fridge: turkey, ham, cheese."

"I'm a vegetarian," she said, her tone implying disapproval of the largely carnivorous offerings.

That's why Kit hasn't been eating meat, Beth thought, forcing herself to smile graciously. "No problem. The avocados on the windowsill should be ripe and there's lots of salad stuff. Veggie burgers in the freezer, too, Kit."

"Thanks, Mom."

"I'm heading out to the studio so I'll be out of your hair, and Nanny's on her way to the beach with the girls. After she starts her laundry, that is," she added, winking at her youngest.

Neither Kit nor Karen bothered to disguise their relief at Beth's announcement.

After helping Nanny with her bags, Beth gave her a kiss and a hug. "I'm glad you're going to spend time with Dad. Come and see me when you get back from the beach to say goodbye, okay?"

As she walked along the path to the studio, Beth began making a tally of her upcoming garden chores. At the summer's end, many of her perennials were dried and sold to a local greenhouse for seed and to use in fall wreath making workshops. The owner was always glad to buy any of the unusual varieties she grew. In addition to the stemmed flowers, she grew a number of hydrangeas in shades ranging from deep crimson to fairest blue. These too were picked and dried, their blossoms prized by local people who created wreaths and decorative arrangements.

Every day when she left the studio she picked a basketful of flowers and hung them in the barn's drying room. The work that lay ahead, however, would take several hours each day: cutting back, weeding, separating, transplanting, and the endless picking that would fill many wheelbarrows with fragrant, colorful blooms. The gomphrena and strawflowers were already crackling and crisp in the August sun. Beth calculated that she could put off the process for another week, but then she'd have to get to work.

She had just put the brush to the canvas when the phone rang.

"Hey, doll, how's things?"

"Rick. Oh, God, I'm sorry. Did you come by? I mean, I forgot all about our meeting this morning."

"So I noticed. I was there on the dot of eight, too."

They had arranged to meet early this morning so that he could begin the process of listing and cataloging the paintings for the Lynch show.

"Oh, Rick. I'm sorry. You should've let yourself in and made a cup of coffee."

"No, thank you, dear. Although I couldn't say for certain, that moldy jar of instant coffee you keep out there might prove to be lethal. Not to worry, I've been sitting here at ye olde quaint coffee shop drinking gallons of their excellent mocha supreme and I'm just tucking into my fourth cranberry corn muffin."

"Where are you, at Begley's?"

"The very establishment. Mr. Begley himself has been taking care of me."

"Want me to come down?"

"Not unless you want to tote all your paintings with you, dear girl. No, no, no, I'll be along directly, if I may expect to find you there?"

"I'll be waiting."

Rick spent several hours fussing around the studio. Beth endeavored to work despite his constant interruptions. Every time she set down her brush in response to his chatter, he would shoo her back to her easel with, "Keep at it, girl. Don't bother with me." Then, two minutes later he would call her again.

Finally, hands on hips, he declared, "That's it, I'm set. Unless there's anything in the house?"

"No, I'd rather not use them, unless you really think we should?"

"Let's not. You've got quite a bit here. You have been very productive this summer, haven't you? I can't get over it. Why, this little Quaker lady is priceless. Quite the finest work I've seen you do in ages. Lynch was right, you have a talent for portraiture."

"You haven't seen the subjects." She laughed, always uncomfortable with praise.

"Nonsense. These are spectacular and, Bethie, stop selling yourself short. We'll have to practice receiving accolades gracefully, my dear. For receive them you will, that's guaranteed. There's no need to be demure. What's young Lynch say about these anyway?"

"He hasn't seen most of the latest paintings, but he will tomorrow night. We're going out to dinner."

"Oh, ho! Aren't we getting cozy?"

"No, we are not!"

"Well, listen, I'm off. I'll send Leroy over to pick up this last batch for the framer Monday or Tuesday, okay?" Kissing her, Rick declined her offer for lunch, tugging at the waist of his creamy beige slacks. "Look at my waistline after all those muffins. These are my best summer linens and the button is about to pop."

He flew out before she had time to call his attention to the black smudge on the back of his white tee shirt.

It was well after two when she returned to the house to find Kit and Karen on the terrace, the remains of lunch on the table beside them. They were laying sardine-like on her favorite chaise, Karen cradled between his legs, his arms draped around in front of her. As Beth approached, her son hopped up, clearly uncomfortable. Karen stayed put.

"I'm making lunch. You two want anything else?"

He grinned sheepishly. "All set, Mom."

"Thanks, Mrs. Hadley."

Karen's attempt to pull him back down on the chaise proved futile. He hopped up to clear their lunch dishes and followed his mother into the kitchen. Expression inscrutable, Karen lay back, closed her eyes and lifted her face to the sun.

"So?" He watched her as she assembled the ingredients for her sandwich: avocado slices, alfalfa sprouts, lettuce, tomato slices, and mayonnaise.

"So, yourself." She smiled, looking up from her task.

"So don't you have anything to say?"

"'Bout what?"

"You know, about Karen. Karen and me, just now."

"What's there to say? She seems nice."

"No, she isn't. She's kind of a bitch, really."

"Then why are you going out with her?"

"I'm not sure. It's more like she's going out with me."

"Sounds a bit one-sided."

"She's okay, I guess. What are you doing the rest of the day?"

"Painting, maybe a little work in the garden, why?"

"Need any help?"

She stopped stuffing the pita pocket, setting the knife down and turning to face him. "Should I? Are you looking for an excuse to stay home?"

"Maybe. She wants me to take her to Newport, shopping," he whispered.

"Oh, I see. Kit, you can use me as an excuse if you need to, but I'd recommend you tell Karen the truth. It might not be as easy, but it's usually the best policy in situations like this. Believe me."

He nodded. "I hear you." Kit disappeared and a few minutes later, Beth heard the Volvo backing out of the drive. She smiled. Newport had won the day.

After lunch, she settled in for a nap in the sun when Kit appeared around the side of the house.

"I'm back!"

She laughed, closing her eyes.

"If you still want help in the garden, give a yell. I'm going up to my room to start getting organized. Dad gave me money to get some stuff before I go to school."

"Good for you," she called, but he had already disappeared. After years of organizing her children, they were finally taking over. It was a bittersweet moment.

CHAPTER 34

Saturday flew by. Beth painted, gardened, and ran errands. She was looking forward to the dinner with Graham whom she hadn't seen for over a week. He was taking her to Moby Dick's, a popular waterfront restaurant two points up the coast from Windy Harbor. That morning he had called to ask if she would like to go by boat and Beth had happily agreed. She loved the ride along the shoreline, docking at the restaurant's wharf, the return trip even better with the moon lighting their way. If the sky remained clear, it promised to be a beautiful night.

She dressed in beige linen trousers and a short-sleeved blouse, a sweater draped over her shoulder and a windbreaker in her hand. They met at the docks at quarter to seven. As he helped her into the boat, she noticed flecks of gray in his dark wavy hair. No one was ageless, not even Graham. Beth paused and smiled up at him.

"Good to see you," he said quietly.

He had a nervous habit of pushing his wire-rimmed glasses up the bridge of his nose. Beth recalled that same gesture from the first time she met him. Impulsively, she leaned forward and hugged him. "This was a great idea."

A confused smile lit up the usually solemn face. "Shall we go, then?"

The sun sank behind the rooftops of the harbor as he guided the boat along the coast. At Beth's request they took a detour along the east branch of the river. As they drove through the marsh, he slowed to allow them to peer into the clear water, spying blue crabs, fish and eels, moving soundlessly through the gently undulating spartina. At the river's mouth, he opened the throttle and the whaler covered the remaining distance along the coast bringing them alongside the restaurant's dock five minutes before their seven thirty reservation.

Graham requested an outside table on the porch.

"This is lovely." She sighed, sipping a crisp chardonnay. "Just what I needed."

Graham ordered seltzer water for himself.

"Tough day?"

"Tough week." And, you don't know the half of it, she thought. It felt good to be talking to a friend. She realized it had been nearly three weeks since she had seen Clarice. She had a sudden urge to confide in Graham, to tell him about Jack. Would he understand or would he be shocked and outraged?

Her raw emotions and conflicted feelings seemed to be playing tricks on her. All the dodges and deflections she usually employed around Graham seemed silly tonight. What was wrong with her? While the revelation about Jack's relationship with Lesley had been a relief, it had left her feeling vulnerable. She felt an inexplicable longing to reach out to her old friend. The friend she had kept at arm's length for half a lifetime.

"Hello? Earth to Beth."

He had obviously been talking and she had missed it. Beth looked up, mortified to find the waiter watching her as well.

Blushing, she stammered, "Sorry, my turn?"

"Want a few more minutes? I can come back?"

"Have you ordered yet, Graham?"

He shook his head. "Ladies first."

Flustered, she scanned the menu, her cheeks burning red. Graham glanced up at the waiter. "Why don't you give us five."

"No, I'm all set, really. I'll have the swordfish." Chin up, she handed over her menu.

He ordered, then waited for the waiter to disappear. "Want to talk about it? It might help. I'm a good listener and the soul of discretion."

She managed a half-hearted grin. "Thanks, but I can't, not now anyway. Rain check, though?"

"Absolutely." He reached across the table and squeezed her hand.

Surprised, she pulled her hand away and grabbed hold of her wine glass. "How about you? It's been almost two months. How do you like being back?"

"I've decided to stay, for a while anyway. I'm enjoying the gallery and seeing old friends."

"You and Alan have seen a lot of each other, I hear."

"He's looking better, isn't he?"

"Thin last time I saw him, but then, I don't see him that often."

"So I hear. He complains about it constantly."

"Some things never change, do they?"

He nodded, eyes twinkling with warmth.

"We're going through with the divorce, Mary and I." As he spoke, his fingers played with the ice cubes at the bottom of his glass. Suddenly piercing eyes looked up at her. "And don't you dare say too bad, because it isn't. We've never belonged together, not from day one. Sexual attraction does tend to mask incompatibility for a while, doesn't it?"

"I wouldn't know."

What a liar she was, thinking of her behavior this summer.

"None of it was Mary's fault. The blame is all mine.

"I doubt that."

"True, I married her because I couldn't have you. What chance did we have?"

She looked away, unable to meet his gaze. "Here we are," said the waiter, presenting their salads with a flourish. "Ground pepper for you, Ms?"

They spent the rest of the meal chatting about painting, the trials of middle age, and Graham's plans for the gallery; safe topics, which Beth introduced one after another whenever the conversation began to lag. It wasn't until they strolled down the dock to the boat that she seemed to run out of small talk and she realized at the same time, that three glasses of wine had left her more than a little tipsy.

As they headed for the whaler, her heel caught on the rough dock and she stumbled. Graham caught her, then left his arm around her waist. This time she did not pull back. Once she regained her balance, she circled her arm around him. The soft warmth of his sweater against her cheek felt comforting.

He helped her into the boat and grabbed a blanket, which he threw around her shoulders.

"Thanks," she murmured, facing him, his expression unfathomable in the shadows.

Clouds had rolled in obscuring the stars and moon. Darkness made for slow going. Graham maneuvered the boat cautiously, no trace of the reckless speedster of years past. Many a night after too many beers, Beth had feared for her life with Alan and Graham at the helm racing home in the pitch blackness of a moonless night, but not tonight. As the boat puttered slowly through the night, she felt safe, her knees rubbing against his as they headed home.

Finally, the harbor lights appeared, the windows of village homes winking like cats' eyes, bodies hidden in the inky blackness of the starless night. Graham headed toward the wharf's spotlights that illuminated the channel.

Once docked, Beth let her blanket drop as she stood up. Folding the cover and stowing it beneath the bow, she leaned forward and helped him tie up. As she turned, their eyes met and his expression even in the half-light was unmistakable.

Suddenly, she was very glad she had brought her own car. As if echoing her thoughts, he said, "Why didn't I pick you up? Some date, huh?"

As they stood next to her car, she smiled, gazing up at him. "It's been a wonderful evening, Graham. Thank you."

"I'm not ready to let you go." Friendly, he wasn't pushing her. "I don't suppose I could entice you into coming back to my place for a nightcap?"

"Thanks, but I've got to get an early start in the morning. Kat's leaving Monday and we have a crazy day ahead of us packing and all."

"Still go to the Meeting?"

"Yes, but not tomorrow, I'm afraid. Both the Meeting and Mother have been put-off, I'm ashamed to say." Not Jack Talbot though. "That's the price you pay, I pay, for leaving everything until the last minute. Last year, when Kat was a freshman, we were super organized and had everything packed weeks in advance. The anxiety level seems to be lower this year. I've grown accustomed to her leaving and it's made me lax in my duties."

"I doubt that. You'll miss 'em, won't you?"

"It's awful. The house feels so empty."

"I would be more than happy to step in and fill the void." His tone was light-hearted, but his piercing eyes searched hers for signs of encouragement.

Beth's first impulse was to pull away and hop into her car, but instead she reached up, and her arms circled his neck as she kissed him, a long, lingering kiss that left her breathless. Just as quickly, she pulled away.

"I really have to go, thank you."

"My pleasure," he whispered as he closed the car door behind her.

CHAPTER 35

No Meeting for worship, no visit to her mother, but at two o'clock Beth headed for Hestor's Way and Jack, drawing supplies and a thin pad of paper on the seat beside her. As she turned down the gravel road, the cottage's roof visible among the scrub pines at the far end of the street, she felt her body stir.

He was already there, pacing just inside the door. He had taken quilts from the hall closet and laid them on the living room floor. Beth took her time gathering her things, collecting her thoughts and emotions along with her supplies. She took so much time that he finally appeared in the doorway, his expression impatient and questioning behind the screen door. Run, Beth, run, a voice screamed out to her; run now before it's too late.

Instead she waved, smiling up at him. How different things would be if it were Graham waiting behind the screen door, she thought, waving hello as she made her way up the walk, feet crunching on the clamshell path overgrown with crabgrass and dandelion.

He sensed the change in her immediately. His eyes questioned as they stood in the dim light of the front hall and he drew back, holding her at arm's length. "What's wrong?"

"Nothing," she lied, reaching up to smooth tousled strands of hair from his forehead. "I brought these." She held open the case, pad tucked under her arm. "Still want me to do it?"

"Not now." He took the things, set them on the hall table and lifted her, wrapping her legs around his waist as he carried her to the living room. The same tender longing, the same desperate desire as he undressed her with practiced hands. His hands played over her and ripples of pleasure coursed through her body.

For an instant, she tried to pull away. His lips on her neck traveled down, opening the blouse, only partially unbuttoned. Instead of the tee shirts she usually wore, Beth donned light summer blouses for their Sunday trysts because blouses prolonged the exquisite pleasure of the undressing, buttons slowly giving way to insistent hands and lips. Finally, he drew her to him and she returned the embrace, lost in her desire with no will or inclination to pull away.

Only later, as they lay spent in each other's arms, did she focus on the subtle change in both of them. The passion had been there, but something was missing. A connection, a bond, indefinable, yet crucial, had been broken. His fidgeting beside her told her he sensed it too.

In the rapidly dwindling light she dressed as Jack reached for his jeans, languidly pulling them on. Then, he slumped back against the sofa and stared out the window. She was aware of how few words had passed between them since her arrival, the whispered murmurs in the heat of passion absent in the stillness.

Not inclined to break the silence, Beth padded out to the hall and retrieved her paint supplies and a glass of water, then returned to sit opposite him on the floor. She drew him as he lay solemnly gazing out to sea, bare-chested, jeans half-zipped, arms akimbo resting on the faded mauve cushions of the summer couch.

"Kat leaves tomorrow, huh?" His voice startled her and she jumped nearly upsetting her glass of water.

"She does. She'll be back in a few days over the Labor Day weekend, but that's it. How about you?"

Try as she might, Beth seemed unable to hold on to a single feature long enough to put it to paper, not the wide, angular chin, nor the piercing dark eyes and even the sandy hair looked as if it belonged to a stranger.

"I'm not playing soccer. Ineligible. Too old, remember?" The words hung in the air between them.

"Oh?"

"Last week. They recruited me for the lacrosse club, no age limitation there. Dad thinks I'd be better off starting Harvard without the pressure of sports on top of the academics anyway."

"He's probably right." There, finally she'd gotten his jaw and the overall contours of the recumbent body were beginning to take shape.

He shrugged, sitting up.

"Oh, Jack, please don't move! I've already started you lying down."

"Why are you taking pictures? You take lots of the other people you draw and paint."

"This is better I think."

"Don't want anyone to know your dirty little secret?"

His bitter tone frightened her. "Is something wrong?"

He leaned forward, head bowed, almost touching the floor between his legs. "I'm sick of this."

Me, too, she thought but said nothing, waiting for him to go on. He didn't.

Her hand that held the charcoal shook and she paused, placing both hands in her lap, black smudges staining her skirt. He liked her in skirts, so he could reach between her legs to her soft wetness unencumbered by pant legs and zippers. He would reach up with both hands and slowly bring her panties down her thighs, before lifting her skirt to press his manhood against her. By this time, their bodies ached for one another.

"Maybe it's time we ended this? What do you think?"

Shrugging, he turned away. "If that's what you want."

"Jack, what is it? Is it Lesley? Are you feeling guilty about seeing me when you're dating her? Is that it?"

He looked directly at her for the first time. "You know about her, then?"

"Yup."

"I've been wanting to tell you. It just kind of happened, that's all."

"Jack, you don't have to explain anything to me. I'm glad for you." Partially a lie, partially the truth.

"I feel like a scumbag, you know? Coming here with you, then taking her out to the movies."

"Stop it. You're beating yourself up for doing exactly what you should be doing. Falling in love with someone your own age."

"But, I'm not in love with Lesley. I'm in love with you. This is such bullshit. I'm a coward. Lesley probably thinks I'm practically a virgin like everyone else. If they only knew. Christ." He rose and grabbed his shirt. "I gotta go."

"Jack, wait!" But he was gone, leaving her to lock up. She closed her sketchbook without a glance at the unfinished drawing. She would dispose of it as soon as she got home.

CHAPTER 36

Monday morning, Beth, Kat, and Nanny rose before sunup and piled into the car. They stopped for breakfast at their favorite diner just north of Boston and by eleven had Kat checked into her dorm. Kat left almost immediately and ran across campus to her practice. Beth and Nanny bustled around the dorm room, making the bed, hanging curtains, and making ineffectual attempts to unpack Kat's things.

"I knew there was a reason we should have come yesterday," Beth said, flopping down on the freshly made bed. "That's enough, Nan. She'll have to do the rest."

"Looks pretty good, much better than her room last year."

"You're right, Nan. Let's go watch a little of the practice and then say our goodbyes, okay?"

"I thought we were staying for dinner?"

"Nope, Kat said she'd rather we go along so she can eat with the team."

"Oh," Nanny said, disappointment evident in her tone.

"Don't worry, sweetie," Beth said. "There will be lots of chances for you to come and stay. When she comes back up after Labor Day things will be calmer. Right now Kat needs to catch up with her buddies. If you like, we can eat in the cafeteria before we head home."

Nanny's face brightened.

Later that night as Beth lay reading in bed, the phone rang. "Hi, it's me. How's the separation anxiety?"

"Bearable, thank you. If you had children you wouldn't joke about it either." Silence. "Oh, Graham, I'm sorry, I didn't mean that. What a stupid, insensitive thing to say."

"It was, but you're forgiven. Did you and Alan take her up?"

"No, just Nanny and me."

"Any update on his prognosis?"

"I really don't know. You probably see and talk to him more than I do."

"We never talk about the cancer."

"I'll phone tomorrow and see how things are going."

"You free at all this week?"

I'm free all the time, she thought, but said, "What did you have in mind?"

"Honestly, I hadn't thought that far. I'd just like to see you."

"Come for dinner, then. Tomorrow? Both kids are staying at Alan's so we'll have the house to ourselves."

"Sounds good to me, what time?"

"Seven okay?"

"I'll look forward to it. Night, Beth."

Chapter 37

After a morning spent running errands in preparation for her dinner with Graham, Beth took the wheelbarrow to the far end of the garden and began an afternoon of flower harvesting. Cutting blooms at their peak, she layered them gently in the wheelbarrow and gathered flower and herb seeds, which she shook into bags, labeling them as she went along. Over half of next year's annual garden would come from those seeds, but she also gave away seeds to friends and neighbors. Many times over the years, she had been encouraged to market the varieties she cultivated and developed, but she preferred to enjoy gardening for the hobby it was, no deadlines and none of the headaches of running a business.

It was a clear, sunny day, the temperature in the nineties. Ocean breezes kept the garden relatively cool as she worked. She had just made the third trip to the barn with a full wheelbarrow. There she piled all on benches until she could return at the day's end to hang them. As she exited the barn, she spied Kit in the Volvo tearing up the drive. She shielded her eyes against the sun and paused, sitting on the empty wheelbarrow, watching as he hopped out of the car and headed toward her. As he neared, she could tell by the set of his jaw and the furrowed brow that he was furious. In his left hand he held a folded paper.

Dear God, oh, Alan, what have you done now? she thought, calling out, "Hey, stranger, how are you?"

He said nothing until he stood directly over her, eyes blazing. "How do you think I am?" He threw the paper in front of her on the ground.

Beth gasped. On the ground lay the unfinished drawing of Jack. "Kit, where did you get this?"

"You do something like this and dare to ask me where I got it?"

"Kit, please."

"I got it from your studio, if you must know. See your lover, if that's what you call him, told me about you and him. Stupid, idiot, trusting son that I am, I didn't believe him." Tears welled up in the dark eyes, pushing away the anger for an instant, pain visible beneath the rage.

"Oh, Kit."

"So he told me to go look for proof in your sketch pad. Told me just where to look, like he knew the studio better than me."

"Kit, please, let's go inside and talk, okay?"

"No. I don't want to talk about this. I won't talk about it. I'm just here long enough to get some of my things. I'm moving to Dad's. I can't even look at you."

"Oh, God, Kit, please, just a few minutes." As she reached out, he recoiled from her touch.

"No, my mother is screwing my best friend and I'm leaving!"

He stalked off, shoulders set. "And don't follow me into the house. I only need fifteen minutes."

Beth sank back down on the wheelbarrow and hunched over, sobs wracking her body. A short time later, the Volvo roared out of the driveway.

The sunset jolted her. She had been there crying for hours. She shook herself and stood, leaving the wheelbarrow and carrying her tool bag to the terrace door. She had barely stepped inside the house when Graham knocked. Gazing up at the clock, she saw it was ten minutes after seven. She had done nothing about dinner.

"Beth, my God, what's happened?"

His face told her all she needed to know about her appearance. She collapsed into his arms, allowing herself to be led to the couch in the family room. Between sobs, she poured out the whole story, ending with a description of the scene with Kit.

"Oh, God, Graham, I'm so sorry. I have no right to burden you with this. I can't imagine what you must think of me and I don't blame you if you want to go.

I'm afraid there's no dinner." Fresh sobs overtook her as she leaned against him, his arms circling her, patting her softly.

Finally, he stood and bent over, taking her up in his arms. He carried her upstairs and set her gently on the chair in her bathroom. While the bath ran, he peeled off her mud-and grass- stained gardening clothes and led her to the tub.

Strange, Beth thought, following him. He's never seen me naked, yet I'm not embarrassed or self-conscious in the slightest. She allowed him to wash her, to scrub her back, to gently towel her off and finally to dress her in warm sweats as if she were a two-year-old.

In clean clothes, her body relaxed after the bath, she began to feel like herself again. When he came to sit beside her on the edge of the bed, she found she could look him in the eye."Thank you. I am pathetic. You can make your escape now."

He stared at her for a long time without speaking, expression unreadable. "I don't think you're pathetic and I'm not going to run away. I love you, Beth. I've always loved you. To be honest, I don't know how I feel about 'us' right now, with all you've just told me, but I won't run away. No matter what happens, Beth, you have my friendship. Understood?" She nodded, afraid to speak. "And no more crying, it does terrible puffy things to those beautiful eyes. Come on, I'll make us some soup. You do have cans of soup around somewhere, don't you?"

In spite of her aching heart, she laughed and followed him downstairs. She toasted some English muffins, while he "doctored" some cream of asparagus soup.

As they sat at the counter sipping the hot, creamy soup, Graham looked up. "Feeling better?"

"Much, but, oh God, what a mess I've made of things."

"Why did Jack tell him anyway? Do you know?"

"No. Well, maybe. Jack's always been bothered by the secrecy. From the beginning, a part of him has always wanted to be open about us, even though he knew it was crazy. It's been difficult the last few times we've been together."

She set down her spoon and held her head in her hands, rubbing her eyes, unable to look at him. "He's got a girlfriend. Her name is Lesley. I was happy about it and told him so. I'm ashamed to say that I was a little jealous, but ultimately I knew that Jack and I couldn't go on. Can you imagine the Talbots? Oh, God, the Talbots. Do you suppose he's told his parents?"

"Probably not." Clearly he had no basis for his assumption beyond the wish not to upset her.

"Somehow my not being angry about Lesley made him angry. I don't know why. He said he was feeling guilty for not telling her about me. He's probably told her, too, by now. He stormed out of the beach house and I haven't seen him since.

"Of course, that's not that unusual. Since we started seeing each other, Jack hasn't come around the house much with Kit and his friends. All summer they've been speculating about where he goes, what he does, so we agreed we should only see each other on Sundays, away from Windy Harbor, at Mother's beach house in Sayles Cove. Oh, Graham, what have I done?"

"You've had a love affair with a younger guy. Hey, it happens every day, my sweet. Usually it's the old geezer and the young babe, but hey, no reason it can't go the other way, is there? Think about it. That's where the label cougar arose."

"Why doesn't that make me feel better?"

"Just an old-fashioned girl, I guess." That remark coaxed a flicker of a smile. "And look at it this way, you're closer in age than Alan and Chloe."

"Very comforting, however, Chloe wasn't one of my children's best friends."

"A complication, yes, but, he'll get over it. Kit's a man. Probably more hurt that you didn't tell him than about the affair itself."

"I doubt that very much."

"Don't forget, he's been the man of the house these past few years. Let him cool down. He'll come back after a couple of days. I'll wager it's pride more than anything."

Head buried in hands, she thought about her flowers. On top of everything else, she would probably lose many of them, too.

They talked a while longer, then Graham gave her a snifter of brandy and put her in bed. He cradled her in his arms until she slept.

Just before drifting off, she cried, "Oh, what will Kat and Nanny think? Never mind the rest of the world."

"Hey, relax. Jack may have told Kit and that's as far as it'll go," Graham whispered, kissing her forehead.

CHAPTER 38

Beth rose early and plunged herself into her work. She was determined to salvage what she could of the previous day's harvest so she spent the morning hanging flowers in the barn's drying room. The previous night had been cool and dry so most of the blossoms were still fresh. The discovery brought no joy after the events of the past days. Late morning found her in the studio working on a portrait of Milly Kittredge, the post mistress.

Graham had left a note on her pillow. *I'll have that dinner tonight, even if I have to cook it. Love, G.* The note was now tucked in her pocket acting as a kind of talisman. Whenever her spirits began to flag, she reached down and touched the bulge in her jeans. The reminder of Graham's kindness kept her from bursting into tears.

Earlier in the day she had carried on a somewhat normal conversation with Rick, where they arranged to meet with a customer in Bay Port. Porter Lang had commissioned a landscape from her several years earlier and his wife had asked for "another Hadley" for her birthday. He wanted to get together and talk about possible subjects. They scheduled a meeting for Wednesday of the following week.

Just as she was putting the finishing touches on Milly's thick, salt-and-pepper tresses, Alan burst through the studio's back door. Her first thought was concern. He looked even thinner than the last time she had seen him: hollow cheeks, yellow skin, and another ten pounds missing from the once rugged frame. His expression soon banished her worry and she braced herself, waiting for the onslaught. There was little doubt from his demeanor about the reason for his visit.

"How could you?" Thin arms waved in front of her and for an instant Beth feared he might strike her.

"You've heard, then," she said, turning away, leading him to a chair. She was certain she couldn't have this conversation standing up and Alan looked as if he might keel over at any second.

"Heard? Of course I've heard. Jesus Christ, Beth, what do you take me for?"

Her head began throbbing as the brandy caught up with her. "Alan, I have no idea what you mean. What do I take you for? Frankly, this is none of your business, and if you want to talk to me you'll have to stop shouting."

"Fine, is this better?" He lowered his voice half a decibel. "I'm Kit's father for Christ's sake, and it is my business. He's a fucking mess and no wonder. I've had to get out of my sick bed to come over here. Beth, I want answers."

Her remorse of the previous night was now replaced by weary annoyance. Calmly, she replied, "Alan, I haven't got any answers. I'm just as concerned about Kit as you are."

"Ha! Fine time to think about that."

She glared at him. "If I could spare Kit this hurt I would, but I can't. It happened."

"I'll say."

Ignoring his sarcasm, she said, "I need your support, Alan."

"For what?"

"For what to do next."

"It is still happening, according to what he told Kit."

"Okay, whatever's happening, it has nothing whatsoever to do with Kit and you of all people should know it. It is just an awful coincidence that Jack is his best friend."

"Spare me, would you please. Don't use that line of reasoning to justify your, your—"

"Go ahead, say it. Robbing the cradle? Old enough to be his mother? You should be an expert on the terminology. You've probably heard it all."

"Is that what this is about? Is this thing with Jack to get back at me for marrying Chloe? Is that it?"

Furious now, she glared at him. That was Alan all over. Always assumed that everyone's actions and behaviors evolved from him.

"Believe it or not, Alan, this has nothing whatsoever to do with you. Jack and I started, well, we began seeing each other because of a mutual attraction. The same indefinable thing that draws every man and woman together. Love? Lust? Need of affection? I don't know, but we had it. Maybe we still do, I don't know after all this…but this is between us, Jack and me, and it has nothing to do with you or the kids. I know it's difficult for you to believe this, but I really am over you. Once in a while the old hurt returns, I admit it, but not often. As I told you on the Fourth of July, the love I felt for you is gone and so is the anger. That's the truth."

He sat back as if she had slapped him, the frail body trembling.

She waited a few minutes to collect her thoughts before continuing. "I am committed to trying to get along with you for the sake of the kids and I hope you can make the same commitment, at least until they are on their own. I'm not asking you to understand about Jack, but I am asking for your support right now as the other parent in this family. When you left, I spent half my life crying, the other half in a rage, but I never denounced you to your children. Never. Believe me, I said plenty in therapy, but to the kids you were always their father and a good man. I'm asking you now to please give me the same consideration."

"Oh, God, Beth, what a mess I've made of things. I've driven you to this."

There it was again. Him, him, him. "Alan, this is my life. I'd like to own it warts and all, if you don't mind. I did this. I had the affair. I'll take all of the responsibility."

"Did it again, didn't I?" He smiled. The Alan of twenty years ago peeked through the hollow mask for a second. "So? What are we going to do? Correction, what are you going to do, if you don't mind me asking?"

She did, but answered him anyway. "Well, first, I want to talk to Kit, and then Jack. Do you know if Jack has told anyone else?"

"Not that I know of, but, at least Kit didn't think so. Might've told that girl of his, Lana?"

"Lesley."

"Are you gonna keep this up? I mean, seeing him?"

"No, I don't think so. We were drifting apart anyway."

She stopped, not wanting to confide in her ex-husband while at the same time realizing that it was comfortable talking to him. Remnants of the past intimacy?

"Okay, don't worry, I'm behind you, babe. Kit will get over it. He's a man now." He reached over and took her hand in a claw-like grasp.

She almost said, "That's just what Graham said" but held her tongue, unwilling to tackle that subject just now. "Thanks, I appreciate your support. Really I do." She squeezed his hand before extracting hers. "How are you feeling?"

"Shitty, but I go in for my check-up soon to see if the chemo's done the trick. Doctor says my body's responded well so far."

"That's good news. What about your work? Does he think the paints and shellacs and all could have caused it?"

He looked at her with a blank stare.

"I asked you about that before, remember?"

"Yeah, I forgot to ask, but I'll check."

He was lying, but she let the matter drop. She wasn't his wife anymore. It was none of her business. Besides, carcinogenic or not, he'd never give up his work. That would kill him.

They talked for a while longer, then he rose, stiff-legged and weak-kneed. "I'd better get going."

"Where's your car?" she asked, moving to his side, her arm around his waist preventing him from keeling over. As he leaned into her, she could feel every rib pressed against her.

"Car's right outside. If you get me there, I can make it the rest of the way. Kit's home. He'll help me on the other end."

Once in the car, he looked up, giving her a wan smile. Clearly in pain, he was trying hard not to show it. "I'll talk to him, Bethie. Get him to come over. You should give him a call. Better get hold of Talbot before he spreads this all over town. I'm not going to tell Chloe. She'd blab it for sure. No one's hearing this from me, okay?"

Thanking him, she stepped back from the car and waved as he pulled away. Instantly, her shoulders relaxed and she let down the steely façade she always erected when dealing with Alan. What she really wanted to do was to sit down and have another good cry, but instead she forced herself to go in and clean her brushes. No more painting today.

She headed back to the house for a sweater and her car keys. She needed a long, restorative walk on the beach.

When she returned home, he was waiting for her in the kitchen.

Chapter 39

"Hi." Voice tentative, eyes lowered, he shifted his feet, the sawdust on his boots sprinkling the tiled floor.

"Hi, yourself."

She came to sit beside him at the counter. He was covered with paint from the job, flecks of colonial gray in his hair and streaked across his face, work shirt and jeans, gray crescents under every fingernail.

"I'm on my lunch break."

"Want me to fix you a sandwich?"

"Already ate while I was waiting." He blushed. "I mean, not your food. I brought my own and ate it."

"You've fixed yourself enough meals here to know this kitchen's open to you anytime you're hungry, Jack. Always has been, always will be."

"Yeah, for friends of Kit and Kat's. That sure leaves me out now."

"No, it doesn't. Kit's angry and hurt, but he'll calm down. You'll get beyond this, you'll see."

"I'm sorry. I never should've told him."

"Yes, you should. He's your best friend."

"And I'm fucking his mother."

Startled at his choice of words, she stared at him.

"Sorry, crude huh, but then I'm a crude bastard, aren't I?"

"No."

"Guess I've made a pretty big mess of things?"

"We both made a mess of things. It's as much my fault as yours, probably more mine. Have you told anyone else besides Kit?"

"No, I almost told Lesley last night, but she was going on about school. She's going to Bates. Anyway, she was so happy and excited, I didn't want to spoil things."

"Wise. Want my opinion?"

"I know, don't tell anyone."

"There are good reasons and you know it."

"So, does this mean we can't be together anymore?"

"I don't know. It's probably not a great idea."

"I want to keep seeing you. If I have to, I'll stop seeing Lesley and then we can be together and I won't feel guilty to both of you at the same time."

There's more to it than that, she wanted to say, so much more. "I'm not sure it's a good idea."

"You've already decided, haven't you? You've made your choice."

"Excuse me?"

"You've chosen Kit over me."

"No, I haven't. Of course, I'm sorry for the hurt I've caused him and wish I hadn't. I'm trying to find a way to make it up to him."

"What about me? What about my hurt?"

"Jack, I am thinking about your hurt. I'm thinking about everyone: you, Kit, myself, our families, our friends, everyone. This would be very hard on everyone who knows and cares about you. Think of your parents. They would view me as ruining your bright future and my friends will regard me as a, well, I don't know, but it wouldn't be flattering."

"That's what's important? What your friends think?"

"That's not what I said. I'm thinking about you, too."

"Well don't. I'm thirty-three. I can take care of myself."

Beth felt as if she spun inside a whirlpool as the conversation spiraled down into a black hole of despair. She rubbed her temples and closed her eyes.

"Want me to go? Is that it?"

"No," she said softly, touching a paint encrusted sleeve. "I don't want you to go. I never want you to go. That's the problem."

As if her words released a pressure valve, his whole body relaxed. "Please don't make it be over," he whispered and leaned forward, kissing her.

Beth responded and returned the kiss, heart breaking at the thought of losing him.

"No! We can't, you have to go."

"When can I come? Tonight?"

"No. You can't come here."

"Next Sunday, then?"

"No, we can't."

"Please, just one more time." He reached for her again as she struggled to keep him at arm's length.

"If I meet you Sunday, will you promise not to say anything to anyone? I'd like to talk to Kit. But, Jack, this Sunday will be the last."

He nodded, eyes regarding her with sadness, then hopped off the stool. "Gotta get back to work."

Her sandwich had no taste and she no longer felt hungry. Half eaten, she wrapped it, then placed it in the fridge and went to her room for a rest. Napping was impossible. Her emotions played havoc with her usual midday tranquility.

Finally, head throbbing, she rose and dialed Alan's number. Chloe answered and Beth asked for Kit. "Yeah, he's here somewhere, hold on."

"Beth, he says he'll have to get back to you."

"Chloe, I need to speak with him now. Tell him to come to the phone please."

Silence. Finally, Chloe said, "Sure, okay, I'll try."

After several more minutes, he said, "Hello."

"Kit, please, we need to talk."

"I've got nothing to say to you."

"Listen, please, Dad and I have spoken. We agreed he wouldn't tell Chloe about this."

"So what?"

"So, if I have to, I'll come over there and find you. We need to talk. Please."

"What for?"

"What for? Because you're my son and I've hurt you. I want to at least try and explain, to make things up somehow."

"Well you can't."

"I thought we were going shopping this week for school things."

"Dad will take me."

"Kit, Dad's too weak to take you and you know it."

"I don't need anything."

"Yes, you do. You had a whole list of things."

"I said I don't want anything."

"How's Nanny?"

"Fine. She's never here. Spends all her time at Carrie's."

Beth realized she hadn't any idea where her youngest had been for several days. In only a few short weeks, she had turned into a disconnected, neglectful parent. For over three weeks, Beth had deflected Clarice's repeated requests to get together and their last conversation had been strained. Clary was clearly miffed by her evasion and had practically hung up on her. It couldn't be helped. Beth knew Clary to be the one person who could see right through her and she couldn't risk having her pry the truth about Jack out of her.

"Kit, would you please come home and talk to me? Or I can meet you somewhere?"

"I can't. I've got too many things to do."

"What about tomorrow?"

"No, Dad needs me."

"Please, Kit." She was struggling vainly to hold back tears.

He knew her well and heard the change in her voice. "Okay, but I can't stay long. I'll come over around ten."

"Thanks, sweetie."

"Gotta go, bye." He hung up before she could utter another syllable.

Beth raced through the house and cleaned. She prepared a salad and dessert for dinner. Her part was easy as Graham was bringing the rest of the meal: lobster, corn, and bread. By three, satisfied with her preparations, the table set, she was too restless to sit and relax so she retreated to the studio.

CHAPTER 40

It hadn't been her intention to paint. In her agitated state, she assumed it would be impossible, but as soon as she stepped inside the door, she went straight to the Hoosier cupboard for her brushes, paints and palette. The hush of the lonely building soothed her, stroking her battered psyche. Setting up a blank canvas, she went to work and a painting magically sprang to life on the blank white surface.

It was a view of Hestor's Way. The idea had begun as a sketch drawn while she waited for Jack their first time at the beach house. Unlike most of her paintings, where she relied so heavily on photographs, Beth used nothing but the rough sketch to guide her hand. Soon the shingled house emerged.

It had been a clear, sunny day when she had done the sketch, but now the cottage looked quite different. The sky behind it was dark with an approaching storm, the sea inky black and in turmoil. Waves crashed with hurricane force onto the beach behind the house. As the scene began to take shape, it frightened her. Driven by unseen forces, she kept on, eyes riveted to the canvas, trance-like.

So rapt was she in her work that when his hand touched her shoulder, she jumped, crying out. As she lunged forward, he caught her and the easel before they could topple over. "Whoa, sorry I startled you."

As if coming out of a trance, she collapsed against Graham, exhausted from her efforts, her energy sapped away.

"You okay?"

Unable to speak, she allowed him to lead her to the couch, where he took the brush from her hand, carrying it to the sink. When she collapsed against him, she had daubed his khakis with a wide streak of black paint, but he didn't appear to notice.

After cleaning the brush, he lay all the paint tubes and her brushes on paper towels and rinsed out the jar and set it on the edge of the sink. While he worked, Beth watched, grateful for his steady presence.

"This mopping up after me is getting to be a habit, isn't it?"

"Come on, there are two lobsters on your terrace awaiting their doom. We'd best not prolong their agony."

He held out his hand and pulled her to her feet. In the fading daylight, they walked arm in arm back along the garden path. They spoke little, but as they approached the terrace he turned and kissed her on the forehead. "Still want to do this or would you rather I took my clawed friends and disappeared?"

"No," she whispered and rested her head against his chest, his warmth reviving her. "I mean, yes, yes, I do. At the moment, I'm almost happy, if you can believe it. Some hostess, huh?"

"Doing fine by me."

He led her into the house. The meal and wine improved her spirits immeasurably and she began to feel herself again. By the time they returned to the family room, Graham with coffee, Beth still nursing her wine, she felt relaxed and calm.

She related the events of the day. Graham listened, but made little comment except to wish her luck in the morning. As he refilled her wine glass, she said, "Whoa, if I didn't know any better I'd say you were trying to get me drunk."

"Never." He laughed. "But it would do you good, I'll wager."

She took a sip. "I don't know about that."

"That was quite something you were working on out there. Have you been at it long?"

"No."

She found she couldn't bring a clear image of the painting into her mind and didn't want to discuss it anyway.

"Gonna put it in the show?"

Eyes closed, she rubbed her temples.

"Wrong subject. Sorry."

"Not wrong, just disturbing. I don't know what happened to me out there today. It was almost like I was possessed. It was like someone else held the brush and I was watching."

"I'm sure lots of artists feel that way."

"Well, not this one. Of course, I have moments which I might arrogantly describe as inspirational, but nothing like this."

"It's a remarkable painting, Beth, however it was created."

"Thanks," she said.

Taking her glass and setting it on the table, he reached out and pulled her gently to him.

"You were right, you know."

"Oh?"

"About it being my life and not your fault that I screwed it up."

"Excuse me?"

"The drinking, messing things up with Mary. They were all my doing. I made those choices, Beth. And, I never should have burdened you with all that garbage. I'm sorry."

"Graham, you don't have to apologize."

"Yes, I do, my darling. I love you and I need you to know that what I feel for you is real, not some feeble attempt to escape from a fucked-up life."

"Considering the current state of my life, I'm not sure I'm the best person to hitch your wagon to." She smiled up at him.

Kisses grazed her hair and cheeks and finally he found her lips. Beth closed her eyes and felt twenty again, conscious of nothing save the touch of the man she had loved in secret for so many years. Moaning softly, she pressed against him, grateful for his warmth and love. Shutting out the world, she gave herself to him.

They made their way upstairs, discarded clothes trailing behind them until they reached the bedroom, fully aroused and naked save the condom, slipped deftly on as they slipped through the door. His hands were everywhere, on her breasts, moving up her thighs to the soft, moist wetness, lifting her, wrapping her legs around him. He entered her, hands cradling her buttocks and they moved together, pressed against the doorframe. Finally, moving to the bed, he lowered her. Their bodies moved in perfect synchrony as they brought each other to climax again and again, each time wanting more. Each time the wrench of separation felt almost unbearable.

Finally, exhausted, they lay bodies entwined, his kisses reassuring her, his words of love healing the ache of loneliness felt for so long. If Jack had been a desperate passion, Graham represented love, an abiding, steady presence. At that moment, she wished for nothing more than to stay in his arms forever.

CHAPTER 41

Beth found his note when she woke up. *I'll call later. Good luck with K., G.*

A spotless kitchen greeted her, the only evidence of their meal the huge splatter ware lobster steamer upturned in the sink's drying rack, a half-eaten berry pie in the refrigerator.

Juice and two Advil later, she felt better, but not much. With a pounding head, she wandered around the house, wondering what to do with herself.

The phone rang.

"Okay, dear friend, this is it. If you don't have dinner with me tonight, I'm coming over there and sit on your doorstep."

Beth laughed. "Hi, Clary, I'm sorry. It's been crazy."

"How about the Bayside?"

"Too many familiar faces. We'll be interrupted all night."

"You're right. Rudy's then? Ben ate there last week and says food is still pretty good. Cheap, too."

"Sounds perfect." She arranged to pick Clary up at seven and rang off.

Shortly after ten, Kit appeared. He looked thin, as if he'd dropped ten or fifteen pounds in the past few days. She refrained from remarking about it for fear of upsetting him.

She followed him to the terrace. Kit slumped in the chaise, eyes half-closed. Beth sat beside him in one of Alan's porch rockers. "So? How are things at Dad's?"

"Okay."

"How's he feeling?"

"Better."

"Chloe doing okay?"

"I guess. She's hardly ever home. She's working on some big project so she stays on campus most nights with a friend."

"Oh."

Silence. Kit gazed across the yard, the far end of the field seeming to hold great fascination. "I never meant to hurt you, Kit. If I could take back this summer and start again, I would. You and Kat and Nanny are my whole life."

"Why couldn't you find someone your own age?"

"It just happened."

"The affair?"

"I suppose."

"I mean, Mom, look at Dad and Chloe. People of different ages get together, I realize that, but did it have to be Jack? Why did you have to pick him? Do you have any idea how uncomfortable that makes me?"

I didn't pick Jack, he picked me, she thought. "I know, honey, and I am so sorry. I have no right to compromise your friendship. It was very selfish of me."

Resigned, the fight knocked out of him, he said, "I talked to Dad about this."

"Oh?"

"Yeah, it helped."

"I'm glad. I'm glad you and Dad are close again."

He nodded. "Me, too. That's the main reason I've decided to stay home this year."

"What?" She felt as if she'd been kicked in the stomach."

"Mom, don't get upset, okay? Lots of kids do it. I talked to my advisor at Bowdoin this morning. They have a deferment process I can go through if I get all the paperwork in."

"Oh, Kit, don't do this."

"Mom, I knew you would react this way. Dad said you would be mad. He is fine about it. Why can't you be?"

"Because I know how much you wanted this, how much you've been looking forward to this year. What about Charlie, your roommate? Where will that leave him?"

Kit and his roommate from South Carolina had been calling each other all summer making plans.

"His name is Chester, Mom, and he'll be fine. We were in a quad, remember? He'll have two other people. Probably be glad to have his part of the room to himself. Maybe they'll assign someone else to the room?"

"Is this because of me? Because of this thing with Jack?"

"Uh-oh, Mom, now you're sounding like Dad. You're doing what you always say he does, making everything about him. This has nothing to do with you or Jack Talbot."

There it was. The first flash of anger since their conversation began. Kit spit his friend's name out as if it were poison.

"I want to do it. I'm not ready for college. I want to work for a while and be close to Dad."

"What will you do?"

"Help Dad with the woodworking. He really needs me. If things get slow, I'll find something else."

"You're set on this, aren't you?"

"Yup."

"You won't change your mind next week?"

"Nope."

"How about trying preseason and making the decision after that?"

"Mom, I've already made the decision. I'm not going. Mr. Koenig, my advisor, didn't think there would be any problem with the money or anything, so it won't cost you and Dad anything. If it does, I'll pay you back."

They talked a while longer and Beth gave him her blessing. Then, they discussed issues related to the deferment, forms, and letters that she and Alan would have to sign. At one point he said, "If they don't grant me the deferment, Dad thinks we can use his illness to plead our case."

Finally, he rose and hugged her. "Mom, I gotta go. It'll be fine. Don't worry."

"I know it will, sweetie." She walked him to his car. "Will you live here?"

"Maybe. I'll see how long I can stand Chloe. She's been okay, but kind of weird. I'd like to stick it out for a while, until Dad's feeling better. He needs me right now."

"I know he does." She hugged him and wanted to scream, "I do, too," but instead whispered, "I love you."

"Me, too." He smiled at her, hurt still evident in his eyes.

"Kit, don't let this destroy your friendship with Jack."

"It has."

"He needs you, too, more than ever. You know how worried he's been about college."

"Let him talk to Lesley or one of the other guys, not me."

"Kit, you've been friends your whole life. Friendship like that doesn't come along very often."

"Mom, I don't want to talk about this, okay?"

"Okay." She touched his arm gently. Enough for one day, she thought as she watched the Volvo drive off. Relieved that she hadn't lost him completely, she was nonetheless devastated by his decision about Bowdoin and furious with Alan for not warning her.

Resisting the urge to phone Alan to chew him out, she made a sandwich and went out to the studio. She spent the remainder of the day with the phone disconnected, painting, sleeping, reading, and straightening up. Finally, in the late afternoon, she propped her paintings around the studio and began circling the room studying each one. With only a few exceptions, all of the pieces chosen to hang in the Lynch show would be new ones. In comparison to her recent work, her earlier stuff looked flat and lifeless, as if they'd been painted by a completely different artist.

At six, she stopped and hurried back to the house to change into jeans and a sweater. Only a few minutes late, she arrived at the Rollins' to find Clarice, as usual, far from ready. Beth came inside to enjoy twenty minutes of Rollins family chaos, kids shouting and dinner preparations progressing willy nilly. She and Ben attempted to carry on a conversation above the din, until Clary appeared. Then Ben shooed them out with, "I can handle this, girls. Go."

"I love it when he's domestic," Clary whispered, taking Beth's arm as they strolled out to the car. "It's a huge turn-on."

"Everything Ben does is a huge turn-on to you." Beth laughed, nudging her as they separated, each to her own side of the car.

Clary laughed. "Guilty as charged."

Rudy's was crowded and smoky, but they found a table in the back room, away from the bar and the greatest concentration of smokers. Rudy's didn't have a non-smoking section and it wouldn't have mattered if they did. The ventilation system was nonexistent.

"Okay," Clary began, drumming her fingers on the marbleized gray Formica. "Why have you been avoiding me for the past month?"

"I haven't."

"Oh, yes, you have. Two drafts, Marla," she called over her shoulder to the waitress who had just waved at them. Rudy brewed his own draft beer, creamy dark ale that was delicious. "What gives, Beth? Come on, you can tell me."

"It's nothing. I've been busy, that's all. Painting furiously with the show coming up. Either that or running around sketching and taking photos."

"Beth, hello? This is me, your best friend you're talking to, not Mitzy Chabot down at the Stop and Shop. Something is going on. Either you tell me or I'll start guessing."

What a fool I was to come out with Clary, Beth thought. Of course she would give me the third degree. Clarice was like a bloodhound hot on the trail and she would not rest until she had the truth.

There was no way she could confide in her. Clary and Ben were good friends with Ed and Molly Talbot. No matter how much she understood, and Beth had no doubt Clary would understand and sympathize with her, she would never look at Jack Talbot the same way again.

Suddenly, protecting Jack seemed terribly important to her. Maybe it was because she needed to preserve the image Clary had of him, the same one she herself had had only a short time ago. That idealized image of the child man to all the mothers who had known him since toddlerhood.

"You've been seeing someone, haven't you? Come on, Beth, tell."

Swallowing hard, she said, "Yes, I have. I've been seeing a lot of Graham."

"I knew it! I've been telling Ben for weeks that that was it. Why the hell have you been keeping that a secret? We've seen a good bit of him lately and he hasn't said a thing. Why all the big secrecy? Oh, I get it—Alan. Alan's why you've been keeping everything hush-hush?" Clary waved for two more drafts.

"It's everything, not just Alan. I'm not ready to discuss Graham or my love life with the world. Don't you think we should order? You know how I get after a few beers."

Conversation ceased long enough for them to order two "fish in the bag" dinners, fish cooked in parchment paper with a medley of summer vegetables and rice pilaf on the side.

"So is it serious?"

"Things are always serious with Graham."

"He is intense, isn't he?"

She nodded.

"I say go for it. His divorce will be final soon. After living with that bitch for what, fifteen years, he'll think he's died and gone to heaven with you."

She laughed, relieved at the turn their conversation had taken. "I doubt that."

After exhausting the subject of Graham Lynch, they caught up on the kids and their other summer activities. Clary loved to talk about her work and wanted to know about Beth's painting.

She had heard about Kit's deferment and actually supported it.

More relaxed and light-hearted than she had felt in many weeks, Beth chided herself for avoiding the friend who made her laugh. Clary also listened to everything she said and responded honestly and enthusiastically to her happiness. When she dropped her off, Beth declined Clary's offer to come in. "Clary, let's do this again, soon, okay?"

"Absolutely, and listen, when you two decide to come out of the closet let me know and we'll have a double date."

Beth promised, giggling as she drove off, relieved to have satisfied Clary's curiosity while keeping Jack Talbot a secret.

CHAPTER 42

Beth spent the remainder of the week arguing with Alan, mostly about Kit. Although quite willing to support her son's change of heart, she had serious misgivings about his father's role in the matter and refused to stand by while Alan usurped Kit's life to serve his own needs.

Graham had been called back to Chicago for a meeting with Mary's fleet of divorce lawyers, all friends and partners from her firm. Lonely and restless without his steady, comforting presence, she grew more and more anxious as Sunday neared.

Friday night, as she prepared for bed, the phone rang. It was Graham, still stuck in Chicago. "How's it going?"

He sounded weary and sad. Determined to keep her worries to herself, Beth responded with as much cheerfulness as she could muster. "All's well. Kit and I had a good talk. He's decided to take a year off before starting college, to work and help his father. It's taken me a few days to adjust to the idea, but I'm getting there. Right now I'm grappling with disappointment more than anything else. All our hopes and dreams that we thrust on our kids, pretending all the while they're not ours, but theirs."

"Not sure if I've ever mentioned this, but I traveled for a year after high school. Best thing I ever did. Wasn't ready for college. Would have been a complete waste at that point in my life."

"I do remember you talking about that, and look how well that turned out."

They both laughed.

"How's everything in Chicago?"

"Shitty, but I never expected it wouldn't be. I won't be home until Tuesday or Wednesday. Can I have a rain check on Sunday supper?"

"Of course, where are you staying?"

"At the apartment. Mary's at our weekend cottage. She's involved in a case out there. She'll probably be back in the city Monday. We have separate bedrooms. Have had for years actually. Might be a little tense, but I'll survive. Her law partners are blood suckers. They're making all sorts of outrageous demands. They're even asking for a piece of the Gallery. Do you believe that?"

She didn't, but said nothing. If she put aside the hurt, her divorce had been relatively easy, friendly, amicable and civilized. Alan had been generous in every way and seen that she and the children were well provided for.

"I know you wanted me to be there Sunday when you get back from your meeting. I'm sorry, Beth."

"I'm a big girl, I can handle it."

"Have you seen him?"

"Briefly," she replied, reluctant to talk about Jack.

Responding to the change in her tone, he changed the subject. "How's the painting going?"

"Well, I pulled everything out the other day to look things over. I hope you will be pleased."

"I'm sure I will. You've been doing some incredible work this summer. Your public will be thrilled."

They talked a while longer, then reluctantly rang off.

Saturday night Rick and Gary took her out to dinner. Before departing for L'Auberge, Gary's favorite restaurant, a half hour inland, they strolled out to the studio, glasses of wine in hand to look over her latest work.

Both men were dressed impeccably, as always, in linen suits, Rick's a pale sage, Gary's beige, a crisp, white, open-collared dress shirt setting off his dark tan. Gary prided himself on his masculine bearing and gait, despite a tendency for flamboyant gestures when excited. Nervously, he flicked back his full head of thick, blond hair as he led his companions around for nearly half an hour.

"Breathtaking," he pronounced after completing the studio tour. Ordinarily stingy with his compliments, Gary waxed on, heaping praise upon painting after painting.

Slack-jawed, Beth exchanged winks with Rick.

"You know, sweetheart, he's right. They're magnificent. What's happened to you? Have you had an out of body experience?"

"Love, I'd guess." Gary stood back, hand on hip, smirking. "Am I right?"

"Is he right?" Rick turned to her, eyes wide.

Blushing unexpectedly, Beth said, "Is it that obvious?"

"Yes," they chorused.

"Who, who?" Gary cried, grabbing her by the elbow.

"Naughty, naughty, Beth! Rick joined in, taking the other elbow. "Fess up."

She hesitated.

"It's Lynch, isn't it? God, I knew it," Rick cried, triumphant.

"Yes, well, we have gotten kind of friendly."

"So, after all my orchestrations, you were a shoe-in for the exhibit no matter what?"

"No, this happened very recently and had nothing to do with them giving us the show. In fact, if we'd been dating when the decision was made, he might have been less encouraging. Graham's an old friend. We've just been getting reacquainted, that's all."

"I'll say," Gary remarked, staring at the picture of Hestor's Way. "Looks like a dangerous liaison to me."

"He's still married," she said, hoping that might discourage Gary's uncanny intuition for uncovering secrets. "It's kind of messy right now."

"Hmmm, this looks like more than adultery to me," Gary continued, still staring at the painting. "Looks almost like—"

Glimpsing the look of terror on Beth's face, Rick intervened. "Time to eat, kiddies. We're going to your restaurant, Gary my love, so let's get a move on before they give our reservation away."

"Yes," she concurred. "We only have twenty-five minutes."

The dinner, to which they arrived ten minutes late despite Gary's driving thirty miles over the speed limit the entire way, was delicious as always. In the center of the kitchen, at the chef's table, they enjoyed "off menu" entrees prepared especially for them by the chef, Paul Bovare. The two men kept her entertained throughout the meal with accounts of their latest trip to New York, the plays they had seen and the exhibits they had taken in.

As the dessert dishes were cleared away, Gary said, "We even saw your ex's stuff at the Fowler." Ignoring his partner's warning glance, he blithely continued, "He's done some incredible pieces, hasn't he? Surprised he's not a billionaire. Think you could get us a deal?"

Gary didn't care a wit about Alan's furniture, but always jealous of Beth and Rick's friendship, he seldom lost the chance to needle her.

She nodded, smiling. "Alan's work does get better each year. He's always pushing himself in new directions. It's his greatest strength as an artist and teacher. He encourages his students to stretch and grow, to experiment with new styles and techniques. Our son is taking the year off to work with him."

"What, Kit's not going to college?"

Rick loved her children like a benevolent uncle, and took pride in their accomplishments. Gary was indifferent to children.

"It's only for one year. He's applied for a deferment from Bowdoin. His advisor is sure they'll grant him one and we've completed all the paperwork. Close your mouth, Rick dear. He'll be fine."

Later on, as she kissed both men goodnight, Beth silenced yet another protest from Rick about "Kit's missing out on life." As the Mercedes pulled away, she suddenly ran toward it waving. Gary braked and rolled down the window.

"Rick, Gary, please don't say anything about Graham just yet, okay? Alan doesn't know and I suspect Margot Lynch hasn't heard either. We've only—"

"Just begun," Gary sang out, finishing the lyric of the familiar song.

"Something like that," she said, laughing and patting the car door, stepping back to let them pass.

CHAPTER 43

Even for a birthright Quaker devoted to silence, the Meeting House was unusually quiet. So quiet Beth feared her fellow worshippers might overhear the thoughts screaming in her head. There were only twenty besides herself in attendance. Many members were away on vacation and were away at Yearly Meeting. Beth had forgotten about Yearly Meeting and was disappointed not to find Constance Bicknell in the assembly. She had hoped to talk with Constance about her mother.

Hestor had taken a turn for the worse in the last few weeks. Her daughters feared they wouldn't have her much longer and they wanted Constance to visit. Even though Hestor wouldn't know her old friend, they both felt the visit was important. Constance had been asking to go and Beth had been putting her off. Now, the doctors informed them, there was no longer time for putting off. She resolved to phone Constance as soon as the elder returned from Yearly Meeting.

Try as she might, she couldn't settle her thoughts and her mind raced for almost the entire hour during which no one felt moved to speak. Thomas Albro's announcement broke the silence, a relief from the endless conversations she was having in her head.

Rationally she knew what was best for both of them, but she didn't know if she could go through with it. And, now there was Graham, whose arms she had fallen into out of uncertainty and confusion. She wasn't at all sure she could trust her feelings there either. Perhaps she was simply retreating into his safe arms, hiding from the tattered remains of her relationship with Jack.

The faces of Molly and Ed Talbot haunted her. The proud, unsuspecting parents would be driving their son to Harvard, so full of hopes and dreams for his future. If they knew about their liaison, she felt sure they would view her as the wicked seducer, a cougar, who had led their son astray. What about Kat and Nanny? What would their reactions be? It was all too horrible, especially when she realized at the core of her being, that she still went weak at the knees whenever she thought about Jack. Was it love? If it was love, it was the kind that would bring nothing but pain. She would close the door now, even if he could not.

After Meeting, she met Lanie and they drove to Friend's Home discussing their mother.

"Bad week?" Lanie said, Beth nodded.

Both had received calls from the staff. Hestor could no longer walk and had been having small strokes all week.

"How did she deteriorate so fast?" Lanie's question went unanswered.

They found Hestor sleeping, a new set of bedrails up. Lanie rang for a nurse.

"She's been rolling out of bed," Emma Peebles explained, coming in to sit with them. "She's got dreadful bruises on her sides and we were afraid she'd broken her left hip, but it's okay."

"What does the doctor say?"

"Keep her comfortable. There's not much else to do."

Beth took her mother's thin, knobby hand in her own. Hestor opened her eyes and Emma whispered, "I'll leave thee together. Come find me if thou needs me."

"Hi, Mama." Beth smiled at her beloved parent as Lanie came to sit at her elbow.

Hestor's pale eyes stared blankly for a minute, then darted from one daughter to the other. For an instant her eyes focused and appeared to be pleading, beseeching them for something, but just as quickly the moment passed and her expression became once again blank and unseeing.

"Oh, Mama." Beth sobbed, burying her face on her mother's breast. "We love you so much."

Lanie's arm slipped across her sister's back as she bent to embrace both of them.

Beth buried her face in the soft, flannel bedclothes. She no longer smelled like Mama. She smelled like the hospital—institutional laundry soap and disinfectant mingled with an ever present scent of decay. But, she was soft like Mama, the comforting softness that had cradled them throughout their lives.

After a while, Beth sat up and smoothed wisps of hair from Hestor's cheeks, their rosiness gone. Suddenly, she felt dampness on her fingers, and looked down to find the alabaster cheeks streaked with tears.

"Oh, Beth, do you suppose she hears us? She knows we're here and we love her, don't you, Mama?"

They moved slowly through their usual ritual of cleaning up and reading aloud to Hestor. Finally, the sisters departed shortly after two. Beth begged off lunch and asked Lanie if she would mind being dropped off for an earlier train. She felt guilty, knowing that her sister needed her, that they needed each other; but she wanted to get to Hestor's Way. She needed to be there early to prepare herself.

The sisters agreed to talk in the next day or so to decide what to do next. Beth intended to go back for a visit Tuesday and perhaps again on Thursday with Constance if the old Quaker was up to it. Lanie agreed to meet her Tuesday at the station and they hugged goodbye.

Before parting, Lanie asked, "How's everything going?"

"Up and down," Beth said, realizing that she hadn't even told Lanie about Kit's decision.

"Beth, you have that look. You know, the ready-to-crawl-out-of-your-skin look. What's wrong?"

"I can't talk about it right now. I promise I'll fill you in later, okay?"

"Promise?"

Beth nodded and turned to go.

"Good luck," Lanie called, watching her drive away before disappearing into the station.

She drove toward the cottage as if possessed. She had no awareness of scenery, passing cars, or the speed at which she traveled. As she headed down the dirt road, she breathed a sigh of relief finding the driveway empty. Relieved to have a few precious minutes to collect herself, she hopped out of the car, opened up the house and went out to the porch. Thick fog blanketed the beach and waves broke just above the low tide mark. She left the screen door ajar and kicked off her sandals, descending the steps onto the sand.

She walked a half mile down the beach, the fog still thick and unyielding. As she headed back, she spotted him walking toward her. At first, the mist made it difficult to read his expression, but as he drew near, she saw that he was smiling.

"I followed your foot prints," he called out, returning her wave.

Beth's heart constricted. How would she ever say goodbye?

Even under the cover of fog, they were careful, their greeting formal, no touching, not even a handshake as they walked back to the cottage. Once inside, however, the restraint vanished and his hands were all over her. His lips banished all thoughts of her carefully rehearsed words of goodbye. She returned his kiss, her whole body letting go of the tension of a week spent at war with her emotions.

She hadn't intended to make love. She had told herself to keep things calm and rational, to talk to him, reach an understanding, then walk away. How foolish she'd been, to think such a scenario was possible after the past month. To think their relationship could be extinguished with a few words of reason.

Afterwards, they lay on the couch instead of the floor, his arms wrapped around her, rough hands fondling her breast. His lips grazed her neck, arousing her again.

"No." She sat up and snatched her clothes. Turning away, she pulled on her blouse and skirt.

When she finally gazed back, his eyes revealed his hurt. How would she find the words? "I'm so sorry, Jack. We can't do this anymore."

"Beth, look what just happened. Can you really say we can't after that?"

"It's just not right. Not for you, not for me, not for the people we love. Not anymore."

"I love you."

"I know. I love you, too. That is what makes this so hard." She reached down and touched his cheek. "I can't do this to Kit. What about your parents and the rest of your family?"

"They'd get used to it, when they realized how much I love you. I want to marry you, Beth."

She smiled down at him. "Oh, my love, don't give yourself away so easily. You have a lifetime ahead of you."

"Not without you."

"What about Lesley?"

"That's different."

"What about marrying her?"

"Not if you say yes. If you say yes, there is no Lesley. If I could be with you all the time."

"You're leaving for Cambridge next week."

"Not if you say you'll marry me."

"Jack, I can't marry you, not now, not ever. Someday, you'll understand."

"Never happen."

"What would your parents think about you marrying the mother of your best friend?"

"Who cares?"

"You do."

"I could reach for you right now and start kissing you and you'd make love with me again."

"But you won't," she said, watching him, the awareness of the power he held over her apparent in his look.

"Why not?"

"Because, in your heart you know I'm right."

"Bullshit. I don't want Harvard, I want you. I'm ready to give up everything for you. Everything."

"But, I'm not," she whispered, bending to kiss his forehead. "I won't give up everything for you, Jack Talbot, even though the sight of you sends liquid fire to the very core of my being. Now, come on, get dressed. I've got to go home and you do, too."

They stood in the back hallway a few minutes later, each reluctant to break away. "So this is it?"

"Yes," she stated emphatically. "This is it. I hope someday we can be friends."

"Doubt it." His eyes challenged her in the dim light of the hallway.

"You'll get to college and forget all about me. Believe me, you will."

"And, if I don't? What happens then?"

Taking his hand, she answered softly, "Go on, I'll lock up."

"You've got it all worked out, haven't you? This is all your decision, not mine."

"Someday you'll realize it was your decision, too. Goodbye, Jack, take care of yourself." Standing on tiptoes, she kissed him lightly on the cheek.

He caught her arm and pulled her to him, kissing her and refusing to let go. Beth struggled momentarily, then gave in, her arms around his shoulders, hands stroking the hair on the back of his neck.

As she yielded, he let her go and gazed down, eyes triumphant. She pushed away and ran from the cottage. At her car, she stopped, called back, "Lock up."

Then, not trusting herself to meet his gaze, she hopped into the car and drove away. Not until she reached Windy Harbor and turned toward the village center did her breathing return to normal and her heart ceased its relentless pounding.

Chapter 44

While Beth had spent the previous week missing Graham and assuming everything would be fine, she found his return unsettling. Sunday's encounter with Jack had left her shaken. A restless emptiness settled over her, coloring everything she did. She no longer trusted her heart. She had to fight to return his embrace, the weight of her betrayal almost paralyzing.

Thrilled to see her, it seemed as if the strain of his week lifted when Graham laid eyes on her. Feeling guilty, Beth returned his embrace, keeping her conflicted emotions to herself. Two days earlier, she had made love to Jack all over the living room at Hestor's Way. Now, as she held Graham, her every gesture seemed a lie. She felt like such a hypocrite.

Finally he released her. "You look lovely today. Lovely and mysterious, alluring, as if you are full of secrets?"

She laughed and avoided his eyes as they strolled toward the airport parking lot. "Let's talk at home."

"No kids?"

"They're still at Alan's. Nanny will move home at the end of the week."

"Kit still determined to take the year off?"

She nodded. "The deferment was okayed today. He's very excited and you know something, much as I hate to admit it, I'm glad. I think it's the best thing for him right now. Please remind me of that in the dead of winter when he and his father are ready to kill each other."

"He's gonna work with Alan, then?"

"Yup."

"Lucky guy to be working under the master."

"We'll see," she said, thinking back to the time she had helped Alan with projects. Simon Legree came to mind.

Once at home, she tossed up a shrimp scampi, made a salad of baby greens and sliced French bread to go with it. Graham poured Beth a glass of wine. They sat at one end of the dining room table enjoying the simple meal, talking about her painting and Graham's plans for the gallery's fall season. Restricting the conversation to small talk seemed the most comfortable for both of them.

Later, after they cleared the table, Graham helped her clean up, then they retreated to the living room for tea. "It wasn't quite as simple as I expected in Chicago."

"I'm not surprised."

"We've been married a long time."

He's going back to her, Beth thought, not sure whether to feel relieved or devastated. She set down her cup and faced him.

"It felt hollow and empty after all the fighting, you know?"

She nodded.

"We spent last night talking until three. It was odd. Now that everything is over, we're friends again."

"No second thoughts?"

He gave her a quizzical look. "We weren't that friendly. No, it's just, the whole thing shook me up more than I care to admit. Mother's cross examination this afternoon didn't help either."

"She liked Mary?"

"So, so. In the beginning, when we were first married, they were bosom buddies, but as time went by, relations cooled. They're both strong people, with their own ways of doing things, so it was inevitable that they'd clash. Of course, Mother took my side when the trouble started. Never mind that I was a disgusting drunk and Mary needed her support more than I did. I could shoot Mary right in front of Mother and she'd claim it was Mary's fault. Mother still thinks I'm ten years old, I'm afraid. Thank God I'm moving out of her house next week. Give us both some distance."

"Does she know about us?"

"She knows I've been seeing you, but thinks we're old friends."

"Sounds like maybe that is what we should be for a while."

"Whoa, where did that come from?"

Before she could stop herself, she blurted out, "I slept with Jack again, when we met on Sunday."

He stood up and went to the window. For a moment, Beth feared he might leave.

Finally, still standing at the window, he cleared his throat. "Boy, this is one of those times when I wish I was still drinking. Wanna tell me about it? Why did it happen?"

Not especially, she thought. "I don't know why it happened, Graham."

"Wanted it to go out with a bang, did you?"

Beth fought back tears. "That was uncalled for."

"Yes, it was. I apologize. Can you tell me why? After us? Is the change I sense in you because you're planning to set up house in Cambridge together?"

"I just told you, it's over."

"Are you keeping your options open?"

Hurt and confused by his sarcasm, she replied, "I don't blame you for being angry, but I'd rather not sit here and get beaten up. I didn't have to tell you. I could have lied, but I wanted you to know what you're getting into."

"And exactly what am I getting into?"

"A mess, I'm a mess."

"You've really broken it off?"

"Yes."

"Why did it happen, Sunday I mean?"

"I don't know. It just did. I can't explain it and what's more, I'm not sorry."

"So is this likely to happen every time you cross paths with Jack Talbot for the rest of our lives?"

"No."

"How do you know that?"

"This conversation is spinning around in circles. I'm exhausted and I'm sure you are too."

"I'll go. By the way, Clary and Ben invited me to come Saturday night to the beach cookout."

"Wonderful."

They arranged to meet at the Point of Rocks at five for a beach cookout. He bent to kiss her cheek.

CHAPTER 45

Despite all the elements of a Greek tragedy, Saturday evening's beach cookout proved to be one of the season's most memorable. Not only did Graham come, but Alan and Chloe as well, along with a number of teenagers and a few of Chloe's artist friends. Kit brought Karen along and Jack, Lesley Patterson, a curvaceous, blue-eyed blonde, the latter's jeans and summer jersey hugged her like a second skin.

Beth had seen little of Graham the previous week. They canceled their planned beach walk and he had stopped by the studio Friday to take some photographs of her paintings, but departed quickly. Clearly hurt and angry about Jack, he was as unsure of Beth's feelings for him as she was herself. By tacit agreement, they had taken time off rather than risking another painful confrontation.

Saturday night, they put on a friendly front for friends and family. When she arrived at the docks, Graham came to greet her, kissing her before stooping to help with her cooler and bags. After a week of raw emotions, his greeting made her feel safe and she gratefully returned it. Their little drama was not lost on Clary and Ben who stood a short distance away.

When they reached the Spit, Graham suggested a walk and she agreed. "I've missed you," he whispered as they set off. The sand was still warm under their feet as he slipped his arm around her waist.

"Me, too," she returned and draped her arm over his.

"Where are we?"

"Good question. I've done a lot of thinking and all I can tell you is that I'm having a really hard time trusting my feelings, or perhaps it's my libido I can't trust."

He laughed.

"Graham, I've loved you for so long. Now, we're at a place where we could actually be together and what do I do? I don't know. Maybe I need time to let the summer fade away before we go on? The selfish part of me needs and wants you desperately, but I'm not sure that's fair to you. I know I'm not ready to marry again. Not right now at least."

He turned and pulled her close, kissing her. "So, I'm to be a kept man, am I?" His long, graceful fingers cupped her chin and lifted her lips to meet his.

"No, and let's not get carried away, okay? I haven't even told the kids about us."

"They know we've been going out, don't they?"

"Yes, but I'm not sure they're ready to find us naked in the dunes. Let's head back."

Arm in arm, they approached the others. Beth spied Alan and Chloe and waved, thinking that now was as good a time as any for Alan to learn about her relationship with Graham.

"Gang's all here," Clarice called out, sensing the tension in the air. "Beth, come sit by me and help me get things ready. You, too, Chloe."

The men were out of earshot, building the fire when Clary whispered, "Did you get a load of Lesley, the bombshell? How do you suppose she got into those jeans? She'll have to cut them off, don't ya think? Glory be, what a bod. Where's Talbot been hiding her?"

Neither woman responded.

"Hey, Beth," Chloe asked, turning to her. "Are you and Graham an item?"

"Sort of. Yes, I guess you could say that."

"'Course you can say that," Clary said. "Go ahead. You of all people have a right to be happy, dearie. You and Graham are an item and a hot one from my observations."

Clary's voice carried beyond their circle.

"Sure, that's great." Chloe nodded, but looked vaguely uncomfortable.

Beth decided a change of subject was in order and asked Chloe about her upcoming exhibit.

The sunset was glorious. They all sat back and took time to enjoy it, sipping an extra drink while the chicken baked.

The warmth of the fire and four beers relaxed her and as darkness descended, a pleasant sense of euphoria settled over Beth. After everything had been cleared and packed, she came back to the fire, sat beside Graham, and leaned against his shoulder. He slipped his arm around her and lightly kissed the top of her head. Other couples around the huge fire pit were similarly engaged, but all eyes seemed to be on them. Alan glared, Kit and Nanny looked surprised, but not uncomfortable and Clarice and Ben genuinely pleased. Jack sat apart from the others, his expression inscrutable, his arms draped over Lesley's shoulders. It appeared that Lesley had plans for the evening, but her partner seemed only vaguely aware of her presence.

Ben saved the day by beginning a story that was picked up and continued by others. It was one of their cookout traditions. Someone began a story, then others picked it up and ran with it. Clarice was always threatening to record the long, rambling tales and write them down for posterity. Each storyteller picked up where the last left off, continuing the general plot line. Each new segment incorporated the same characters and followed a somewhat logical sequence while embellishing on the tale. People listened carefully, joining in whenever the mood struck them.

Ben started with a yarn about a hapless fisherman who had lost his nets at sea, only to return to port despondent and penniless, to a house full of children and a nagging wife. The saga continued with several love affairs, one with a mermaid, and the introduction of an anonymous benefactor who finally came to the fisherman's rescue, buying him new nets. His loyal crew stood by him and the nagging wife deserted him, but at the end of the tale, the fisherman was back on his feet and prosperous.

Alan's contribution was a side plot about a vengeful widow, one of the fisherman's spurned lovers, who tries to learn the identity of the benefactor so she might abscond with the money instead. Chloe followed her husband's segment telling of the fisherman's poor, neglected daughter who must take up all the work after the mother's desertion. Then, Clary ended with a successful fishing trip and promise of a romance between the fisherman and the newly appointed harbor mistress, the first woman in village history to hold such a position.

The ripple of laughter in response to Clary's story telling broke the tension that had been slowly building as the story progressed. In the silence that followed, punctuated only by the crackling of the fire and the occasional call of a foghorn in the distance, Ben rose. "Getting late, folks. Who's ready for the ride back?"

Beth and Clarice waited with the younger children, who always begged to stay until the last trip across the channel. Nanny and three of her friends waded at the water's edge talking and giggling. Clark, Clary's youngest was having one last pirate adventure with his buddies behind them in the dunes.

The two women sat shoulder to shoulder on the beach talking quietly. "Quite a night, huh?" Clary said.

"Yup."

"Could have been a disaster."

"Yup."

"Did you see Alan's face when he first saw you and Graham together?"

"I'm afraid I did."

"I thought he was gonna keel over. Never took his eyes off you all night."

"Guaranteed I'll get a call first thing in the morning, I can almost recite what he'll say word for word. How could you? In front of the children? My oldest friend, blah, blah, blah."

"I'd hang up on him. Better yet, tell him to go to hell, then hang up."

Breaking into peals of laughter, the two women clung on to each other.

"Seriously, Beth. Don't you dare take anything from Alan."

"I won't, don't worry. I've gotten pretty good at dealing with Alan's tirades. You'd be surprised."

"No, I wouldn't. What's going on with you and Graham anyway?"

"We're very good friends," she answered, chuckling. "And you can quote me on that."

"He divorced yet?"

"No, but soon. I don't think he's quite ready to jump into another serious relationship right now and neither can I."

"Listen here, Beth Hadley. You can pussy-foot around this good friends and not being ready and all that garbage, but I have eyes, girl. The man's crazy about you. I bet if you asked him, he'd marry you tomorrow, bigamy be damned."

"Looks can be deceiving."

"What's that supposed to mean?"

"It's complicated."

Ignoring her, Clary went on, "And I might add, you're crazy about him. For you to be all over a man with your kids sitting three feet away, you've either got to be in love or completely insane."

"I wasn't all over him."

"The hell you weren't. I thought Ben and I were bad, but you guys. The only couple who had you beat was Talbot and his young bimbette. Where'd lovely Lesley come from anyway?"

"You asked me that before and I don't know. Why didn't you ask her?"

"She didn't come up for air long enough to talk to anyone."

"All right, all right."

Beth realized she had snapped at her friend, but Clary was right. Lesley had been all over Jack from the moment they had finished dinner, pulling him away from the fire, trying to entice him up into the dunes where most of the other couples had already retreated. Despite all her coaxing, her date refused to leave the fire. He remained in the same spot all evening, directly across from Beth. Acutely aware of his presence, Beth hadn't trusted herself to meet his eyes.

"Here's Ben. Come on, kids. Come help Beth and me with these bags and coolers."

As they started across, Ben leaned down and whispered to Beth, "Be forewarned, there was a slight skirmish on the other side."

"Oh, God, what happened?"

"Nothing major," he said, patting her shoulder. "Just Alan flexing his muscles, but you might find Graham a little out of sorts."

"Oh, Lord." She sighed, leaning back against the console. Once on shore, the boat was tied up at the dock and everyone piled into the cars, Nanny and Carrie into Beth's and Clarice and Ben took the rest of them. Graham stayed behind.

She asked Nanny to wait and walked over to Graham's car at the opposite end of the grassy lot.

Slipping his arms around her, he asked, "Everything all right?"

"It's me who should be asking you that question. Ben said Alan created a scene. Graham, I'm so sorry."

"Don't be, it was fine."

"Did the kids hear it?"

Her cheeks burned with shame and indignation. "No. It was just Ben, Chloe, and the two of us. It's understandable, Beth."

"No, it isn't. He has no right."

"Look, the man still loves you. He will always love you. He'll get over it. Don't worry. Person you should be upset about is Chloe. I felt bad for her standing there listening to him ranting on about me staying away from 'his wife.' Sensitive guy he ain't."

"It's unbelievable, isn't it? He leaves me after a year-long affair with Chloe. Oh, forget it. I've got to go. The girls are waiting. I'll call you, okay?"

He pulled her close. "Do I get a kiss?"

"I love you," she whispered and reached up to kiss him.

As he pressed against her, she found him fully aroused, lips already moving to her neck and shoulders. "Time to go before I really get into trouble," she said softly, breathless and not waiting for his reply before sprinting across the parking lot.

Giggling, then silence greeted her as she slipped into her seat. Time to talk to her children about Graham. "All right, girls, let's go home."

More giggles and more whispers.

CHAPTER 46

Beth rose at dawn Sunday and took an early morning walk on the beach. Afterwards she and Nanny went to Meeting together for the first time in months. It was comforting to have her daughter beside her. Nanny's soft arm in sleeveless summer tee shirt pressed against her own on the crowded bench. A mist shrouded morning, the fog was so low that it wafted through the open windows, bathing worshipers with its salty caress.

Beth closed her eyes and endeavored to clear her mind. Alan had called while she was out walking. "He really wants to talk to you, Mom," Nanny had informed her, but Beth had hustled her daughter out of the house before the phone could ring again with a "Don't fret, pumpkin; I'll call him as soon as we get home tonight."

After the service, Constance Bicknell called to them. "So good to see thee, Nanny. Thou must come to Meeting more often. We need thy youthful spirit."

Nanny nodded, smiling.

"Constance, I've been trying to reach you all week."

"Oh, dear, I am sorry. After Yearly Meeting I went to visit my daughter. It was the twins' birthday. They're sixteen now, can you believe it?"

Beth smiled, remembering Constance's two grandsons as toddlers, identical tow-haired boys sitting solemnly beside their grandmother during the Meeting. It had been years since she had seen them.

"Hard to believe, Constance. It seems like only yesterday that I had them in my First Day School class."

"The place has never been the same after those little hellions. Lord, forgive me. What did thou want of me, dear?"

"It's Mother. She hasn't much time."

"Oh, dear. It's been over two months since I've been up to see her. It's the driving, you see."

"I know, Constance, that's why I thought you might like to drive up with me one day this week?"

"I'd love to. What day?"

"Earlier in the week is better for me as Kat will be home for Labor Day Weekend. But I'll be happy to work around your schedule."

"My dear, when you get to be my age, there's not much of a schedule, I'm 'fraid. Most of my friends are dead, my children are busy. You name the day and I'll be ready."

"Tomorrow, then?" she said, knowing what the reply would be. Constance was busier than anyone she knew despite her statements to the contrary.

"Oh, dear, that would be Monday. Well, let's see now, I have service group on Monday until three."

"How about Wednesday?"

"Now lemme think. There's the food drive and the book sort, and my quilting group, guess I could miss it."

"Constance, when exactly do you have a free moment?"

"How about Tuesday?"

"That'll be fine. I'll pick you up around ten?"

"Perfect, my dear."

"She won't know you and she can't speak. The last few times Lanie and I were there she slept most of the time."

"She will always be 'Hestor with the wind in her hair' to me, my dear. Please don't fret on my account."

"Thanks, Constance."

As she bent to kiss the weathered cheek, lavender talc tickled her lips.

CHAPTER 47

As they headed toward the Providence train station, Nanny turned to her mother. "So, what's up with you and Mr. Lynch?"

"We're old friends."

"Looked like you were more than old friends last night. How do you think that made Dad feel? You guys were making out right there in front of everyone."

Swallowing hard, Beth replied, "You're right, we are more than old friends. I've been meaning to talk to you about him. As for your father—"

"Are you getting married?"

"No."

"Someday?"

"I don't know, Nan. Right now Graham's friendship is important to me. I hope you guys will get to know him better, too. He's a wonderful man."

"He's Dad's friend. Couldn't you have picked someone else?"

"We don't always get to choose who we love, sweetie. I know how you feel about Dad, but this is my life. I'd like Graham to be a part of it. Is that so bad?"

Nanny shrugged and gazed out the window. When they reached the station, she hopped into the backseat, after barely acknowledging her aunt.

Lanie, never one to be ignored, said, "Hey, Nanna Banana, why the long face?" When this elicited no response, she turned to her sister. "What gives?"

Beth's sharp look warned Lanie off and they drove the rest of the way in silence.

Hestor was much the same. Nanny crawled into the bed alongside her and slung her arm over her grandmother's middle. As she smoothed wisps of hair aside, she whispered softly and kissed the gaunt cheek.

A new nurse came in and told them there had been little change, but otherwise the visit was uneventful.

Later, as they ate lunch in a sandwich shop—Nanny's choice—Beth told Lanie about her plans to bring Constance up Tuesday.

"Lot of good it'll do," was Lanie's response, but she agreed it was important for Constance to have the chance to say goodbye.

When they dropped Lanie at the train station, she made one more attempt to draw her niece into conversation. "So, peanut, you're starting school soon, huh?"

Nanny shrugged.

"Have I done something to offend my favorite niece?"

"It's not you, Lanie, it's me," Beth answered quietly as she stared straight ahead.

"Mom's got a boyfriend."

"She means Graham," Beth said quickly, afraid that Lanie might misunderstand and blurt out something about Jack.

"What's the problem? Graham's a great guy. Not jealous, are you?"

'No, why?"

"Then what's wrong, for goodness' sake? I should think you'd be happy for your mom. Uh, oh, wait a minute. This isn't about Alan, is it? You're not worried about your dad, are you?" Nanny's silence clearly told Lanie she had guessed correctly.

"Nan Hadley, I'm surprised at you. After all your mom's been through, you could cut her a little slack, don't you think? Your dad's married now, remember? Do you expect your mom to stay single and miserable forever?"

"Dad's not happy. He still loves Mom and wants to get back together, but she won't. He told me."

"So, what do you think? Your mom should drop everything and take him back? After all the hurt and pain he's caused her?"

Nanny's eyes welled up with tears.

"That's enough, Lanie." Beth sighed. "You better go or you'll miss your train. Nan and I will take care of this."

"I'll see you Thursday. Then we will plan something, okay, sweet pea?"

When Lanie announced her plan to visit for three nights over Labor Day weekend, she received a half-hearted nod from Nanny. Then, kissing them both goodbye, she hopped out of the car.

"Remember, sister of mine, I want a date for the Labor Day dance and don't even think about opting out! We're going!"

CHAPTER 48

After driving for fifteen minutes in silence, Beth said, "Want to talk about it?"

"There's nothing to say. Dad's sad and you won't help him. He almost died and you wouldn't go and see him. Now you won't give him a second chance. When he needs you most, you've gone behind his back with his best friend."

"Oh, sweetie, you've been dragged into the middle of this, haven't you? Listen to me. You were so young when Dad left. I wanted to spare you, so I didn't share my feelings and my pain with you the way I did with Kat and Kit. I never really told you what I was going through. I knew how much you loved your dad and I didn't want to change that. Maybe I was wrong not confiding in you more about my side of things?

"Nanny, Dad and I will never be together again. It may be Dad's wish. If it is, I'm sorry for him, but it is definitely not mine. I care about your dad and I'm glad he's feeling better. I'm really sorry his marriage is not working out, but Dad hurt me deeply, too deeply to ever go back. His leaving very nearly destroyed me. If I hadn't had you three kids in those first months I'm not sure I'd have had the courage to go on living. When Dad married Chloe, he left our marriage behind, sweetie. He took my love for him, too. I'm sorry, but it's never coming back."

Nanny was sobbing so Beth pulled to the side of the road and leaned over, putting her arms around her. "I'm sorry, sweetie."

"I just want us to be a family again." Nanny sobbed, her head pressed against her mother's chest.

"I know, I know," Beth said, fighting unsuccessfully to hold back her own tears. "I miss our family too. Sometimes I miss it so much my heart aches."

After they both had a good cry, Beth started the car. As they drove up the driveway, the last vestiges of daylight flickered along the horizon's edge. Beth stopped the car and mother and daughter held hands, gazing out across the pond, watching the sun set.

Later, as they walked through the door, the phone was ringing. Alan. Ignoring the harangue already in full swing on the other end of the line, Beth eyed her daughter from across the room.

"Alan, Nanny and I just walked through the door. We've been to visit Mama and we're hungry and tired. Can I call you in the morning?"

He started to protest, but she said, "How about meeting at Begley's for breakfast?" knowing full well that that would appease him. Alan loved to go out to breakfast. She had, too, before the divorce. He agreed and as she hung up, Beth looked up at her daughter. Nanny gave her a crooked smile, her eyes still full of sadness."

CHAPTER 49

Proud as a peacock, Alan sat in the sunlit front window of Begley's, waving to passersby and calling hello to Jan, the waitress, even though she had seated them only minutes earlier. Look who I'm with, his every gesture screamed. We're back together, everything is fine.

Beth looked around to find a room full of eyes staring at her. "This wasn't the best place to meet."

"Nonsense, everyone's minding their own business. We can talk freely."

Stifling the sarcastic remark on the tip of her tongue, she said, "So? What's so important it warranted ten frantic messages on my machine?"

"Beth, Beth, can't we just talk? Enjoy a few minutes of each other's company?"

"Alan, what do you want?"

"You know exactly what I want." He leaned across the table, voice a hiss. "My wife's screwing around with my best friend and flaunting it in my face."

The statement was so ridiculous she didn't know whether to laugh or cry. "Alan, do you hear yourself?" she said quietly, thankful the din had resumed to muffle their conversation. "First, as I seem to need to remind you on a regular basis, I am no longer your wife. Second, Graham is far from your best friend and even if he were, so what? Lastly, what I do in my personal life is no longer your business."

"It is when it affects our children."

This was too much. Beth felt red hot rage creep over her. "I quite agree," she answered through clenched teeth. "You have used Nanny in a shameless way, filling her full of your tales of woe, painting me as the cold-hearted villainess who won't take you back!"

His eyes scanned the room. "Lower your voice."

"I will not lower my voice," she replied, although she did, a little. No one seemed to be paying attention. "You better start right now to repair the damage you've done, and I'm serious. To give Nanny false hopes about something that is never going to happen is unconscionable. We are never going to be together again."

"Never say never." He grinned sheepishly.

"Never, never, never."

"Let's get Jan over here and order. Shall we?"

They both ordered muffins and coffee, then waited until Jan had disappeared before continuing. "Look, babe, we got kinda off the track on the Graham situation."

"There is no Graham situation. My relationship with Graham is absolutely none of your business."

Jan arrived with their orders. Sensing the tension, she practically threw the food on the table and disappeared.

"Don't you think you at least owe me the courtesy of a brief explanation? Okay, maybe it's none of my business, but the guy's a good friend and you are my ex-wife. We do share custody of our children. I think I should know a little bit about something that's gonna have an effect on their lives."

Seething now, she wanted to slap him. He didn't give a damn about the effect on the kids, he was worried about his pride and his self-interest. Controlling her anger, she replied, "I will talk to the kids if and when it seems appropriate. I've already talked to Nanny about this and will talk to Kit and Kat soon. This is between me and them, so please stay out of it. Graham has been nothing but wonderful to me this summer. I intend to keep seeing him, if that's what you want to know."

"Have to keep seeing him now anyway, don't you? Wouldn't want to jeopardize the show, would you?"

"Alan, I'm going to pretend I didn't hear that. Look, I have to go. Here's money for my food and yours." She threw six dollars on the table and grabbed her purse.

He grabbed hold of her arm, but she shrugged out of his grasp. "Wait for me outside, please."

She exited the shop with Alan on her heels. He caught up halfway down Main Street and took hold of her arm again. "Beth, come on, please don't make a scene."

Eyes blazing, she stopped and turned to face him. "You're the only one making a scene. I will not stand around listening to your hateful comments. If you think my getting the show had anything to do with my relationship with Graham, you're even more delusional than I imagined. How dare you insinuate that I slept my way into that show. And how dare you accost Graham after the cookout the other night, telling him to stay away from your wife? You have no right, Alan, no right at all. It's bad enough what you did to Graham. Have you even thought about how Chloe must've felt listening to your tantrum?"

"She doesn't give a shit, believe me." The bitterness in his voice stopped her for an instant and she glimpsed the pain in his gaze.

Softening, she said, "Alan, I care about you, I really do. You are the father of my children, but I don't love you anymore and never will. It's a small town, we're going to run into each other. So, you have two choices, you can either accept that and try to make the best of it, or you can go on harboring these ridiculous fantasies that do nothing but cause pain to your children and yourself. If you persist in using Nanny this way and berating me for things that are none of your business, you will lose my friendship and Graham's too."

"You have to admit your conduct this summer hasn't been the most motherly. You barely broke it off with you know who then you take up with Graham."

"That's enough."

At least ten people had stopped and were now staring at their little drama. Beth turned and practically sprinted to her car, ignoring his pleas to stop.

Chapter 50

Too agitated to paint, Beth spent the morning cleaning the house and weeding the gardens around the terrace. Nanny had left a note, *gone sailing with Betsy, be back at five* so she had the house to herself. A little after one, she was sitting at the kitchen counter eating a sandwich when he knocked on the back door. He entered without waiting for an invitation.

He knows my habits well, she thought, sadly. "Jack, hi. Kit's not here. He's still at his dad's." The look on his face told her he wasn't looking for Kit.

"Why couldn't you just be honest with me? Why did you have to use Kit and all that other bullshit? If you were screwing around with him, why couldn't you just tell me?"

"Jack, I don't think we should have this conversation."

"Well I do. I want to know."

"I didn't lie to you; I just chose not to mention Graham. He's an old friend with whom I've just become involved."

"Does he know about us?"

She hesitated, and then told the truth. "Yes, he does. I did not tell him anything but the barest details. He wanted to help after Kit and then Alan exploded at me."

"You could have told me."

"I'm sorry, I wanted to, but then there was never the right moment."

Angry tears welled up in his eyes and she wanted to reach out to him, to take him in her arms and tell him everything was all right, but it wasn't. Nothing was right and nothing would ever be right again between them. She had betrayed him as a mother and rejected him as a lover. Neither role fit anymore. "I gotta go. I'm leaving for college Monday anyway."

"Good luck. I know you'll do well."

"Who gives a shit? Not you."

Yes I do, she thought sadly, watching him slam out the back door. Yes I do, Jack Talbot, more than you'll ever know.

CHAPTER 51

As they drove out the driveway of Friend's Home, Beth looked over to find her companion's eyes brimming with tears. She reached across and squeezed her hand. "Thank you, Constance."

"Hestor has been my dearest friend for eighty years. Don't know what I'll do when she's gone. Haven't seen much of her lately, but she is such a part of me."

"I know. Dad died when Lanie and I were so young. She's been mother and father to us for most of our lives."

She sniffled, hand trembling as she dabbed at her eyes with a yellowing lace hankie. "If only I could've kept her with me until the end. We had so many happy times together."

"You sure did."

Conversation ceased, both of them comforted by the silence as they drove home.

When they neared the outskirts of the village, Beth asked, "Can I take you anywhere? Any errands to run?"

"No, dear, thank you. Home will be fine. She did look well, didn't she?"

Beth nodded. "Mama is still a beautiful woman."

"May she go in peace, poor lamb," Constance said, more to herself than Beth. "I don't think I'll go again, dear. Do you think that's wrong?"

"No, Constance, I don't."

A few minutes later, she stopped the car and leaned over to kiss the wizened cheek before hopping out to help the old Quaker into the house.

Constance lived in the same duplex she had shared with Hestor for over thirty years. Half of a restored Victorian, the landlord, a quiet, generous soul, lived in the other half. A bachelor in his late fifties, he had watched over "his two ladies" with more than the usual custodial care, checking on them every day. Without him, both women would have found it impossible to live independently for as long as they did. Nowadays, Dory Grant did almost everything for Constance except cook. Before Beth left, she settled Constance in her parlor for her "afternoon rest."

CHAPTER 52

Labor Day weekend arrived, heralding the official end of the summer. Lanie breezed in Thursday evening and Kat late Friday. Rob did not accompany her nor did her daughter mention him all weekend. Beth thought it best to let the subject alone until her daughter felt like sharing.

Lanie's presence always threw the household into delightful turmoil. Their aunt liked to be on the go every minute, playing tennis, seeing old friends, wandering through her favorite gift shops and she liked her family to accompany her on all outings. In an effort to spare Beth, who was trying to complete garden chores, Kit spent Friday driving his aunt from place to place so she could catch up with old friends and "see the sights." Kat took over mid-afternoon and niece and aunt had a spirited, but friendly game of tennis.

They arrived home, sweaty and ready for a swim and to find that Beth was fixing supper. "Hey, sis, the ocean looks delicious. Come on down for a dip with us."

"You've had quite a day for yourself. I'll bet Kit's seen places he never knew existed." Beth set down her towel and wiped her brow.

"He loved every minute of it. Besides, he's the one who kept pushing me to go into this shop and that. He's a closet tourist, Bethie. What are you doing in here anyway? I told you, I'm taking you all out tonight."

"Lanie, you don't have to do that. I've just taken out some chicken and I'm starting a salad."

"It's a done deal, big sister, so put the chickie back in the fridge. I've made reservations at Moby's at seven and we're going. Kit's gonna pick up Nanny, then he'll swing by and get us. Now get the hell outta that apron and into your bathing suit. The surf awaits!"

When her mind was made up, there was no budging Lanie. Since they were children, she always got her way. No one, not even their parents wanted to face the consequences if she didn't. Laughing, Beth scooped up the vegetables she'd been chopping and slipped them into a plastic bag while Kat wrapped the chicken.

Kat gave her a secret look that seemed to say, "surrender is the only option."

"Here, Mom, I'll take care of the rest, go get into your suit."

Beth smiled and followed her sister upstairs to change.

As usual Lanie was right, the ocean was delicious. The three spent nearly a half an hour swimming and riding the waves. They brought soap and shampoo and showered in the beach club's outside stalls. Afterwards, the two sisters sat on the wide, wooden benches of the clubhouse porch talking and gazing out to sea, watching Kat swim laps.

"So who've you got lined up for my hot date tomorrow? And don't tell me 'Graham the gorgeous' wasn't successful or I'll have to snatch him away from you."

"Oh, that's right. I almost forgot, Graham called this afternoon. He did say something about someone."

Instantly, her sister's green eyes lit up with curiosity. "Come on, come on, give!"

"He's bringing an old friend. His name is Carlos something. They went to college together."

"Oh, a Latin lover! I'll go out tomorrow morning and purchase a sinful red dress and some castanets."

"Lanie, be serious. Graham says he's a great guy, but I haven't told you the best part."

"He's drop-dead handsome?"

"No." Beth ignored Lanie's disappointed groan. "I mean, I don't have the faintest idea what he looks like. No, the best news is, guess where he lives? Boston.

Graham invited him down for tomorrow night 'especially to meet the gorgeous, very eligible Lanie Whitman, a fellow Bostonite."

"Oh my God, he didn't make me out to be a charity case, did he? I mean, he didn't tell Mr. Gorgeous, Mr. Perfect, Mr. Dream-Come-True, that I was some little spinster, too pathetic to find herself a date on Labor Day weekend, did he?"

"Relax, he knows you're in town for the weekend, that's all. Graham gave me no account of his physical description, so don't get your hopes up."

"Oh, Carlos, where have you been all my life?" Lanie crooned.

As they watched Kat make her way up the beach, she changed the subject. "Do the kids know about you and Graham?"

"A little, they've seen us together."

"Thought so."

"Oh?"

"Both Kat and Kit mentioned him today."

"What did they say?"

"Not much, just that you'd been seeing a lot of him and they wondered how well I knew him. I think they sense he's more than a casual acquaintance. Is he?"

Beth waved to Kat as her daughter headed for the shower. "Yes, he's more than a casual acquaintance, but after everything that's happened this summer, we're taking it slow."

"Does he know about the other one?"

"Yes, which is one of the reasons we're taking it slow."

"Geez, that must've been rough. What about the kids, do they know?"

"Only Kit, but I'm going to tell the others, at the end of the weekend."

"Do you thing that's wise?"

"Probably not, but it's something I need to do, for Kit's sake, as much as anything. He shouldn't be shouldering all this alone. They're close and he needs his sisters' support."

"I guess so, especially Kat's, I'd imagine."

"Someone mention my name?"

Kat came up behind them and rubbed her aunt's shoulders. Lanie patted her hands.

"I was just telling your mom what a beautiful woman you've turned out to be. Just like your auntie."

"Uh, huh. Fine, keep your secrets, but we better get going if we want to make our reservations."

CHAPTER 53

Saturday morning, the two sisters sat at the kitchen table drinking tea.

"Thanks again for last night."

"My pleasure, I love Moby Dick's. There's nothing quite like it anywhere, is there?"

Beth nodded and patted Lanie's hand. "It's good to have you here, little sister. I wish you'd come more often."

"Perhaps I will. Carlos and I will purchase a weekend house after we're married. He's fabulously wealthy, I'm sure of it."

Giggling, Beth poked her. "You'd better behave yourself tonight. No dancing on the tables and no castanets. This is Windy Harbor. I have to live here after tonight."

"Oh, pooh, when have you known me not to behave myself? Well, maybe a couple of times here and there, but I've matured. These days I'm the very model of decorum."

The phone rang, interrupting them. As Beth rose to answer, Lanie freshened their tea cups and brought milk from the refrigerator for Beth, who still took her tea "the English way" with plenty of milk and sugar.

Beth winked at her sister. "Hey, Clary."

"Has Lanie arrived?"

"Oh, yes."

"Why are you keeping her all to yourself?"

"We'll be at the dance tonight. Me at the Labor Day Dance. Can you believe it? After three years, I'm re-entering harbor society with Graham Lynch at my side. He's found a date for Lanie, too."

"Don't make me sound so pathetic," Lanie said. "Hi, Clary, see you tonight," she called.

"Tell her hi for me. We'll be waiting with baited breath to see her and Mr. Wonderful. Listen, hon, Ben and I made a reservation for the buffet at seven. Want to join us?"

"Thanks, but we're eating out beforehand. Quieter, you know? We'll be there around nine, okay?"

"Whew," Lanie said as Beth rejoined her. "Talk about the third degree."

The pot calling the kettle black, Beth thought. "She's just excited. She loves the Labor Day dance and has spent the last three years futilely trying to get me back to it. Guess we should've asked Ben and her to dinner with us."

"No way! I want Carlos' undivided attention."

Beth sipped her tea and gave her sister a wry look.

"You know, I've had such a good time, I think I'll head down again before it gets cold and stay the weekend at Hestor's Way. If I'm lucky, Carlos may accompany me. I haven't been there in so long."

"We've got to come to a decision about that this fall. It's getting pretty run-down. We either have to put some money into it, or it may topple over in a really good storm."

"You know how I feel about it, Beth. I've wanted to sell for years. It's you who has wanted to hold on."

"I know, but I'm ready now. After everything this summer, I know I could never stay there again. The boys have worked hard this summer clearing lots of storage space in the barn. If we sell, we can have everything moved to the barn, then sort through things at our leisure."

"Okay by me. Why don't I plan to come down in mid-September and we can talk to a realtor. What do you think?"

Voice shaky, she replied, "That'd be great, if you have the time."

"Hey, don't get weepy on me, sweetheart. This is supposed to be a fun weekend, remember?"

"Sorry."

"What are your plans for the day? Why don't you come with me? Phyllis and Eddie would love to see you and there's plenty of room on the boat." Lanie was going deep sea fishing with a school friend and her husband, who ran a charter fishing business. "Besides, you'd be a buffer. After a couple of hours of Phyllis droning on about little Eddie's soccer trophies and what a genius little Betty Sue is, I'll be ready to jump ship."

"Her name is Betsy Ann, Lanie. Thanks, but I'll pass. I've got lots to do around here. I'd like to get a little work in, and then I'm going to the beach with Kat and Nanny."

"Well, I'd better stir my stumps, or Eddie will accuse me of letting all the fish get away. Wait until Phyllis hears about Carlos. She'll be green with envy."

Beth rolled her eyes.

"Have you seen Eddie lately? If his beer belly gets any bigger, he'll have to hire a crane to hold it up!"

Waving her off, Beth went up to change. As Lanie drove out of the driveway, grinding the Volvo's gears every inch of the way, Beth gathered her things. She wrote a note to the girls and asked them to call her when they were ready for the beach, then headed out to the studio.

Their beach day turned into "old home week" as Nanny and Kat disappeared with their friends leaving Beth to chat with an ever changing retinue of passersby, many of whom she had not seen in years. Labor Day weekend was definitely not the time for a peaceful, relaxation at the beach. Midafternoon when Alan joined her, Beth knew for certain the outing had been a mistake. The girls were having a ball, but she most definitely should have stayed home.

"Hey, babe, how you doin'?"

Shielding her eyes, she looked up to see him, chair, beach bag and umbrella in hand. His legs looked impossibly thin in trunks now several sizes too big. She wondered absently how he would ever keep up his suit while swimming.

"Hi."

"Mind if I join you?"

Yes, yes, yes, she thought, yes, I do mind. "Where's Chloe?"

"Who knows? I thought she was here, but damned if I can find her." He stood, waiting for an invitation.

"I'm going to be leaving soon."

"That's okay," he said and unfolded his chair.

"Alan."

"Relax, I won't bite you. I'll stay a few minutes to catch my breath, then move on. Haven't got my old energy back yet, I'm afraid."

"How are you feeling?"

"Pretty good. Kit's been a life saver."

"I'm sure he has." She gazed out to sea.

"So I hear Lanie's in town?"

"Yup, just for the weekend."

"How is she?"

"Great."

"I'd love to see her."

"We're going to the dance tonight. Are you going?"

"Wouldn't miss it. That's one of the few things Chloe and I agree on—dancing. We both love it. Of course, you know I love dancing. We used to cut quite a rug, didn't we?"

Beth continued to stare out to sea, and offered no response, refusing to be drawn into a conversation about the past.

"Yeah, well. Lotta good it'll do me tonight, my dancing, I mean. I'll probably get winded after half a dance and have to be carried off the floor. Then Chloe'll get pissed and go off with some young guy."

"Alan."

"Yeah, yeah, I know, sorry. Not your problem. Where're the girls?"

"Off with friends. I probably won't see them again."

"They both goin' tonight?"

"Kat is, I'm not sure about Nanny. She'll probably go if everyone else does. Besides, Lanie has already made her promise to save a dance for her."

"So who you goin' with? Lynch?"

"Yes," she replied through gritted teeth and braced herself for a confrontation.

"You guys decided to go public, then?" Silence. "How about Lanie, who's she going with?"

"Graham's friend from Boston."

"Oh, who?"

"Someone named Carlos; I can't remember his last name."

"Carlos Ricci, I'll wager. Graham's college roommate."

"Yes, that's it. Do you know him?"

"Yeah, great guy. Good-looking, too, as I recall. Lanie will be salivating."

Beth gave him a sharp look and stood up.

"Hey, I'm kidding, you know that, but you have to admit Lanie can be a bit aggressive with men."

"I have to go. It's getting late and I have lots to do. I'm going to find the girls."

He grabbed hold of her wrist. "Beth, please don't go yet. Stay just a few more minutes." His eyes pleaded, desperation in his gaze.

"I can't really." Gently she extracted her hand. "I'm sorry."

She turned away, hiding her tears as she strolled down the beach, refusing to look back. When she returned with Nanny and Kat, he was gone. The girls decided to stay, so she packed up and returned home to shower, change, and lay out her clothes for the evening.

CHAPTER 54

"Wow!" Beth exclaimed as her sister waltzed into the family room. Lanie had been scurrying back and forth from bathroom to bedroom for over an hour, and Beth had begun to despair at her ever being ready. "I'll look like a country bumpkin beside you. You're gorgeous!"

True to her word, Lanie had gone straight from Phyllis and Eddie's boat to Lizzie's, a small women's dress shop two villages away, in wealthier Old Harbor. The dress was not red, but a shimmering, luminescent blue-green. The sheath, worn with simple black pumps, perfectly complimented her light auburn, shoulder-length hair, which she had pulled back to softly frame her face. Its mid-thigh length showed off her slender, shapely legs to their best advantage.

"Think I need a wrap?"

"Only if you want an extra prop. It's a pretty warm night. Then again, we will probably be out until after midnight so it might get chilly. I have a sweater that would go with the—"

"Heaven forbid. No, no, if I get chilly, Carlos will drape his jacket over my shoulders, or better still, wrap me in his arms and, is that the doorbell?"

"Yes, it is," Beth said. "And don't worry," she added, noticing the look of panic on the other's face. "If he's a friend of Graham's, he'll be great."

Lanie grabbed her hand and held her back. "You look beautiful, big sister," she whispered. "I hope Graham realizes what a lucky man he is."

Beth opened the door to find Graham standing on the stoop. Handsome in a navy sport jacket and beige khakis, his blue oxford shirt changed the color of his hazel eyes to a deeper, richer green. He wore a bright, flowered tie that looked remarkably similar to the pattern of her skirt.

Noticing the similarity, he held up the tie, grinning. "Hey, we're a match!"

His smile always melted her heart and Beth found herself smiling back, wanting to throw her arms around him. In truth, Graham rarely smiled, so when he did, it was something to cherish.

A shorter, darker man, impeccably dressed in a beige linen suit stood beside him, waiting expectantly. Alan had been right, Carlos Ricci was handsome. From his demeanor, it appeared that he knew it. A strutting peacock came to mind.

Graham kissed her cheek as he passed into the front hall. "This is Carlos. Carlos, my beautiful Beth."

"Hello, Beth."

His voice was deep, sensual, every syllable oozing charm as he took her hand. As soon as politeness allowed, she extracted her hand. "Come in, please."

Beth led the way to the family room. For an instant, she wondered if Lanie might be hiding. Then, her sister burst through the door from the kitchen, her dramatic entrance not lost on Carlos, who stepped forward to shake her hand.

"I've heard so much about you, Elaine."

"All good, I hope," Lanie replied, her voice shaking.

She's petrified, Beth thought, watching her beautiful sister. In spite of all the bluff and bravado, Lanie was like a love-struck school girl on her first date. Not for the first time, she wondered how happy her younger sister really was living all alone in Boston.

"Please, call me Lanie. No one's called me Elaine since the third grade."

"Lanie it is then."

Clearing her throat, Beth said, "Lanie, you remember Graham, don't you?"

With effort, Lanie tore herself from Carlos' deep, brown eyes. "Of course, Graham, wonderful to see you."

Graham shook her hand a bemused expression playing across his features. "You've changed since we last met. Last time I saw you, you were wearing love beads and dread locks, I believe."

Lanie laughed. "Not me, you're thinking of Beth. Beth was the quintessential flower child, still is, as you can see."

She gestured towards her sister's peasant blouse and full, gathered skirt of gauzy cotton, its print a riot of summer flowers. Her hair, loosely tied back with tortoise shell combs, fell over her shoulders. In sharp contrast to the city chic of her three companions, Beth looked like a warm earth mother.

"Lovely, as always," Graham said quietly, his eyes attesting to the sincerity of his words.

"Real knock-outs, both of you," Carlos added, turning to his date.

"Would you like to sit for a few minutes?" Beth asked.

"We'd better go," Graham said. "Our reservations are for seven thirty."

They ate at a small French restaurant in Old Harbor, the *Moulon Rouge*, once a favorite of Graham's. They all agreed it had seen better days, the food mediocre, and the service slow. Mediocrity notwithstanding, they enjoyed themselves, laughing and conversing easily throughout the meal. Lanie warmed up after a glass of wine and spent most of the meal flirting shamelessly with Graham seated beside her and Carlos, seated across from her. A few times Beth thought she spied her sister's hand slipping under the table and there appeared to be foot activity as they sipped cappuccino.

Several times she caught Graham's eye in silent amusement at the antics of their companions. Not for the first time, she thought how easy it was to be with Graham and how much she enjoyed his company.

CHAPTER 55

When they arrived at the country club shortly after nine, the dance was in full swing. Many revelers had dined beforehand on the club's lavish buffet, but Beth was glad they had decided to eat elsewhere. At the club, their meal would most certainly have been delicious, but also subject to countless interruptions, not to mention the possibility of landing at a table with Alan and Chloe, the first people they spied upon entering the room.

"Hey, Beth, Graham, over here," he called, gesturing.

"We're just saying hello, not sitting," she whispered, as Graham led her toward the table.

"Hi, Lanie," Alan said, rising to peck his former sister-in-law's cheek.

Lanie allowed herself to be kissed, but did not reciprocate, pulling back stiffly with barely a nod. Undaunted, Alan turned to Carlos, shaking his hand, but found the other's attention directed elsewhere, in fact, riveted on his wife, or rather his wife's chest. Clearing his throat, he added, "I'd like you to meet my wife, Chloe."

"Hi," Chloe said, rising. "Good to see you all. You too, Graham."

She came around the table to give Graham a kiss, a familiar gesture he clearly had not encouraged and one Beth felt sure he had never received before. It appeared to be staged for her benefit and Beth had to admit, Chloe pulled it off beautifully.

In red, what little there was of it, Chloe's sleeveless dress fit her slender body like a second skin, every curve, every muscle outlined in sharp relief. The neckline plunged to her waist, satin cords in a laced pattern from neck to waist, the only thing keeping her ample breasts in check. As it was, there was enough cleavage showing to guarantee every male's eyes would be on her or more specifically her chest, whenever Chloe stepped onto the dance floor. Diaphanous red stockings and red stiletto heels already abandoned under the table completed the ensemble. Wisps of blond hair fell around her face and the rest she had tied back in an elaborate French braid. She looked fabulous and, like Carlos, she knew it.

Truth be told, Chloe and Lanie were overdressed for the informal dance where most men were in sport coats, the women in skirts and blouses or simple summer dresses; however, no one was complaining, least of all Carlos, who looked ready to rip Chloe's laces apart and take the plunge.

Clary saved the day. Out of the throng, she emerged and grabbed Beth by the elbow. "Come on, guys. We've got a table outside. It's a little quieter at least."

Waving to Alan and Chloe, they allowed themselves to be dragged through the crowd to where Ben sat on the porch with several of the Rollin's neighbors. Introductions were made and then the men went off to get drinks for everyone.

Clary gave Lanie a hug. "So good to see you again, dearie! Carlos is pretty hunky, huh?"

"Yes, he is," Lanie said, morosely. "But I'm afraid I'm no match for the whip woman."

"Chloe's a trip, isn't she? Where do you suppose she finds those clothes?"

"Forget her." Beth slid her arm around her sister's waist. "He's plenty interested in you, little sister, although I'd watch him. Seems a bit wolfish to me."

"Mr. Rogers would seem wolfish to you. Carlos can paw me anytime!"

"Lanie!"

"Come on, you two, don't start. Have you seen the kids? Kat's here with a bunch of her friends and Mike and Janelle condescended to sit with us for fifteen minutes or so."

"What about Kit and Nanny?"

"I know Nan's here. She and Carrie are running around somewhere, most likely bothering the dishwashers in the kitchen. Carrie says Nan's sweet on Kevin Higgins."

"Oh?"

"Now, Mother, calm down. As for Kit, I bet Karen will drag him in before long. Mike said that gang went to the Foc'sile for dinner. They'll be here soon, you wait."

As Carlos, Ben, and Graham returned with drinks, the teenage crowd descended. The Labor Day dance was the only dance of the summer where adults and kids mingled. The rest of the time, there were kid dances every other Tuesday, and adult dances once or twice a month, on Saturday evenings. After spending their summer avoiding their parents, the "kids" joined them and always seemed surprised at how much fun it could be rubbing elbows with the "old folks."

Jack neither looked at Beth nor acknowledged her presence. His behavior was not lost on any of those who knew about the affair. Graham, Lanie, and Kit all stared back and forth from Beth to her former lover with worried eyes. Soon the teens retreated to their own table at the opposite end of the porch and the tension eased.

The girls all wore light sundresses in varying pastel shades; Kit, Pete, and Jack wore sports shirts and ties, but no jackets. Karen was glued to Kit's side and her fingers clutched his arm in a vise grip. Lesley was similarly draped round Jack. Pete brought up the rear with freckle-faced, wholesome Judy Wilcox, a new relationship for him. They looked a little less chummy than the others.

"Do you think Karen could hold on any tighter?" Lanie whispered as they watched the retreating couples.

"Hush," Beth said, silently agreeing with her.

"Shall we?" Carlos asked, holding out his hand to Lanie.

A few awkward moments ensued as Ben and Clary followed Carlos and Lanie to the dance floor, leaving Beth and Graham standing alone. Finally, he circled his arm around her waist and he leaned toward her. "I'm not a great dancer, but I'll try."

Smiling, she returned his embrace. "I'd love to."

The floor was jammed, the throng gyrating to Bob Seger's *Old Time Rock and Roll*. Graham hesitated for a moment, and then they plunged in. He danced just as she remembered from years ago, awkwardly, his long, gangly limbs, each with a life of its own, flailing out in discordant rhythm with the music. He did somewhat better when they held hands, dancing in rock and roll fashion, spinning her, catching her and leading her round under his arm, moving apart as their hands snaked down one another's arm, clasping hands at the very moment of separation, smiling as they got better and better at each move.

As they danced, Graham became more relaxed and they laughed, experimenting with new steps and movements. Some worked and others failed abysmally, sending one or the other of them flying into a neighboring couple. It was during one of these disasters that Beth ran headlong into Jack. Instinctively, he reached out and caught her, but instead of releasing her to the dance, he held on, hands around her waist holding her off balance as he leaned into her. Lesley's back was to Jack so it took her a few seconds to notice that her partner was no longer dancing. When she turned to find him locked in an embrace with one of the mothers, her sharp, questioning look was lost on him. Eyes held Beth's as his pain and anger bored into her.

Graham endeavored to come between them, his hand on Jack's arm, his voice low. "Let her go, Talbot." But, Jack continued to stare into her and through her, his grip tightening.

"Please, Jack," she begged. No response.

"What's going on here?" Lesley's shrill, nasal query finally did the trick. "Jack, come on."

As he released her, Graham caught Beth and led her to the edge of the floor. Although it had seemed like hours, the entire exchange had taken no more than thirty seconds and had seemingly gone unnoticed by the other dances. Brow drenched in sweat, he gazed down at her. "Wanna take a break?"

"Yes, please."

She allowed herself to be led from the room, grateful for the fresh ocean breeze that washed over them as they stepped onto the porch. Slowly she regained her composure, but the run-in with Jack had destroyed the evening. She suspected it had done the same for Graham. Before that moment, Graham had never seen them together. His expression told Beth that the encounter had hurt more than he would ever admit.

As the evening went on, Alan and Chloe joined them, much to the distress of both sisters. Beth, because of the annoyance of Alan's continual invitations to dance, all of which she refused; Lanie because clearly Carlos was smitten. From the moment Chloe stepped into their sphere, she ceased to exist. Alan didn't help matters. He had stepped onto the porch, arm around Chloe's waist, calling, "Help. Somebody dance with her. She's killing me."

Carlos was only too happy to oblige. Except for one or two dances, where a shred of decency made him return to his date, he abandoned Lanie for "The Breast" as Clary dubbed Chloe. Hurt at first, Lanie soon recovered and danced with Alan, Ben, Graham, Eddie, and any teenager she could get her hands on, including Jack. Beth suspected that despite all the talk about her Latin lover, Lanie was fully doing what she enjoyed most.

It was during Lanie's dance with Graham when the thing Beth had dreaded all night occurred. Clary cajoled Alan into dancing with her and pushed Ben toward the teenagers, saying, "Quick, hon, now's your chance. Ask one of those gorgeous babes to dance." Ben chose Lesley, which left Jack free.

Beth saw him coming the instant Ben led Lesley away. Rooted to the spot, she neither fled nor had she formulated an excuse, so when he held out his hand she nodded and allowed him to lead her toward the dance floor.

He stopped short of the crowded dance floor and took her into his arms while still on the porch deck. Clearly he meant them to remain on the deserted porch and no amount of effort on her part could move him inside.

After the first encounter on the dance floor, she was afraid to speak lest her voice betray her feelings, but she endeavored to hold him at arm's length. Her efforts proved futile. His hand covered her back and possessed her completely as their bodies moved as one with the music.

"No, Jack," she heard herself saying, her voice coming from afar. A stranger's voice, hollow and scared. "Please, no."

In response, he held her tighter and Beth prayed Graham could not see them, prayed that no one could see them, the searing heat of their embrace, revealing all. He felt so good, she thought, the familiar contours of his damp chest like a caress. Her breasts tingled with unbidden desire. She allowed herself one moment of weakness, savoring his familiar smell and the tender awkwardness of his shuffling dance steps, but as his lips moved down to kiss her neck, she broke away, her breathless cry, "No!" lost in the din from within.

Their actions had been hidden from those within and she scanned the porch, Beth was relieved to see that not a soul had witnessed the two of them.

"You feel the same, I know you do."

Jack turned away and pushed his way into the dancing throng. She let him go and breathed a sigh of relief when Graham rejoined her several minutes later. His relaxed, happy expression brought comfort and solace for her frayed emotions. He had not spied them together and she hoped her feigned cheerfulness masked the turmoil that raged within her.

Finally, they danced the last dance, a slow, languid waltz. Graham held her tightly, his lips grazing her cheek, her hair, her neck. Out of the corner of her eye, Beth saw Alan watching them and turned away, closing her eyes.

As the music stopped, she reached up and kissed him. "I love you," she whispered softly as they left the dance floor, arm in arm.

The ride home was quiet. Lanie pressed against the door as far away from Carlos as she could get, Graham silent beside her.

When they arrived at Beth's, Lanie popped out. "Don't bother, Carl dear," she said, slamming the door in his face.

Graham walked Beth to the door. "That's the last time I play matchmaker," he said, laughing, as his arms circled her waist and drew her close. "Carlos has changed. Honest. It's been a while since I've seen him and he's been married and divorced twice in the interim. Do you think this self-absorption could be his midlife crisis?"

She shrugged.

"I'm sorry about Lanie. I hope she wasn't hurt or embarrassed."

"Don't worry about Lanie. She's tough, she can take it. Besides, she's always happiest with the kids anyway. She had a great time."

"Tonight was tough on you, wasn't it?" His touch tentative, his voice strained and tense, he was seeking an explanation of the scene he had witnessed on the dance floor.

"Let's just say, that's the last Labor Day dance I'm attending. Will you remind me of that next year?"

"Next year? That's encouraging. After what I saw with you and Talbot I wondered if there'd be a tomorrow, never mind next year."

A trace of anger had crept into his voice and she regarded him sadly. "Please, Graham, can we not talk about this tonight?"

"Sorry, you're right. Forget it. You came home with me, didn't you?"

"Graham."

"Apologies, uncalled for. End of story."

"Thank you."

"It's funny, I almost feel drunk, though I didn't drink anything stronger than cappuccino."

"It's all that dancing, I expect, went right to your head." Smiling up at him in the darkness, her hand caressed his cheek. The tension in his jaw relaxed under her touch.

There was something innocent and vulnerable about Graham, a fragility that his protective wall of sarcasm could never completely obscure and his vulnerability tugged at her heart.

"We were having such a good time, the dancing I mean, I'm so sorry about Jack." She leaned against him, needing his warmth.

"Enough said," he said, kissed her forehead and drew her nearer. "You were the prettiest gal in the place, oh, quintessential flower child of mine."

She laughed. "What about Chloe?"

"God, she's awful, isn't she? Cute little bod, but what Alan and she have in common is beyond me."

"Please, let's not end the evening talking about Alan!"

"Fine, is this better? I love you, Beth Hadley. I'd marry you tomorrow if you'd have me. Now come here and give me a real kiss."

She did, and only with great difficulty did she tear herself away and say goodnight.

CHAPTER 56

After several wild dances the previous evening, Lanie had cajoled Pete into taking her to the station and he had only too happily agreed. Late Sunday morning, she departed in a flurry of activity with promises to come again soon, and "please to come up to Beantown," called out as she dashed around the house, remembering one more thing she had forgotten.

Much as they loved her, the household breathed a collective sigh of relief as Pete's Mustang pulled out of the drive.

As the week went on, Kat's departure loomed heavily on her mother. Sunday night, Beth requested that all three children eat supper at her house. As they enjoyed blue fish, corn on the cob, and salad from the garden, Kit and Kat, so often separated in different social groups, caught up with each other. Nanny and Beth listened, enjoying the conversation.

After supper, Kat said, "Mom, after we clean up I'm gonna head over to Joan's for a little while. Everyone's there. You don't mind, do you?"

"'Course not, sweetie, but I'd like a few minutes to talk with you three before you go. This might be the last chance we get. Can you hold on for about fifteen minutes? You, too, Kit?"

Having all four of them in the kitchen felt good and for once Beth hated to finish cleaning up. The evening's togetherness underscored the disjointed nature of the summer and how much her little family had been fractured and thrown in all directions over the past months. She hoped her words would not be cause for further division, but they must be said.

She needed to tell them about Graham rather than have them rely on rumor or speculation. Also, she refused to have this new relationship filtered through their father's eyes without her side of the story. The second topic of conversation would be a good deal harder for all of them, but she knew she must tell them anyway. Jack was still so hurt and angry, there was no telling what he might say or do.

When they settled in the family room, she began, "I have to share a couple of things with you guys. Things I should've told you about weeks ago. We've always shared the important things in our lives and I don't want to stop now, however difficult it might be."

Kit turned away, gazing out the window, while Kat and Nanny stared at her with anxious eyes.

"Nanny and I have talked about this a little bit already. You all know Graham. I know Kit and Nanny have seen him a few times at Dad's and the cookout last weekend. You might remember him from when you were a baby, Kat? He's an old friend of Dad's and mine who has been living in Chicago for many years and only recently moved back to Windy Harbor."

"He's married," Kit said. "Dad said. His wife's a lawyer."

"They're divorcing."

He looked away again.

"The divorce proceedings had begun long before he came back here. The reason I'm telling you about Graham is that as Nanny and Kit know and maybe they've told you, Kat, Graham and I have been dating. I guess you could call it dating. We enjoy each other's company, as you saw the night of the cookout. Hopefully we will continue to see each other and I hope you'll all get to know him better. He's a wonderful man."

Kat flipped back her hair, twisting the auburn ponytail around her finger nervously. "Wait a minute, Mom. Are you telling us you're getting married?"

"Not in the near future. In truth, Graham has asked me, but I'm not ready. This summer has been somewhat tumultuous for me and I'm not sure I want to make such a big decision right now."

Kit stood, eyes challenging her. "He's not gonna move in here, is he?"

"No, he's not."

"What's he doing here anyway?" Kat gave her brother a quizzical look then turned back to Beth. "Is he retired?"

"He runs the Lynch Gallery where I'm having my show. That's how we got reacquainted actually. He went through my paintings to plan for the show. Please don't make the mistake your father did. My acceptance for the show has nothing to do with my friendship with Graham."

"God, we'd never think that, Mom. Now, what else did you want to tell us?" At the edge of her seat, her eldest was clearly eager to join her friends. "I mean, that's great about you and him. I'm happy for you. In my opinion, it's high time you started dating again."

"Dad doesn't think so," Kit said, halfheartedly.

"How about you?" Beth asked, turning to her son.

He shrugged. "Doesn't have anything to do with me."

"Kit!"

His older sister's indignant tone made him blush. "Sorry, Mom, I'm glad, too." Half- hearted, but it was a start.

Nanny said nothing.

"The other thing I wanted to tell you is much more difficult," she began, glancing at Kit. Please don't hate me, she thought.

"It's about a relationship in which I've been involved in this summer, before Graham. When I refer to my tumultuous summer, this is what I'm referring to. It's probably the hardest thing I've ever had to tell you girls. Kit already knows about this and I debated not telling you, but I don't feel right keeping things. I should not have kept it a secret. I was wrong about the relationship and very unfair to you. I think it may help Kit if he doesn't have to shoulder this alone. You three can talk about it together if you need to, if not, that's okay too."

"Mom, what is it? Are you sick?"

"No, Kat, I'm fine. In a way, I think that would almost be easier to say." She glanced over at Kit, ashen now, eyes staring at the floor in front of him. "There's no easy way to say this, so I'm just going to come right out with it. I've been seeing someone else besides Graham this summer. He's much younger than me and the relationship is over, but I won't deny it happened, because it did. For the past two months, I've been having an intimate relationship with Jack Talbot."

Kat screamed, "Oh my God!"

"Shocking, I know."

"That's what Dad's been so upset about, isn't it? It wasn't Mr. Lynch it was Jack!" Nanny cried. "Mom, how could you?"

'I'm sorry, Nan. It just happened, that's the way love is sometimes."

"But Jack? Yuck, he's more like your son than a boyfriend."

"You're absolutely right, sweetheart."

Kat rose and began pacing. "How did it start? God, Mom, I can't believe this."

"That's unimportant. What's important is that it's over. While I did want you to know, I'd rather not go into the specifics, if you don't mind. I'm hoping no one besides you, Dad, and Jack will ever know about this, but if Jack decided to tell people I can't stop him. I certainly did not want you to hear about this from someone else."

An hour later, tears, shouting and many questions, the group seemed to have talked it out.

Kat left for Joan's with, "I love you, Mom." Hugging her, she whispered, "I understand, too, I think."

"Drop me off at Carrie's?" Nanny called, and the two sisters left together. Nanny said nothing to her, nor did she give her a hug or kiss.

When she and Kit were left alone, she said, "How about you? None of the guys around?"

"Nope. They've all left except Jack and I'm not up to seeing him tonight."

"You okay?"

He shrugged. "Maybe a little down about not going with the others, to college, I mean."

"It's not too late for second semester. I'll bet we could even see about going now if you've changed your mind."

"Whoa, Mom, no. I want to stay home. I'm gonna move back here for a while though, if it's okay with you?"

"Sweetie, you know it is." She hugged him. "Was I right to tell Kat and Nanny?"

"It's your life, Mom."

"But I hurt you, honey, I'm so sorry."

"I'm okay. We're okay."

He stepped forward and hugged her. Beth couldn't remember the last time her son had really hugged her and she wanted to hold on forever.

"Thanks, sweetheart."

"For what?"

"For not stalking out."

"I'm used to it now."

"I doubt that, but, I appreciate the sentiment."

CHAPTER 57

Hestor died on a rainy day in late September. The trees outside her window were just beginning to turn. Her memorial service was held in the Meeting House, a joyous celebration of her life, the silence continually broken with voices of friends and family moved to speak and share personal stories about her.

Alan, the beloved son she never had, spoke eloquently and brought the entire congregation to tears as he reminisced about "Mother Whitman" and what her love had meant to him. As exasperated as he made her most of the time, Beth knew his words were genuine.

Her mother had adored him. While Hestor refused to meet or have anything to do with the second Mrs. Hadley, there was always a twinkle in her eye for her boy. He flattered and coddled her as her daughters never had, flirting shamelessly with both Hestor and Constance on his frequent visits to the duplex. After the divorce, Constance stopped speaking to him, but not Hestor. Truth be told, she had looked forward to his visits almost as much as those of her daughters, although she would never have admitted it to anyone.

Beth never begrudged her ex-husband's relationship with her mother. His own parents, two selfish, globe-trotting socialites, had never been a part of their lives and had not seen their grandchildren more than two or three times in their entire lives. She knew that in Hestor, Alan had found the mother he always wanted and never had.

Kat and Kit spoke about Gran and about summers at Hestor's Way. They recalled rising to find breakfast laid out on the white enamel table, a blue-and-white bowl with fresh fruit, cereal boxes, homemade bread, fresh orange juice in a thick, crystal glass and a tiny pitcher of cream, a matching blue chipped sugar bowl beside.

"Gran would be long gone," Kat said, tears streaming down her cheeks. "Out tramping over the dunes, visiting with friends or tending to her garden. Long before we were old enough, she treated us like grown-ups. We had freedom at Hestor's Way that would have been unthinkable at home. Whenever I'm feeling low," she said, smiling down at her mother, "I just think about our times with Gran." Then, she choked up, unable to continue, and her brother took her hand.

As Beth watched them, standing alone in the hushed silence of the crowded Meeting House, she thought she had never been prouder. After several minutes, Kat was able to go on and they sat down together, emotions visibly overwhelming them.

Constance spoke next. "My Hestor, my beautiful friend for over eighty years. Go in the Light, as thou hast livest in the Light. I will love thee for…. for…" Tears spilled over her as Constance stood, both hands grasping the bench in front of her for support. "There hast never been a friend like thou," she finished and dropped to her seat, her whole body appearing to collapse around her.

Dear Constance, Beth thought, regarding her sadly. Don't leave us, too, old friend.

Graham attended Hestor's memorial, but stayed in the background and allowed Alan the role of patriarch. From afar, he watched his old friend accompany Beth from the Meeting House, his arm circling her waist.

As Alan led the way, Beth and Lanie held hands and appeared only vaguely aware of their surroundings. By the time she greeted people at the house, Beth had regained her equilibrium and broke away Alan's cloying embrace, her irritation evident. Watching her every move, Graham breathed a sigh of relief and caught her eye for an instant. From across the room, she returned his smile before her attention was diverted by another well-wisher.

Finally, the last of the guests departed and Graham approached her. "How are you doing?"

"Tired." She smiled, leaning against him. "Ready for bed."

"Can you go up now?"

"Soon. You go on. I'm fine."

They exchanged looks as Alan's voice boomed from the family room.

"Don't worry," she added, reading his thoughts. "I'm shooing him out, too. Lanie's staying with me and the kids are here. I'll be okay."

He drew her to him and kissed her forehead. "I love you," he whispered, just as Alan burst into the kitchen.

As Graham moved to pull back, she held on and drew him closer, burying her head in his chest. "Me too," she whispered.

Alan turned on his heel and left the room.

Chapter 58

Beth spent the month of October cataloging and sorting her work, touching up and finishing a few projects. Rick dropped in almost daily to pick up paintings for other exhibits, one in Boston and two in New York. With Graham's help, she spent an entire day selecting the forty-three paintings for the Lynch Gallery show. Those had been set aside or sent to the framer. Rick begged to be allowed to take "Hestor's Way" to New York, but Graham had insisted that it and all of the portraits be included in the Lynch show.

The frequent squabbles between agent and gallery manager made Beth feel like foam in a tumultuous sea, buffeted back and forth with neither man paying her any heed. After one such skirmish, she stalked out of the studio. Red, orange, and green leaves, sodden after an early morning shower, covered the path making the going slippery and she started toward the house. Her abrupt departure shamed the men into a temporary truce.

Later, Graham found her sitting at the kitchen counter pretending to read the latest *New Yorker*. He pulled up a stool and sat beside her. "I'm a jerk, what can I say?"

"Don't say anything," she replied, nose buried in the "Talk of the Town."

"Beth, is everything okay? Have I done something? I mean, besides this infantile arguing with Gould?"

"It's not that." She sighed, pushing the magazine aside and turning to face him. "It's just, I don't know, as it gets closer to the show there seems to be pressure everywhere. Pressure from you and Rick to get everything ready, pressure from

Alan's twenty calls a day reminding me to do this or that. Pressure to please you and to be good company when all I really want to do is be alone. The show's over a month away. I don't think I can take this for another six weeks!"

"Look, sweetheart, things are almost set. Let's put it aside, forget about it and take off, go somewhere, to the Cape, to Vermont, anywhere. Or we could be completely decadent and go to an island?"

"There you go again, planning my time for me. Let's do this, let's do that. I have a life, Graham, and I managed it quite well before you appeared on the scene, thank you very much. I don't need you holding my hand through every decision and every crisis."

"No, you let Alan do that."

"Where did that come from?"

"Look, Beth, whether you realize it or not, you're still married to Alan. He hovers constantly. God, he sees more of you than I do."

"It's only natural. He's the father of my children. We've talked about this before, Graham."

"Yeah, but that was in the beginning when you described your amiable arrangements for the kids' sake. What you failed to mention was the constant meddling, the late night calls, his popping in unannounced. If I'd known Alan would be in the bed with us, I'm not sure I would've been so quick to hop in in the first place."

He was right. Alan had been dreadful the past few weeks. Still, his words cut into the fragile flesh of her emotions and she snapped back, "Well, you can just hop right out."

"Is that what you want?"

"Yes. That's what I want. Alan's annoying and intrusive, but he's not in my bed. And what's more, he never will be, but right now I don't want you in it either. I don't want anyone!"

"Fine, I'll send Don over for the rest of the paintings. Mother always likes them there at least three weeks ahead for photos and pre-hanging. I'm done here. I'll get out your hair." He stalked out of the kitchen without a backward glance.

She knew she should go after him, but instead she sat. Maybe it was for the best. She set the magazine aside and began lunch preparations. As she opened the refrigerator, she heard Rick's car tear out of the drive. He's mad too, she thought. Perfect.

CHAPTER 59

"I'm sick of these braids, Mom. I want to get rid of them," Nanny said as the two of them sat down to dinner.

It was Thursday, the night after Halloween and Nanny and Beth were eating dinner alone. Kit was working with Alan installing a commission piece in Newport, a built in wall system designed and hand crafted by father and son for the library of a restored carriage house. Beth had been hearing about it for weeks, Kit bursting with pride at the completion of his first major project.

Alan had begged Beth to bring Nanny down to see it installed, but she declined. She was tired from a day spent clearing out the garden and she had no wish to drive an hour to hear more of Alan's advice about the show, her work, and her personal life.

"That's a big step," she answered, watching Nanny twirl one of the waist-length plaits around her finger. "It's your decision though. Are you thinking about going really short?"

"I don't know. It's just Margie Hollis looks great with her hair cut. She's like a different person, more sophisticated, more grown-up."

Beth watched her freckled-faced teen as she moved about the kitchen, marveling at how she was growing and changing. Her face had lost its childish pudginess. Recently Nanny had plucked her wild, bushy eyebrows into dainty arcs, softly framing her light brown, almond- shaped eyes. She tried to picture Nanny, a short, cropped strawberry blonde, but couldn't. She had had braids her entire life.

"Maybe Dot will have some ideas for you. You could stop in and see her at the salon, look through some of her books before you decide?"

"Maybe." Nanny looked pensive.

"Is there another reason besides Margie?"

"Kind of, I mean there's Jonathan."

"Jonathan?"

"You know, Jonathan Hastings. He's in my grade. He thinks, I mean, I like him and he… Well, what happened is I heard him tell Margie how much he liked her hair cut."

"Nanny, do you really want to cut your hair?"

"I dunno."

"Well, my advice would be think about it, and then, if you want to do it, go ahead, but don't do it to please someone else, okay?"

"'Course I know that, Mom."

At that moment the phone rang and Beth reached for it. "Hello."

"Mrs. Hadley?" an unfamiliar voice inquired.

"This is Beth Hadley, yes."

"Could I speak to your son, please?"

"I'm sorry, Kit's out for the night. Can I take a message?"

Hesitation on the other end, then, "Well, let me see…"

Something about the voice set off alarms.

"I guess I'd better tell you and you can relay the message in case I'm not able to get back in touch. This is Connor Talbot, Ed's older brother. Perhaps you remember me from a long time ago? I've been living in Texas for the past twenty-five years."

"Yes, Connor, hello, how are you?" she replied, vaguely recalling a tall, lankier version of his brother Ed.

"Not well, I'm afraid. I'm calling with some very bad news. I've just arrived in town this afternoon to help out and I've been asked to make some calls. Ed and Mary gave me a list and your boy is on it."

Heart in her throat, Beth listened, scarcely daring to breathe.

"It's about my nephew, their son, Jack."

Oh God, Beth thought, bracing herself.

"I'm afraid there's been an accident. They wanted Jack's friends to know. His parents are, well, of course you understand."

"I'm sorry, Mr. Talbot, you said an accident?"

"I am sorry, please excuse me. It's just I'm pretty shaken up myself. He was my only nephew. Jack is dead. Happened up at school, a car accident, slick road, inexperienced driver, never knew what hit 'em, poor kids."

Fragments of his voice echoed from the far end of a tunnel. "Happened last night, around midnight. No one's quite sure what they were up to."

An involuntary sob escaped as Beth collapsed onto the stool nearest the phone. Nanny stood beside her, hand resting on her mother's shoulder.

"Is there anything we can do?" she heard herself saying from the other end of the tunnel.

"No, I don't believe so. Just let your boy know. The service will be Saturday at Grace Church, nine in the morning, I believe." She hung up and looked up at her daughter.

"It's Jack, isn't it?" Nanny asked. Her mother's nod unnecessary as they held on to each other.

CHAPTER 60

Beth drifted through the nightmare of Jack's funeral weekend in a semi-conscious state, attempting to support her children as she fought to bury her grief. Grieving as a friend of the family, as a parent mourning a child's playmate was acceptable, but the other, borne of her elicit love affair must be secretly tucked away. She acknowledged her pain to no one, not to Alan or Lanie or her children. Kat and Lanie understood and tried to comfort her, but she pushed them away and focused all of her attention on Kit. Even after the events of the summer, his grief was terrible. The loss of his lifelong friend heralded the end of childhood with a finality easily ignored in past.

As weeks went by, Beth grew visibly thinner. Keeping food down was impossible and she slept fitfully. Her warring emotions, suppressed during the daylight, rose up as soon as she closed her eyes. Ravaged with guilt, she lapsed into profound melancholy worse even that of the months following Alan's desertion. She went back to her therapist, who gave her some relief and a small measure of peace.

Graham's attempts to contact her were rebuffed. All final plans for the show were filtered through Rick, or occasionally Margot Lynch. Still smarting about her son's refusal to include Joan Pilmer's watercolors as part of the exhibit, Beth heard through Rick that Margot was driving her son crazy.

"Have pity on the man," Rick said one afternoon when Graham had phoned the studio. "Mommy's a real martinet when show time draws near. Patch things up, why don't you? Give the guy a break."

Beth ignored him like she had everyone else since Jack's death.

Less than ten days before the show's opening, she drove into town late in the afternoon and parked in the Meeting House lot. She circled the stark white building until she came to the rear door. She knew where Constance kept the key so she fished under the stones and pulled it out and unlocked the door. In the growing twilight she could just make out the outlines of the benches as she stepped into the silent building. As her eyes adjusted to the darkness, she advanced and took a seat on the front bench. The occasional headlight sent dancing shadows across the white walls in the inky twilight.

Leaning back, she breathed in the comforting, musty smell of the old building. What had he meant to her? Had it been love? Surely not the same abiding love she had felt for Alan, the kind that was meant to last a lifetime. Was it indeed a mother's love for her child growing away from her with each passing year? Or was it the greedy, insatiable passion of a lover?

Nothing seemed to fit. Nothing described her feelings or allowed her to pack her love for him away into a neat little box where she could cherish his memory chaste and free of the guilt gnawing at her soul. She had hurt him so much in the end, had caused so much pain to her family and most of all to Kit. Although they continued to see each other in a larger group, the two friends had never reconciled. Now, Jack was gone and they never would.

Kit had barely spoken to her since the funeral and had immersed himself in his father's projects even when Alan could easily handle the work himself. His father had urged him to take time off, to relax and go home to your mother's cooking, but to no avail. He clearly couldn't bear to be near her. Did he blame her for Jack's death? Did he think her unworthy of mourning his friend after all that had passed? No answers came as she sat, softly weeping in the silent room.

An hour later, a light was switched on in the back hall corridor sending a harsh, blinding streak of light through the room. When she spied him, framed in the light of the doorway, Beth thought she was hallucinating.

"Mom?"

"I'm here, Kit."

He took a seat on the bench behind her and rested his arm against hers as the oaky scent of Alan's workshop filled the room. She could hear his breath coming in short gasps as if he had been running. "I saw your car on my way home. What're you doing in here?"

"Thinking, trying to make sense of things." Hoping that someday you'll forgive me and that things will be the way they were.

"About Jack you mean?"

"Jack, you, me, my life, and the impossible muddle I've made of everything."

"Nanny says you haven't been sleeping. She says you walk around all night talking to yourself."

"Sometimes," she answered, surprised that her children had been discussing her as if she were the child, they the parents. Ordinarily Nanny slept like a log.

"I'm really gonna miss him." His voice cracked as Beth felt his hand on her shoulder. A light, tentative touch, unsure of its welcome.

She squeezed his hand. "I know, sweetie. He was a wonderful friend, wasn't he?"

"Yup." Sobbing now, his face wet with tears pressed against her shoulder. "Jack was the only person I could tell anything to and he'd listen and understand. Until this summer."

Her heart wrenched painfully as she lowered her head. "Oh, Kit, I'm so sorry for what I did to you and Jack."

He said nothing, but kept his head on her shoulder. In the silence that followed, mother and son's breathing quieted as they gave themselves over to the healing hush. After a long while, he sat up and withdrew his hand. Beth felt as if her heart had been ripped from her chest.

Finally he spoke. "You miss him, too, don't you?"

She nodded, unable to speak.

"It's ironic, isn't it? You're probably the only one who really understands how I'm feeling right now. I mean, you loved Jack the way I did. It was different, sure, I know, but this sure sucks."

His voice trailed off, but its embrace filled her heart and Beth smiled for the first time in many weeks.

"Want to go home?"

"I'll follow thee," he said, voice husky. They rose together and moved silently along the length of the benches into the light of the hall.

CHAPTER 61

"I'd say your opening night is a resounding success, Mrs. Hadley. Your work is wonderful." Jared Phelps, the New York art critic, smiled, extending his hand to her. "As you are no doubt aware, his is an extraordinary talent. I've followed your husband for years."

"Yes, my ex-husband's work is exceptional, Mr. Phelps, but I'm afraid you've been misinformed," she said, wriggling her elbow out of Alan's grasp as she leaned forward to shake Phelps's hand. "Alan is my ex-husband. We've been divorced for a number of years."

"Oh, I am sorry." He gazed from one to the other, confusion evident in his gaze.

Her assumption had been correct; Alan had let Phelps think they were still married. Preposterous, when would it ever end?

In the brief conversations she had had with Graham over the past week, it was clear that Alan had been working on him, too, wearing him down with misleading accounts of a warming in their relations. As the opening night drew near, Alan had been hovering more than usual and in all the excitement and bustle, she had stupidly allowed it. She would have to deal with the situation and soon.

"I see hundreds of artists every year," Phelps continued. "Your work is remarkable. I'd like to take a limited portfolio back to New York with me, if I may? I believe through my contacts, we could get you a nice little hanging in one of the smaller galleries. Would you be interested?"

"Well, I—"

"Of course she would," Alan interrupted. "Jared, you and I can talk about details later."

Beth gave him a sharp look. "Alan, would you please get me something to drink?"

Her icy glare silenced him. He turned away, for once seeming to be aware that he'd overstepped his bounds.

As soon as Alan was out of earshot, she turned to the art critic. ""Mr. Phelps, I need to make something clear. My ex-husband is a wonderful man. He means well, but I need you to know that he has nothing whatsoever to do with my business affairs and I'd like to keep it that way. I don't want to seem ungrateful, I am very flattered by your request, but I'd rather discuss it at another time, just the two of us. I hope you understand."

"Perfectly, my dear, I am so sorry."

"Don't be."

"Here he comes," he whispered conspiratorially. "Just one more thing for you to think about in the meantime. I'm particularly awed by the portraits. They're quite unusual. Have you more? Also that extraordinary painting, "Hestor's Way." Such power and fury."

She nodded, just as Alan handed her a glass of white wine. "So what did I miss?"

Sighing, she turned away and thanked Alan for the wine. "So glad to have met you, Mr. Phelps."

"Likewise, my dear. I'll be in touch."

As they shook hands and he slipped his card into her hand. She walked away leaving Alan slack-jawed. Spying her three children sitting together in one of the building's four side galleries, she ducked out to join them, glad to escape the crowd for a few moments.

Kat lifted her glass of wine to clink hers. "You're a hit, Mom."

Her eldest looked especially lovely in a short, black sheath, a single strand of pearls and matching earrings her only adornment. Her thick, auburn hair was swept up in a loose chignon, a hint of blue eye shadow accentuating her crystal blue eyes.

Nanny sat beside her, hair swept up and styled by her sister in a sophisticated French braid. She, too, wore a short, cocktail dress, hers midnight blue with silver necklace and earrings and high, black pumps. She looked gorgeous, at least four years older than her fourteen years. Alan had wanted her to go home and change, "looks like a hooker" had been his exact words, but Beth declared Nanny's outfit and hairstyle to be "perfect" and he had backed off.

Kit sat on the opposite side of his older sister. He was dressed in conservative navy sport coat, khakis and blue oxford shirt; almost a carbon copy of his father except for his coloring and build. His father's clothes fit as if they were tailor-made, which they most likely were, especially now that Alan had regained most of his weight. However, his son's clothes hung scarecrow-like on his slender frame. Thinness aside, he looked very handsome and she told him so, then complimented the girls again.

She squeezed in at the end of the bench beside Nanny. "You guys don't have to stay all night. You can take the car and I'll have Graham or Rick bring me home. Why not scoot out for some dinner? I'd sure love to join you, but duty calls."

"Beth. There you are." Margot Lynch advanced toward them, all six feet of her. "Whatever are you doing hiding back here? Your public awaits you, my dear."

Kat rose. "Maybe we will take off, Mom."

Behind her back, Beth slipped her the keys.

"Come along now," the gallery owner said, as she led her away from her children.

With a backward wave, Beth allowed herself to be dragged back into the fray. As they mingled, Margot paused only briefly to speak with people as they moved through the room. When they reached the front of the gallery and Margot said, "I have an ulterior motive for snatching you, my dear. Would you give me just a moment of your time?" Not waiting for a reply, Margot whisked her into her private office and shut the door.

Beth regarded her curiously as the gallery owner leaned back against the massive partners' desk. Her outfit looked straight out of *Town and Country*, Beth mused, taking stock of the beige tweed suit, a silk scarf of bright fuchsia and deep blues at her neck. Her shoulder-length, expertly colored blond hair was swept back from her broad, tanned face. Vermilion lips pressed shut in what Beth decided was a grimace. Graham certainly had his mother's bone structure, the wide jaw, the high cheek bones, the clear hazel eyes that changed with the colors surrounding them. "I'm afraid I've kidnapped you, my dear. Do you mind?"

"That depends on the reason," she replied, not bothering to take a seat. In their few brief encounters, Margot Lynch had not endeared herself to Beth. She had no desire to relax her vigilance by sitting.

"It's Graham, you see. I know he's in love with you. In fact, the attraction has always been there if I'm not mistaken. I remember you coming to the house years ago with that overbearing husband of yours. I always felt he led Graham astray. Did he ever tell you that?"

It was a rhetorical question so Beth listened quietly without reply. She wished she were a hundred miles away, anywhere, but trapped in the gallery owner's stuffy, over-decorated office.

"No matter," Margot went on. "That isn't why I wanted to speak to you. I know people say I'm overbearing and a bitch, but single parenting is never easy. You'd know a little about that, although nothing compared to my years of experience. Graham is his own person, don't get me wrong. I'm not trying to control his life. I, well, I simply wanted to tell you that my son is very vulnerable right now.

"The break with Mary was very painful, I'm not sure how much he's shared with you, but it was ugly. Then, to have him become so enmeshed in your troubles so soon after the nightmare with Mary. If it weren't for this infernal show, this might have never have happened. I blame myself, encouraging him to take over and make decisions when he was still so fragile. I should have let him rest.

"I'm sure you've heard I was opposed to this exhibit. You certainly do not lack talent, but I do strive for balance in the gallery's offerings. Initially Graham's involvement with you seemed to bring him out of his depression. For the first time in years, he seemed at peace. So I supported him and acceded to his wishes. I even pushed Joan Pilmer out, poor Joanie, who has always done well for us. Then look what happens. Frankly, my dear, this past month has been nothing short of a nightmare. Graham's been even more unhappy than he was with Mary. I beg of you, Beth Hadley, if you have no intention of returning his affections, cut it off now. Please don't continue stringing him along like a piece of cheese in this cat and mouse game you're playing with your husband and God knows who else."

Seething, Beth chose her words carefully. "Mrs. Lynch, you appear to have me all figured out, don't you?"

"Oh dear, I see I have offended you. I am sorry."

"No you're not. That was exactly your intention, to offend and drive me as far away from your son as possible. Well, I don't scare easily. My relationship with my ex-husband is none of your affair, nor your son's for that matter, so I won't even comment on it. What happens with Graham and me will be between the two of us, not you, and certainly not Alan. I am truly sorry for causing Graham pain these last few weeks, but it has been a difficult time in my life for many reasons. Now, if you'll excuse me, I have to get back."

Not waiting for Margot's reply, she let herself out of the room. Immediately, she spied Constance Bicknell and three of her friends standing before the old Quaker's portrait and smiled.

"It's you, Constance. She really captured thee, dear." Beth overheard as she neared the group. In the warm embrace of friends, Beth relaxed, letting go of the conversation with Margot Lynch.

CHAPTER 62

Almost ten when the gallery crowd thinned out, a few people lingered, mingling in the corridors, chatting as they donned coats. Lily Babcock waved her checkbook in Margot Lynch's face with demands to purchase three of the paintings. "Hestor's Way" among them.

Margot had directed the wealthy widow to her son. Graham and Rick told Lily that none of the paintings were for sale just yet, but she would be the first to be notified when they became available.

"Probably at exorbitant prices." Lily huffed, as Wilson, her driver, escorted her out wrapped up in a floor-length, moth-eaten mink coat.

After saying goodnight to a young couple from Bay Point, Beth headed for the coat room. She found Graham and Alan conversing in the main gallery. Smiling, she approached them and gazed up at Graham. "I let the kids take my car and I need a ride."

"I'll take you," Alan said.

Beth's eyes pleaded with Graham. "I have my car around back. I'm happy to take you," he said quietly.

"Good," she replied, not glancing at Alan. "I'll just get my things."

When she returned, she found Graham waiting in the semi-darkness of the lobby. Alan was gone.

"He got the message?" she asked.

"He got the message—" extending his arm, "—I thought I got a pretty clear message, too. Did I?"

She nodded, smiling.

"I'm not talking about your needing a ride."

"I know," she replied, taking his arm. "Let's go home."

Please read on to preview chapters from Lee's romance, *Widow's Island*!

WIDOW'S ISLAND
CHAPTER 1

"You can't send that nitwit Peterson to do the job. Jesus, Marty! The last census we sent him out on was so fucked up it had to be completely redone."

"Then who do you suggest, Phil? Margot's on Block Island till August and Ray's wife'd never cut him loose for that long; six months is a long time to be away from the family. That's why Andy'd be so perfect. No wife, no kids, practically no friends, and—"

"Forget it. I'll call Ned. He's the best person for the job anyway."

"Fielding—you gotta be kidding! Penny'd never let him out of his cage for six months!"

"Penny's got nothin' to do with it—they're separated."

"Too bad…I didn't know. Not that it's a surprise; mismatched couple of the century, if you ask me. Mrs. Society and Mr. Limpet. Geez, how'd they ever hook up in the first place?"

"Married when they were kids; baby already on the way. Some people grow up together in those kinda marriages. Some don't. Anyway, Ned'd be glad of the chance to get away, I'll bet. It's been pretty nasty on the home front from what he tells me."

"Still under the same roof? Thought you said separated?"

"He's lookin', but they're still sharing the house. She's away right now, I think, with orders for him to be gone before she gets back. His family's house, you know. 'Bout the only thing he brought to the marriage and Penny wants it. Sickening when you think of all the Pardington millions she has to throw around."

"Good old Ned. Penny's always been a bitch."

"Marty, I haven't got time for this right now," the older man interrupted, feeling like a traitor for gossiping about his friend's marriage. "I'll call Ned and if he can't go, better start packing. Someone's gotta be on the Winward Island by the middle of the month. Nicrophorus americanus, if they're there, will be emerging by then and we want a complete study covering the whole six months till dormancy."

"I'll be in Portsmouth if you need me. Later, Phil."

Marty Robinson left his friend to sort through the disheveled mess on his desk. Phil couldn't remember Ned Fielding's phone number, didn't keep a rolodex or an address book, and his blotter, where the number was jotted down, was buried under a mountain of papers. Shifting the pile back and forth several times, he peeked cautiously underneath each corner. As he moved towards the middle of the blotter, he started a landslide of bills, flyers and grant proposals. The pile picked up steam, scooping up an overburdened vertical file in a downward rush. "Shit!" he muttered, watching the last of the papers cascade over the floor, some coming to rest under the water cooler, others floating into an open aquarium. "Sorry Boris," he said, lunging to remove a stack of Chace Point Bird Sanctuary brochures from the back of a baby snapping turtle, too startled by the sudden onslaught to snap at him.

Turning back to the desk, he spied Fielding's number scribbled on the now-emptied blotter. He dialed. Busy. Leaning back, he closed his eyes for several minutes. It had been a hard year for SENCA, the Southeastern Natural Conservation Agency, of which he was president. The whole region was in a recession and state and federal funding had been slashed. The first thing to go had been Phil's secretary, Edna, who had been with him since the beginning—almost twenty years. They'd been good years, he reflected. He missed Edna. Actually, she'd been ready to retire and he just hadn't bothered to replace her. He could easily hire part-time help, but he figured he'd save money and besides, he hated to break in a new person and have her poking around in his and Edna's stuff.

And SENCA was in better shape than most. They had a generous endowment—lots of folks remembered them in their wills and the money had been invested prudently. King Barlow's gift alone would keep them in operation for twenty or thirty years. And, in addition to the money, he had bequeathed Winward Island—half of it anyway—to the agency in his will. The island had been the one holding they'd neglected, until now.

On an unauthorized day trip, a couple of college kids, SENCA volunteers, had discovered what they believed to be Giant Carrion beetles, nicrophorus americanus, on the island. A rare species of burying beetles, nicrophorus americanus had thought to be extinct until their discovery in recent years on Block Island. Now they might also be present on Winward—the importance of this study dictated that he must send a decent researcher. Ned Fielding was overqualified for this type of field study, but the only man within the agency whom Phil trusted to do the job right.

They hadn't sent anyone to the island since its acquisition twelve years earlier. It was time to conduct a complete census of the plant and animal life, time to map it out and give the island the attention it deserved. Its location along the Atlantic Flyway alone made it an important, extremely valuable acquisition.

He tried Fielding again. This time the phone rang four times before Ned picked it up.

"Ned, hey, it's Phil."

"Hi, Phil!"

"How are things going?"

"'Bout the same. You know about Penny and me, there's not much more to say."

"It's been great having your help at Chace Point this spring. Wish we could pay you more, but…"

"Hey, I've enjoyed myself. Ray and I just got the nest platform up on the spit—East Marsh—and we're lookin' for a new project."

"That's the reason I'm calling. You got a place to live yet, buddy?"

"I think I've got a place out near Watuppa Pond—friend of a friend. Gonna rent for a while, 'till I get things straightened out. Why?"

"Well, if you're free to get away for a while, I have a job for you. Winward Island. Ever heard of it?"

"Yeah, off the coast near Derryville. Barrier Island—we own it, don't we? SENCA, I mean."

"Yup—it's one of our few undiscovered frontiers. We need a complete census, soil samples, beach study, and surveying. Giant Carrion beetles have been found out there, you know."

"No, I didn't. Wow! After Block Island, that should be…"

"Let me qualify my statement. Grad students may have found the beetles last summer. They took some pretty amazing photos, no samples though, just pictures. Only there a few hours. Typical. But listen, buddy, if they're there, we could work with the Block Island people on a recovery plan to bring them back. We need you for that, Ned. What do you say—you game?"

"Sounds good. How much time you talking about?"

"At least six months, maybe more."

"Phil, I'd love to, but…with the divorce and all, I'm not sure I could get away for that long. Can I get back to you later?"

"Sure. I can give you a couple of days, but don't wait too long, buddy. Someone's gotta be out there by the middle of the month, and I'll have to get Peterson or Ray if you can't."

"I'll let you know tomorrow. Thanks Phil."

CHAPTER 2

Ned debated an hour or two before calling Penny at the beach house to which she had retreated—until he "vacated her home." She reacted with typical venom, but Ned, stoic and unmoved, ignored her. They had been living apart emotionally for so many years, a few extra months wouldn't hurt before their ties were legally severed. He just didn't care anymore. Didn't care if she took the house, the antiques, the dog—although he'd miss Haggardy. Penny didn't even like Haggardy. She was keeping him for spite.

"I can't believe how selfish you are, Ned. But then you've always put yourself first, before me, before the kids, before your social obligations, before everything. For God sakes, couldn't you think of me for just this once? How am I going to get on with my life if you leave me dangling here for six months while you're off counting bugs?"

"Do you want to get remarried right away, Penny?"

"Are you kidding? After what you put me through, I'll never marry again!"

"Then what does it matter, really? Six months isn't long after all the years we've…"

"Don't even say it Ned! I will not have our estrangement become public knowledge. In fact, I'm having Martin draw up gag orders to that effect. I will not have my reputation ruined by gossip and I'll thank you to speak to no one about our affairs, past or present, until the papers are drawn up."

"Penny, relax. Everyone knows. It's not exactly a surprise. Can we just let it go for now? I'm going to Winward and I'll be back the end of October, beginning of

November. We can sign papers then, or if you can't wait, I can come back for a day to take care of things whenever you and Martin have things ready."

"What about the settlement?" What about all the details, the division of property, the—"

"You handle it, Pen. Whatever you think is fair. Have it all if you want. I—"

"Isn't that typical! Once again, I have to do it all. Isn't there anything you want?"

"My clothes, tools, and…"

"Yes…here it comes. I knew it."

"Well, if you'd like, I could take Haggardy. He's a…"

"Forget it! Just forget it, Ned! I wouldn't dream of sending Haggardy to some God forsaken island, probably loaded with deer ticks and fleas! Besides, he belongs to me."

"Fine, Pen. Listen—I gotta go. I'll send you an address where I can be reached and I'll call the kids too."

"That's the other thing, the children. Are they supposed to wait six months too; to have this settled, to see you, to…?"

"I'll call them, Penny. If they have strong objections, I won't go, okay? Now, I've really got to go."

"Fine, I'm late for an appointment! You'll be hearing from Martin soon. Good-bye."

She clicked the phone down before he could say good-bye, anything to get the last word.

He put off calling the kids until the evening, but he called Phil and accepted the job. Neither Ned Jr. nor Sydney, his daughter, would care, he knew, but he'd check with them anyway.

CHAPTER 3

Icy pearls of sunlit water fell noiselessly from the paddles as the kayak glided through the channel rounding the east end of Winward Island. With spring, Addie spent her mornings, just after sunrise, paddling in the marshes. A net and several empty burlap bags lay ready, stuffed in the prow beside her feet, should they be needed. But pleasure, not work, drove her to the sea in the early morning hours.

The day was clear and crisp. The April morning air embraced her with cloying chilliness. The marsh beckoned, reaching out to envelop her in its magical green depths, but thoughts intruded, distracting her from the rustling beauty that surrounded her. Usually, she paddled hard for a time, then lifted the paddles and drifted, listening to the sea birds screeching and calling, the fish jumping and the rustle of the spartina…soft and soothing, but today she paddled ferociously as if driven by unseen demons, faster and faster until beads of sweat dotted her brow and her arms burned with the strain of exertion.

Her home was about to be invaded and there was absolutely nothing she could do about it. For twelve years, she had lived alone on the island. Now her sanctuary, her peaceful world was to be taken over, perhaps forever. Who would they send? Would there be more than one? Would they disregard the boundaries and trespass onto her side of the island?

The trustees of her husband's estate had assured her that the conservation agency that shared the island with her would respect her privacy. They owned thirty acres, she twenty. The island was to be kept as a wildlife sanctuary. No building, no camping, no human habitation was planned for Winward Island, the name they had given it upon taking possession. Now they were sending someone to live for six months on her island. Six months!

She knew she was lucky to have the land at all. So many times over those last precarious months, King had threatened to take it away, threatened to will the entire island to SENCA and let them have her cottage, her gardens, everything. He'd laughed and taunted her continuously, knowing that Winward was her only refuge, her only love. She didn't love him, had never loved him. But, King Barlow had died suddenly before he could change his will and his widow had inherited the cottage and its surrounding acreage, the fields, ponds, gardens and thicket. She owned the cove with its many caves hidden beneath the cliffs, where she loved to explore.

The dock was in the cove, the only easy access to the island, hence the reason SENCA had contacted her in the first place, to request permission to use her dock. Recognizing the futility of refusing, she had written back giving her consent and requested that they use the west footpath to reach their property, rather than the more direct path running north to south that traversed her fields. The reply assured her that the agency would respect her privacy, keeping to the western footpath when venturing forth from the dock. "Rest easy Mrs. Barlow," the letter had ended. "Our people will try not to pester you in the slightest way. We are as eager as you are to ensure that Winward remains undisturbed and peaceful. Please contact me personally if there is any problem whatsoever. Phillip K Bodington, director SENCA."

The letter from Mr. Bodington had not reassured her, especially the part about "our people." Was there to be a whole bevy of scientists crawling over the island for six months? Would there also be a steady stream of visitors taking part in the study? Visions of boatloads of college students descending upon Winward made her shudder and the paddle jabbed unevenly beneath the glassy surface of the water, the handle nearly jerking free of her grasp.

Glimpsing a crab, its broad swimming legs catching the sunlight as he paddled sideways through the eel grass, she swung the net, a flawless extension of her right arm and scooped him up, wetting the burlap bag with her left hand as she tossed him in. The action, completed in a few seconds time, appeared to be almost reflexive, after which she continued paddling, worries consuming her still.

After an hour's time, she headed back, a bag full of crabs, heart and mind no lighter, but resigned. Dropping the crabs in one of the pots near shore, she paddled in and pulled the kayak up onto the beach. She kept her fishing scow tied to the dock, but she preferred to drag the lighter craft up onto the beach. That way it could be more easily be carried to higher ground if a storm threatened or she could drag it over the ridge for use in the pond near the cottage. She scanned the surface of the water closely for some minutes before turning to head up the path lined with rose hips and honeysuckle that led back to the cottage.

As she entered the thicket, she heard a familiar screech. She turned in time to spy a huge bird dropping from the vast blue above her, its talons outstretched as it fell. Pulling a leather glove from her pocket, she slipped it onto her right hand, stretching her arm out straight to her side. Sharp talons dug into the leather as the osprey came to rest, grasping her gloved hand. "Gwydyon, son of Don," she smiled, stroking his feathers, "How goes it with you this fine day?"

The fish hawk bowed his head, enjoying the attention, alternately gazing from his mistress to the sea. "I have nothing for you this morning, maybe later." As she talked, she walked slowly along the path through the thicket. When it became clear that no meal was forthcoming, Gwydyon became restless. "Just a minute my friend," she cooed, quickening her pace.

Vulnerable to attack in the thicket, she hated to release him lest his flight be checked by an unforeseen enemy. Without food, he was probably safe, but there were several golden eagles and great horned owls that frequented the island. While they rarely challenged Gwydyon on the open water where he was pestered instead by terns continually lying in wait to steal his catch—they might hazard a skirmish in the brush where his sharp, lashing talons were less effective.

Finally, she reached the open fields. From there, the path ran straight through the meadows to the shingled cottage just visible in the distance. The bird arched his wings, rearing back. Addie released him with an upward thrust and his powerful wings carried him aloft. As soon as he reached a safe height, he circled once, screeching farewell as he disappeared over the treetops towards the open sea.

Walking on, she stared ahead at the whitewashed cottage, her home for the past twelve years. Built seventeen years earlier, at the time of her marriage, the cottage had been winterized when Addie had settled permanently on the island.

Two stories with a wide porch wrapped permanently around its front and sides, the faded white shingled walls were alive with climbing greenery, English ivy crept high under the second story windows intertwined with clematis vines, the blue and white flowers not yet in bloom. The vegetation at first gave the impression of wild abandon, belying the hours of cultivation and care that had put them there.

A two-story barn with a lean-to shed and greenhouse attached stood behind the house to the south. The land gently sloped from the back of the cottage so that the taller, more imposing barn faded gracefully into the receding landscape, rather than overwhelming the much smaller house. Its brown, weathered sides blended comfortably with the woods to the east, at harmony with its surroundings.

As she approached the cottage, a yelp of greeting hailed her as a tawny beast bounded up flinging her front paws around her mistress. Laughing, Addie knelt beside her pet, ruffling the soft fur on the animal's back. "Aran! So you finally decided to wake up! No swim for you this morning!"

Woman and beast went together into the cottage where she fed her pet, fixing tea for herself. Sipping it slowly, she sat at the worn table fashioned with her own hands from wood carted back from the mainland by boat. There was a salvage yard in Derryville she visited when she needed materials for the house and she kept an old pick-up truck on the mainland to use for these infrequent sojourns and for her deliveries of produce and fish. She hated driving, but as her client list had grown, the truck had become indispensable. The drop-off places along the river reached roughly half of her customers; the rest had to be delivered by truck.

During the spring, her days were freer; the garden was not yet in full flower and the fishing still sparse. The Massachusetts climate demanded caution in planting fragile, warm weather crops, but her tomatoes, peppers, eggplants and flowers were flourishing in the warm moisture of the greenhouse. She attended to them first, passing among the rows to give water and pinch back unwanted growth. The greenhouse, too, had been built entirely from salvage materials. Unlike the cottage and barn that her former husband had had built—as a wedding gift to her—the greenhouse and shed had been constructed later on, after she had come to live on the island.

The first years she had survived on the small inheritance King had left her, tending a tiny garden for her own needs. When she began fishing, clamming, and lobstering to earn money, she expanded the garden too. Once she began marketing her produce, she needed a hothouse. Rather than hiring someone to build it, she had undertaken the project herself. It had saved money, but more importantly, it had given her confidence and a feeling of self-sufficiency. Previously she had called upon plumbers, carpenters, electricians and mechanics when things broke and needed repair, but since the completion of the shed and greenhouse ten years earlier, not another soul had set foot on the island. Whatever expertise she required came from books and her own experimentation.

Midday found her weeding and picking early spinach. She had already harvested parsnips and winter carrots and her broccoli, cauliflower and lettuces were well underway. She protected the lettuces at night and when the days were particularly cold, but the thick layer of mulch and the protected enclosure of the garden kept the plants relatively safe from a killing frost.

Until June she sold little of her produce, as most of her clients were seasonal residents, coming to spend the summer at the beach. She had a few year round customers that paid to have anything from her garden yield, as well as a share of her catch. What little money she made before June, however, came from the fish she sold to wholesalers. From June to October she sold only to her regular customers, unless there was a surplus. When summer cottages on the mainland coast were boarded up, she slowed down, moving into her winter schedule.

As the years went by, her customer list grew until she finally had to turn people away. She kept a waiting list of would-be customers only too eager to receive some of her weekly bounty; some offering double or triple the usual charge to be put "on the route." Addie refused to grow bigger, however, since the thought of having to hire help was abhorrent to her.

Each customer received three deliveries a week of fish, vegetables, herbs, flowers and fruit. They paid a flat, weekly fee, the same no matter what they received. When a new customer was taken on, they filled out a form with likes and dislikes. At that time, they selected which plan they desired; only fruit and vegetables, all five items—fish, vegetables, fruit, herbs and flowers, or just fish and flowers. While she attempted to cater to individual tastes, Addie brought a variety of offerings depending on what was ripe or what she'd managed to catch or dig or net on any given day. No one had ever complained and the woven baskets brimming with fresh food were always a delightful surprise.

When the Widow's baskets arrived, dinner was planned around the bounty within them, whether it was steamers and corn, wild raspberries, apples and blue crabs or lobsters, arugula and fresh scallions. Always there were flowers from early spring on; first tulips and daffodils, then iris, lupine and wild sweet peas, then the zinnias, asters, cosmos, marigolds, coreopsis, snapdragons, dahlias, cornflowers and all manner of wild flowers growing in riotous profusion in Winward's meadows.

This morning would be spent repairing her lobster traps in preparation for the following week when they would be baited and set out for the first time. She also needed to make several new baskets as she had reluctantly agreed to take on four new clients this year. Some of the old baskets were worn and split, in need of repair. Fashioned from rushes, dried in the sunroom over the winter, the baskets were strong and water-resistant, their large willow handles smooth and comfortable to hold, even when they were heavily laden with produce. Along with the baskets, she sometimes used burlap sacks for her deliveries if she was bringing large quantities of shellfish.

Each customer was allotted two baskets and several bags per season, the empty one to be returned with the following delivery. If a basket was lost or misplaced, she had begun charging for new ones. Some people feigned loss in order to have one of the simple, but beautiful baskets to take home at the end of the season so she was careful to set aside enough of the cattails and rushes for drying in order to replace worn or "misplaced" baskets. Several times customers had suggested that she might like to sell some baskets to the local gift shops or stores in the city, where they assured her she would make a handsome profit. Addie always demurred.

As she went about her afternoon chores, she began to relax. They would stay on their side and she would stay far away. She knew every inch of the island and every hiding place. Six months and they would be gone. She would find a way to bear it.

Acknowledgements

Most importantly, I would like to thank my dear family and friends, who are always there, no matter where life's travels take me. I love them all beyond words.

I would like to thank the Formatting Fairies, and the unfailing good cheer and encouragement they bestow upon this fledgling author. Special gratitude to Ashley Lopez for designing the lovely covers that encourage readers to pick up each book! A huge thank you to my readers for picking up my books, for writing to tell me you love them, and for continuing to come back for more. It is heartwarming to know you are out there!

About the Author

M. Lee Prescott is the author of dozens of works of fiction for adults, young adults and children, among them **Prepped to Kill, Gadfly, Lost in Spindle City (Ricky Steele series), Jigsaw, A Friend of Silence, and Song of the Spirit**. Her newest contemporary romance series, **Morgan's Run,** debuts in the summer

of 2015. Three of her nonfiction titles have been published by Heinemann and she has published numerous articles in the field of literacy education. Lee is a professor of education at a small New England liberal arts college where she teaches reading and writing pedagogy. Her current research focuses on mindfulness and connections to reading and writing. She regularly teaches abroad, most recently in Singapore.

Lee has lived in southern California (loved those Laguna nights!), Chapel Hill, North Carolina, and various spots in Massachusetts and Rhode Island. Currently, she resides in Massachusetts on a beautiful river, where she canoes, swims, and watches the incredible variety of migratory birds that pass by. She is the mother of two grown sons and spends lots of time with them, their beautiful wives, and her amazing grandchildren. When not teaching or writing (both of which she loves), Lee's passions revolve around family, yoga (Kripalu is a second home), swimming, sharing mindfulness with children and adults, and walking.

Lee loves to hear from readers. Visit her website at mleeprescott.com and Facebook page (mleeprescott). The Facebook page is a "work in progress," but I am working on it with help from friends who know what they are doing! E-mail is mleeprescott@gmail.com

A Note from the Author

Thank you so much for taking the time to read **Hestor's Way**, the first in my *Well Loved* series. Like all my books, Beth Hadley's story is near and dear to my heart. I wrote this book years ago, but set it aside. Just recently, I picked it up, read and reread and thought—why not? So, here it is!

If you like **Hestor's Way** and would be willing to write an Amazon review, I would very much appreciate it! In fact, I will be happy to send my first 25 reviewers a free e-copy **of another of my titles! If** you submit a review, just e-mail me at mleeprescott@gmail.com and I will see that you receive your free copy of whichever title you choose!

If you would like to sign up for future book releases and occasional notices about my books, please e-mail me at mleeprescott@gmail.com and I will add you to the list. I promise I will not share your address, nor will I flood you with e-mails. Do visit my website at www.mleeprescott.com to read more about my books and to hear what's next. **Lost in Spindle City**, the third *Ricky Steele Mystery* debuted last summer, and I am really excited about the sequel to **A Friend of Silence**, the second *Roger and Bess Mystery*, which will be out in April 2015! This summer, I look forward to publishing several books in my contemporary romance series, **Morgan's Run**, set in the United States southwest. The first book, **Emma's Dream**, will be available in June 2015!

Finally, this book has been revised, proofed and edited many, many times, but I, and my intrepid assistants, are human, so if you spot a typo, please e-mail me at <u>mleeprescott@gmail.com</u> and I will fix it. If you'd like to know more about my other books, please scroll ahead to the next section that is followed by sample chapters of **Widow's Island**!

Warm wishes,
M. Lee Prescott

Contemporary romances and mysteries by M. Lee Prescott include:

Mysteries

The Ricky Steele series
Book 1: Prepped to Kill
Book 2: Gadfly
Book 3: Lost in Spindle City

Also featuring Ricky Steele:
Jigsaw

Single titles

Romantic suspense

Roger and Bess Mysteries
Book 1: A Friend of Silence
Book 2: In the Name of Silence (coming in April 2015!)

Contemporary Romance
Well Loved Series: Lassitor's Return (coming soon!)
Glass Walls (coming soon!)
Morgan's Run

Young Adult Historical Romance
Song of the Spirit
Contemporary romances and mysteries by M. Lee Prescott include:

Mysteries

The Ricky Steele series
Book 1: Prepped to Kill

Book 2: Gadfly

Book 3: Lost in Spindle City

Also featuring Ricky Steele:

Jigsaw

Single titles

Romantic suspense

Roger and Bess Mysteries

Book 1: A Friend of Silence

Book 2: In the Name of Silence (coming in April 2015!)

Contemporary Romance

Well Loved Series: Lassitor's Return (coming soon!)

Glass Walls (coming soon!)

Morgan's Run

Young Adult Historical Romance

Song of the Spirit

www.ingramcontent.com/pod-product-compliance
Lightning Source LLC
Chambersburg PA
CBHW061018120726
47910CB00006B/1998